Fair To Middling

By

Kira Shay

FSF Publications

Cover art and design by Scott P. "Doc" Vaughn

e-Book ISBN: 978-0-9961485-9-7
Print ISBN: 978-0-9961485-8-0

Manufactured in the Unites States of America.

First US Printing 2018

www.fivesmilingfish.com

For Loretta

Promise kept

Endless Thanks and Appreciation To:

Will for making sure I kept my promise.

Sidney Reetz, Megan E. Vaughn, and Matthew Bergren for helping me through untested waters and the encouragement to keep paddling.

Scott P. "Doc" Vaughn for the incredible cover art and patience.

Tom Dushku for the edits as well as scanning and formatting the letters.

Shannon and Wade Rimmer for keeping me honest when it came to the details.

And thanks to you for reading!

Table of Contents

FOREWORD
A WORK OF REMEMBERANCE

    Writing this book has been more difficult than I ever anticipated. Even though Grandpa was 92 and lived a full and vibrant life, even though it was his time, trying to put my thoughts together to honor his years with us was nearly impossible. After all, no death is ever easy.

    Especially if it is someone you love.

    I wish I could paint a picture with my words as to the type of man Grandpa was. I wish I could use my vocabulary to describe this remarkable person in a way that you could feel like I do when I think of him. I wish I could convey the sheer amount of love and gratitude I hold for this man.

    The words I do have are paltry and generic and seem somehow insincere.

    Nevertheless, these words are all I have.

    Anyone who ever met Albert Kent Tone knows he was a storyteller. He was good at it too. With a sort of wide-eyed wonder, he would spin tales or tell a joke to anyone who would listen. His favorites were the ones that made people laugh. Grandpa loved to laugh.

It wasn't just the stories themselves, it was the way he told them. His voice was distinct and his laughter infectious. He had wide blue eyes and an easy smile that invited you to talk to him. When he really got going, his thick, calloused hands gestured wildly and his pale face transformed like a child telling you a story. His words were peculiarly formed with an accent that is the result of a childhood of gleaning words and phrases from migrating farmers escaping the Dust Bowl. Some of his more eclectic phrases have found their way into my own everyday speech. I've caught myself telling friends that I had some "rat killing" to do and, so help me, I've described something going off like a "ruptured duck". One of my stories is titled "Wooden Nickels" because Grandpa always warned not to take them.

I entitled this "Fair to Middling" for a few reasons. Mostly because when I called Grandpa, I'd ask how he was doing and he'd invariably reply with "oh, fair to middling." He also raised cotton for a while and, as he explained to me very animatedly several times, fair to middling is an average grade of cotton that's usually used for blue jeans — his favorite attire. He was always so happy to explain his more interesting colloquialisms.

I was lucky enough to talk to him every day. I was blessed to hear his stories about growing up on the ranch before there was electricity. He confided in me about the pranks he used to play on visiting relatives and friends. He recounted his time in the war and how it felt when he met Grandma.

This collection of his life experiences was originally a project suggested by my Grandma Loretta, as a way to keep him busy and his mind off of her failing health. As the writer of the family, it fell to me to record his stories — a unique opportunity that I embraced. Over the following years until his death, I recorded, listened, and questioned the man on all the tales he had to tell.

These stories are my heritage. They are my history. Because Grandpa shared them and because he allowed me to learn them, they have become a part of me.

People say Grandpa was a hero. A cowboy. A kind-hearted family man. He was honest and he, for some unknown reason, was addicted to Fox News. And he always did what he felt was right — which is never easy.

All of these things are true.

But what makes Grandpa truly special was his talent as a storyteller. I can still hear his laughter punctuating his sentences. I still see his smile and that sparkle in his blue eyes when he was about to tell you the punchline to a joke. I remember the stories he passed down to me and I will honor his memory by not only keeping them in my heart, but by sharing them with you.

PART ONE
THE PROMISE

I arrived early on New Year's Day. Well, early for me. Grandma and Grandpa had been up for hours by the time I pulled into the driveway. They not only had their breakfast, but were considering what to make for lunch when I tapped politely on the double French doors separating their living space and the back yard.

"Come in, come in!" Grandma waved me inside. She looked good despite her failing health. She was chipper in a new purple silk blouse and pants. Her gray hair stuck up at odd angles and it looked as though it needed a trim, but her brown eyes shone with happiness. Grandpa sat in his scooter, two inches away from the television with his straw cowboy hat set rakishly atop his bald head. When I walked in I was greeted with genuine smiles and earnest wishes of a Happy New Year.

"Good morning! Happy New Year!" I returned their exuberant greetings.

"We sure are glad that you have come down to

visit us this week. Mighty nice of you," Grandpa said with his country accent. His blue eyes sparkled.

"I wouldn't have missed this for the world," I answered, and I truly meant it. The last time I spent a week with my grandparents was when I was a child. Memories of summers spent in Colorado floated to the forefront of my mind.

Grandma and Grandpa resided in the back room of my aunt's house, off of the dining area and the kitchen. The queen size bed was permanently made and there were two large recliners. Crowding the room were two electric scooters and two walkers — one for each of them. There was an airy hiss every few moments, like the sound of Darth Vader's helmet. It came from Grandma's oxygen machine. Attached to it was a green cord that snaked all over the floor; proof of her excursions to and from the restroom.

The double entry way into the kitchen was battered and banged up from Grandpa ramming into the door frames with his scooter. Every time he hit one of them, I envisioned my aunt wincing and shaking her head.

The TVs in both the bedroom and the dining room blared. The broadcast of the Rose Parade was more than half way over and both of my grandparents watched eagerly and waited to see someone they knew. I settled in to watch with them.

"How are you feeling?" I asked Grandma during a commercial break. Grandpa had dozed off in his scooter with his head dipped forward into his chest. Soft snoring emanated from beneath his cowboy hat.

She shrugged and I noticed that her once plump

figure was frailer that it used to be. "Some days are good and some are not. It gets hard with all of these tests and the doctors' visits." She lifted her chin in Grandpa's direction. "Kent worries too much. It's not good for him to be fixated so much on my illness. I don't know what he will do when I pass on."

"It's not that bad, is it?" The finality in her voice shook me.

She gave a weak chuckle in an attempt to dispel the sudden sense of dread in the air. "No, it's not that bad. It would just do him some good to have his mind on something else. It would do me some good too because he barely lets me rest with how much he worries."

Relaxing a little, I said, "I can understand that. What do you have in mind? What could possibly distract him?"

Grandma peered into my eyes, a quirk of a smile on her thin lips. "You know, I think if you get him to tell you his stories that might work. If he has someone who will listen, it might just get him focused on something other than me."

I glanced over at Grandpa who snored so loudly, I could barely hear the TV. "Sure, I can do that."

Grandma took my hand in hers and squeezed. Her skin felt paper-thin.

"Promise me you'll keep him talking, keep having him tell the stories even after I'm gone."

There wasn't any more laughter or humor. Her demeanor, her tone, and her pleading eyes told me that this was a serious request. I wondered then if she knew how long she had to live or if she just wanted to be sure someone would take care of him regardless. In the end, there was really only one answer I could give her.

"Of course I will. I promise."

With a loud snort that startled him awake, Grandpa let out a surprised noise.

"Did you fall asleep, Kent?" Grandma asked, projecting her voice so he could hear her.

Mumbling under his breath, Grandpa said, "No. I was just resting my eyes."

Grandma nudged me and laughed silently as though I were in on a big joke. I smiled back, but the promise still rang in my ears.

Grandpa blinked a few times and then wheeled his cart around to face us. "I think I'll go to the store. I want to get me some of those black eyed peas."

I frowned. "Why do you want those?"

He regarded me with wide, surprised eyes, "You mean that you don't know about black eyed peas?"

"They're beans?" I responded.

"They say that if you eat black eyed peas on New Year's Day, you're supposed to have good luck all year long. That there is too good of a deal to pass up. I need all the luck I can get my hands on."

I got up out of the chair. "Alright, let's go to the store. We can make them for dinner tonight."

"You two go on. I think I'll rest a bit here," Grandma said. She winked at me and I winked back. Grandpa was oblivious to this exchange. Instead, he hoisted himself out of his scooter to grab hold of the traveling walker. Though he wobbled a little, he was quick on his feet. Before I gathered my purse, he had already made it out the door and was making his way to the car.

"Grandpa, wait!" I called out as I ran after him. "Here, let me drive."

After a short, good-natured argument about who should drive, he lifted himself into the passenger seat, pulling his dead leg in after him. I loaded his cart into the back of the over-sized black truck and we were off.

"Slow down a hare," he cautioned. "I can't count the fence posts."

"What? I'm going the speed limit."

"It's too fast. Trust me, it's better to go slow enough to count all of the fence posts than to be in too much of a rush. You drive like your Great-Grandpa Brownie."

"I do?"

He chuckled a bit. "Yes. Old Brownie drove like a bat outta hell. I about pissed myself the first time he drove with me when I lived in California."

"When did you live in California?" The question came out with more than a little surprise behind it. "I thought you were born in Arizona."

"I was," Grandpa assured me. "Born and raised right here in the Valley. After the war in Europe was finished, I was stationed in California. That's when I saved your Great-Great Grandma Blanche's life."

~ ~ ~

End of the war in Europe or not, Kent still belonged to the military. After all, there was still a war on in the Pacific. According to his paperwork, his orders were to climb aboard a troop train heading to Ft. MacArthur in Santa Ana, California.

There was a chance that he could be shipped off to combat again, but Kent was determined not to think of that possibility. No, he wanted to enjoy the time stateside while he could.

The first thought in his head when he got the assignment in Santa Ana was of his girlfriend Loretta, who lived in Hollywood. He'd get to see her right after he reported in. That thought sustained him through the next three days of being confined on a troop train heading westward.

When he reached Ft. MacArthur, he rushed through his in-processing as quickly as he could. It still took a good two hours before he was finally able to place the telephone call to Loretta.

"Guess where I am," he said playfully once she'd picked up the line.

"Where?"

He could hear the smile in her voice and he wanted nothing more than to see it in person.

"Ft. MacArthur. You think your parents would bring you down to see a soldier that just came home from war?"

"Really?" Loretta squeaked. "You're in California? Just wait until I tell Dad!"

"I don't know how long I'll to be here. They are liable to ship me off to Japan any minute now."

"They wouldn't! Listen, I'll be there in an hour by hook or by crook."

Kent hung up the phone, his heart dancing in his chest. After so many months away, he'd finally get to see the girl he'd been dreaming about.

True to her word, Loretta arrived within an hour. It wasn't her father that brought her though, it was her cousin, Wayne. He was dressed in Navy whites but he shook Kent's hand and gave him a hearty welcome home. Truth be told, Kent didn't pay Wayne too much mind. No, all of his attention was riveted on the most beautiful girl in all of California. Heck, in all the world. Loretta looked smart in a pretty yellow dress. Her dark hair was done up all nice with pins and her brown eyes sparkled with happiness. She embraced Kent with a ferocity of youth and affection.

"I can't believe you're back," Loretta said, her voice breaking with emotion. "I wasn't sure I'd ever get to see you again."

"I'm here now. I don't intend on letting you go." When Kent held her in his arms, he felt like a new man. This is what he'd been fighting for all these months overseas.

Eventually, they did break apart, though they never let go of each other's hands. They walked around the PX and talked about Kent's plane ride back to the states and his long train journey across the country. Loretta told him about school and how the next year she intended to graduate.

"There is one thing that I didn't mention in my letters," Loretta confided quietly as they sat on a bit of grass at sunset. Wayne was still in the PX, giving the two sweethearts some time to themselves.

"What's the matter?" Kent asked, immediately concerned.

"It's my grandmother, Blanche."

"The one that comes out to Arizona in the winter and plays bridge with Mother? What about her?"

"She's very sick. We had to move her back here to take care of her. Turns out she's got Leukemia. That's why my parents couldn't come down to see you. Mother and Dad are at the hospital with her right now."

"That's awful. I am sorry to hear that. Blanche is a wonderful woman."

"Thank you. They are trying to find someone to give her a blood transfusion. She has to have a specific blood type, but there's a shortage of it."

Kent blinked, an idea forming in his mind. "What blood type does she need?"

"O negative."

He let out a quiet exclamation. "Why, I have O negative blood."

Loretta's eyes widened. She leaned closer to Kent. "You do? You wouldn't want to help my grandmother, would you?"

Without even a moment's hesitation he answered, "If I can, damn right I will."

Loretta flung her arms around his neck. "Oh, Kent! Thank you! We have to go get Wayne. He'll take us to the hospital."

They were on their way shortly after. The hope that glistened in Loretta's eyes and the way she clung to his hand the entire ride filled him with an indescribable feeling. Was this what it felt like to be a hero?

The hospital was a quiet place. Kent walked with his cap in his hands, his boots echoing against the shining linoleum floor.

When they were close to Blanche's room, Loretta let go of his hand and skipped ahead of him.

11

She stopped near an open doorway.

"Mother? Dad?" she called into the room. "How is Grandmother doing?"

Her mother's thin voice answered, but Kent could barely hear her. He stopped on the other side of the door just as Loretta backed out of the room followed by her parents.

Her father, Orven E. Brown, or Brownie as most people knew him, was a tall, thin fellow. His dark brown hair was parted and combed back. He wore well-made blue trousers and shiny black shoes. Black suspenders hung from his shoulders, a stark contrast to the crisp white shirt. His jacket laid casually across one arm.

Loretta's mother, Dorothy, was a petite thing. Her modest green dress went well with her tanned complexion and chestnut colored curls. Seeing both her and Brownie together so well-dressed made Kent acutely aware that he was still in his traveling uniform. He looked down at his boots, suddenly self-conscious.

"Kent," Brownie extended his hand to the young soldier. "Wonderful to see you again. When did you get back to the states?"

"A few days ago. I just arrived at Ft. MacArthur this morning."

"Dad, Kent wanted to help Grandmother," Loretta interjected. "He's got her blood type."

The surprise announcement made both Brownie and Dorothy blink at Kent.

"Are you sure?" Dorothy breathed. The hope in her eyes matched her daughter's exactly.

"Of course, I am sure," Kent affirmed. "If I can

help, then I want to."

His confirmation made Dorothy rush forward to embrace him. "Thank you," she whispered softly into his shoulder. She stepped back, tears glistening in her eyes and her hand to her lips.

Brownie put his arm around his wife. "Young man, it seems we are in your debt."

"No, sir," Kent replied. "It's the least I can do. She is one of my mother's very good friends."

When the doctors came and Dorothy explained to them about Kent volunteering his blood for a transfusion, they took him to a separate room — one specifically for drawing blood. They confirmed his blood type and, with his blessing, they proceeded to draw out the maximum donation. Loretta looked on as she held his other hand and whispered how thankful she and her family were for his help. Kent simply shrugged off the praise. It was just the right thing to do.

He waited with Loretta's family as the nurses gave Blanche the transfusion. When it was pronounced a success, Kent breathed a sigh of relief. He'd have to let his mother know what happened. She'd want to know how poorly her friend was doing. He assured the nurses that he'd be back again to give some more blood.

Loretta kissed him on the cheek. "My hero," she whispered in his ear.

Kent blushed.

"Come on, Kent. I'll get you back to the base," Brownie said as he donned his suit jacket.

"Thank you," the young man accepted politely. He gave Loretta's hand a squeeze. "I'll see you later."

She grinned at him, "You better."

Together, Kent and Brownie left the hospital.

"So, you're sweet on my daughter, are you?" Brownie asked, his tone knowing. He opened the door to his Cadillac and climbed in.

"Yes, sir. I think the world of her." Kent answered, more than a little flustered at the older man's directness. He got into the passenger side. Despite his nervousness at what Brownie was going to say to him, he did take the time to appreciate the quality of vehicle he was in. It had been too long since he'd been in any car other than a bouncy military truck.

Brownie started the engine and then looked at Kent for a long moment. "What is it you plan to do now that the war is over?"

Kent did his best not to fidget too much. "Well, sir. I don't rightly know. The military isn't quite through with me just yet."

Brownie backed the Cadillac out of the parking space and peeled through the parking lot. Kent stifled a gasp and grabbed hold of the door as if it would help slow the car down. Expertly, Brownie maneuvered the big vehicle onto the streets. He revved the engine, shifted, and sped off down the road only to suddenly stop at the first of many stop signs along the way.

"You know I own a body shop down in Beverly Hills. All sorts of those movie stars come down to get their cars done. Yes, sir. They all come to Brownie's. Do you know how many times I've painted Jack Benny's car? More than I can count."

"You don't say?" Kent asked. He barely heard a

word Brownie said because he was so focused on not being sick. The last thing he wanted to do was throw up in Loretta's father's Cadillac.

Brownie took no notice of his passenger's plight. "It's not bad work, you know. It keeps the family fed and happy. Just what an honest man needs if they are going to get by in this world. You are mechanically inclined, aren't you?"

"Yes, sir. They trained me as a mechanic in the Army Air Corps." Kent stared out the front window. He couldn't help but think that it would be better not to look at the landscape rushing past, but he was physically unable.

"That's good. Working with your hands is an honest day's work, if you ask me. You know, if you don't have anything else lined up for after the military is done with you, I could use one such as yourself at the shop. If you learned the trade, that is. I'm afraid Lincolns and Cadillacs aren't quite the same as those airplanes you've been around."

A nervous laugh came out of Kent's mouth, "Ah, no sir, I don't see how they would be."

"Please, call me Brownie. No need for that sir business." The car lurched to a stop in front of Ft. MacArthur's gates. "Well, here we are."

The young man was never so glad to be on solid ground. He poured himself out of the Cadillac and closed the door behind him. "Thank you for the ride, sir — er, Brownie."

The older man laughed. "Are you kidding? After what you did for our family, it is the least I can do. Would you promise me one thing, though? Would you consider my offer to come work at the shop? If you and Loretta are serious, it would do me good to know that you'll have a good career to fall back on when you are discharged."

The sincerity in Brownie's voice struck Kent. It was a meaningful offer and one that promised a modicum of security for life after the military; something that had worried him since the war ended. He cast Brownie a grateful smile. "I'll think about it."

Brownie grinned. "Good man. In the meantime, how would you like to come with me out to the races next Thursday?"

"I'd like that very much," Kent said and he meant it. He'd never been to the races before and it sounded exciting.

"Great. I'll get back with you on the details. You best get inside and get some rest. We've put you through the ringer today."

Kent nodded and patted the vehicle twice before heading to the gate. Brownie squealed out of sight before the young man could even get his military ID out to show the guards.

~ ~ ~

"You really did that for Blanche?" I asked as we pulled into a parking space at the grocery store.

"I did. They were ever so grateful. Really, anyone would have done it if they were in my shoes." He shrugged off my amazed tone. "We best hurry and get those black eyed peas. I don't want your grandma to be alone for too long."

As I retrieved his cart from the back of the truck,

I realized that Grandma was right; telling his stories would be the best thing for Grandpa. When he spoke, he was so animated. His eyes got big and wide, as though he was doing his best to be earnest and make sure you believed him. There was something else, too. As he told his stories, a sense of lightness radiated off of him. He was at ease. Worry wasn't bogging him down. When he escaped into these memories it was a break for him.

We purchased the black eyed peas and some other groceries for dinner. When we returned back to the house, Grandma was asleep. Grandpa settled into his own recliner as I put the groceries away. By the time I was done, he was snoring loudly.

I watched them both for a long moment before shutting off the TV. I would keep my promise to Grandma, but it would require some planning on my part, especially considering how much Grandpa worried about her.

Dinner that night was grilled chicken, salad, and, the real star of the day, black eyed peas. Grandpa hoovered around the kitchen as I prepared the meal.

"Boy, I sure am excited to try those black eyed peas," he said.

"You mean you've never had them before?"

"No. I've just heard about them."

Concern shot through me. "You don't know how to cook them?"

Grandpa shrugged. "Can't be that hard. I suppose we just heat them up in a pot like any other bean. These here are canned, so we won't have to soak them, I don't think."

"Sure. Maybe we'll add in some salt and pepper

too?" I didn't know how to cook black eyed peas, and Grandpa's guess sounded about right. I emptied the can of beans into a pot and cranked up the heat.

It wasn't long before dinner was ready and the three of us gathered around the kitchen table.

As we all got our plates situated, I said, "Grandpa, I have something I want to ask you."

"What's that?" He focused on drowning his salad in Thousand Island dressing.

"I want to record your stories."

His brow furrows in confusion. He set down the salad dressing and raised a calloused hand to his ear. "You want to what?"

A little louder, I said, "Record you. I want you to tell your stories to me and I will record them with my computer. What do you think?"

Leaning back in his chair, he considered the offer. At last he asked, "You don't think I'd break your camera?"

I choked back a laugh and assured him, "No, you won't break my camera."

A relieved grin causes all of the worry lines on his face to turn into laugh wrinkles. "Alright then, when do we start?"

"Tomorrow after breakfast," I said, glad that he was excited about the project. Out of the corner of my eye, I saw Grandma smile.

"How are your black eyed peas, Kent?" she asked.

"I don't know yet." Hurriedly, he took a big forkful and scooped it into his mouth and I did the same, eager to see what luck tasted like.

Dirt. It tasted like dirt.

Grandpa must have had the same thought that I did because the way his mouth moved to chew seemed to be on the verge of spitting it all out. When he finally swallowed, he let out a soft curse. "Kira, what on earth did you put in those beans?"

Choking down my own mouthful, I replied, "Just salt and pepper. Are they supposed to taste like this?"

Grandpa regarded the heaping pile of beans on his plate with worry.

Grandma laughed at us.

PART TWO
ENLISTING

"Just make sure you speak into the mic," I explained.

Grandpa nodded. "Alright. That's this deal right here?" He lifted up the small penlight-sized microphone. It looked miniature in his large, weathered hands.

"Yep, that's it."

He had gotten dressed up for the recording event with a pale blue button down shirt and his favorite bolo tie; the silver one with large bits of turquoise embedded in the metal. His cowboy hat rested on the table next to him as if he were debating on whether or not to wear it. The thin wisps of white hair around the sides of his head were combed and smoothed down.

The remains of breakfast were cleared from the kitchen table where we set up to record. Grandma situated herself at the end of the table, just out of camera range. She looked tired in her pajamas and uncombed hair, but she watched her husband with a patient smile as he wiped at his mouth for any stray toast crumbs.

I settled myself behind the camera that was hooked up to my laptop and glanced at the sheet of paper with the questions I came up with the night before. "Okay, I'm gonna start recording." I pushed the button on the laptop.

Grandpa couldn't quite figure out where to look. He fidgeted with the microphone and asked, "Is it on? Are you really recording me right now?"

"Yes, it's on. Now, focus on me, Grandpa. First question. Where were you born?"

He leaned forward towards the camera, forgetting the microphone in his hands completely. "I was born in Mesa, Arizona in 1923." Having given his answer, he leaned back in his chair. "How did I do?" he asked anxiously.

I gave him a thumbs up. "Perfect. But you don't have to lean forward every time. That's why you are holding the microphone."

"Oh." He continued to fidget with the mic, twirling it with his thick, calloused fingers.

I needed to get to a story that he'd like to tell, one that he could get wrapped up in. One that would make him less conscientious about the camera.

Grandma must have had the same thought, because she suggested quietly, "Why don't you tell her about how you got into the military."

Grandpa glanced at me, uncertainty in his face.

"Yes! Why did you decide to go into the military? Was it before or after Pearl Harbor?"

After a reassuring nod from his wife, he leaned

forward once more to stare into the camera. He spoke loud and slow, careful to enunciate just right for the recording. "No, it was after the attack on Pearl Harbor. I had just graduated high school, the one over there in Gilbert."

~ ~ ~

"You know what I'm not going to miss? Football practice with Coach Trenton," Ron chuckled before taking a swig of his Coca Cola. "Hey, now that we've graduated, what's your plan?" he asked Kent.

It was late May and the heat was just getting started in Arizona. The two young men sat under a large mesquite tree on the banks of the Salt River. Several of their friends laughed and splashed in the water. Kent and Ron let the warm breeze dry their skin as they ate sandwiches and drank Coca Cola out of glass bottles. The celebratory picnic included 20 of the 23 senior graduating class from Gilbert High School as well as a few others.

"I'm not too sure yet," Kent admitted. His eyes were on a sprightly brunette chatting with her friend, Velma, who had been in Kent's class. Jane was how she introduced herself. He recognized her from around town.

Ron said, "I was thinking of helping Mr. Tisdale. He says he needs help changing some of his grapefruit trees to lemon trees. Says he'll pay me 75 cents an hour to tape lemon blossoms to the grapefruit blossoms."

Kent nodded and took a bite of his sandwich. When he swallowed, he said, "Yeah, I did that last year. He wanted to change some of those trees to navel orange trees. It's really hard work, especially in the dead of summer before the monsoons hit. Those groves are sweltering without a breeze."

Ron shrugged. "Well, the pay is good, anyway."

"You know, Johnny Bowdon said there was an opening at that new airfield being built. They are looking for people to help construct the runways and what have you. I think I'll give that a try."

"Johnny Bowdon?" Ron asked. "I thought he was going down to South America. He boasted about it enough these last few months."

Kent smirked at Ron's statement. "He still plans on it. I guess the construction company he works for has a contract for part of that highway to connect North and South America. They're sending down volunteers every so often to keep work going on it. Could be that he will leave any day."

Jane cast him a look out of the corner of her eye. He caught her gaze and held it. She smiled at him.

"Well, maybe they will give you his job then," Ron said as he raised his coke in a salute.

Kent clinked his bottle against Ron's. "Here's hoping." They each took a long swig. After finishing his drink, Kent set the empty bottle down and wiped his mouth with the back of his hand.

"Excuse me, I've got to go see about a girl," he told his friend.

Ron chuckled and waved him off.

Kent arrived at the airfield with his old classmate, Johnny Bowdon. Johnny adjusted his hat up and down on his forehead as he explained, "The company is Ashland Construction. I'll introduce you to the man in charge, a fella by the name of Chuck Andrews. He's the one you got to impress if you want a job."

The two walked briskly past the squadrons of soldiers marching and through some of the hangers where airplanes rested under the shade. Kent stared at the planes with wide eyes. They were so big on the ground compared to when they were in the sky.

All too soon the majestic machines were out of sight. Kent and Johnny stood before a rather rotund man with a cigar in his mouth.

"Mr. Andrews, sir, this is the fella I told you about. Kent Tone. Kent, this is Mr. Andrews."

The man squinted in the morning light at the tall, lanky redhead before him. He held out his hand and Kent accepted it with a firm grip. "Nice to meet you. Johnny here says you are looking for employment. Is that so?"

"Yes, sir. That's so."

"You live close by, Kent?" Chuck asked all the while sizing the boy up through his squinted gaze.

"Yes, sir. Not five miles away. My family owns a farm off of Higley and Baseline."

"Farm boy, hmm? You quick on your feet?"

Kent cast a confused glance at Johnny before responding, "I suppose I am."

"Good," Chuck rumbled. "We're in need of a stake puncher. What he does is run ahead of the grader machine. You know what a grader is?"

"It is the machine that levels out the ground so a foundation can be built."

"That's right. We're laying the foundation for the runways. Your job is to run ahead of the machine and clear off the blue pegs so that the grader operator can see them. Think that's something in your wheelhouse?"

The young man smiled widely. "Sure, I can do that. It sounds easy enough."

"You'll have to go sign up with the labor union in Phoenix. Their dues are 25 dollars. I can't hire you unless you go through them. I'll expect you to report the day after tomorrow ready to work."

Chuck turned around, obviously done with the conversation.

"Thank you, Mr. Andrews. I do have one question. What can I expect in pay?"

The large man puffed on his cigar and swiveled back around. After a long moment of consideration, he answered from around the cigar, "The standard rate is a dollar and a quarter an hour. Is that sufficient?"

Kent's eyes went wide. "Yes, sir! Why that'd be just fine!"

Chuck plucked the cigar from his mouth. "I'll see you Wednesday morning at six o'clock then. Johnny, you'd better report to Larry."

"Sure thing." Johnny clapped his friend heartily on the back. "Congratulations!"

Still a bit in shock, shook Chuck's thick hand gratefully. "Thank you, Mr. Andrews. I will see you first thing on Wednesday."

All the way home, he couldn't keep the grin from his face. A dollar and a quarter an hour was more than he'd ever made before. He'd be rich! All that was left was the small matter of the labor union. Twenty-five dollars was much more than he had squirreled away in savings.

"I'll have to ask Dad," Kent reasoned out loud. "If I'm making a dollar and a quarter an hour, then I can pay him back in no time."

It wasn't long before Kent arrived back home. Once he put away his riding gear and stabled his horse, he went to find his father.

Albert was in the hay barn, shifting the bales left over from the last harvest to make room for the coming crop.

"Hello, Dad," Kent said and immediately began to help move the bales.

"Back from the airfield, are you?"

Kent nodded. "Yes, just a few moments ago."

Albert paused, waiting for his son to continue.

Setting the bale in his hands squarely on the new stack, Kent said, "Mr. Andrews expects me back on Wednesday morning and he'll pay me a dollar and a quarter an hour."

His father smiled at the news. In that instant, they looked almost identical except for the signs of age gracing Albert's face. "Congratulations, my boy."

"Before I can start working, I have to sign on with the labor union."

"The labor union?" Albert echoed. "Why is that?"

"Mr. Andrews said he couldn't hire me until I had signed on with them. Their dues are a lot though."

"How much?"

"Twenty-five dollars." The answer hung between them. The sun beams highlighted the dust in the air.

Albert coughed and lifted another hay bale.

"Can I borrow the money? I'll pay you back with interest after a couple of weeks of working."

When the hay bale was placed, Albert told his eldest son, "Of course. I'll give it to you after supper tonight."

"Thanks, Dad," Kent said and continued moving the hay. Only a few bales were left. "Oh, and can I borrow the car to go into Phoenix tomorrow?"

Albert answered, "I don't see why not."

Early the next morning, Kent took the Buick and drove 30 miles to the union headquarters on Jefferson St. in Phoenix. He parked the old, hulking vehicle and made his way into the tall brick building through a thick wooden door.

It was dark inside and full of cigar smoke. The lights were electric, but they were dimmer than candle light. Kent's footsteps echoed off of the wooden floor against the tall, bare walls. On the other side of the expansive room was a counter with a glass window and a hole cut out of it. Behind that glass sat a balding middle aged man with thick spectacles perched on his hooked nose.

"Hello," Kent greeted the man through the dim haze. "I'm here to join the union."

The man blinked. "Alright, Sonny. You know to join, you must pay yearly dues."

Resisting annoyance at being called Sonny, Kent said, "Yes sir. I have that right here." He dug into his pocket for his billfold and withdrew the cash his father had loaned him.

The man held out a form and a pen. "Please fill this out and I will process your payment."

Kent took the pen and began detailing his information on the form. When he finished, he signed the bottom with a flourish and presented it along with the money to the balding man.

"Thank you," he responded in a bored tone. "Congratulations, you are now part of the Phoenix Labor Union."

"That means I can go to work?"

The man didn't even look up as he responded. "Report here tomorrow morning at seven o'clock and we will send you to where we need you to go."

Kent's brows furrowed. "Wait a minute. I've already got a job out at Williams Field."

The clerk shook his head. "If you're part of the union, then you have to come here and we will send you to the jobs we want you at."

Kent crossed his arms over his chest as he got his argument ready. "I live a good 30 miles east of here. If I come here for work, you're liable to send me clear over to the West Valley, maybe even Luke Airfield."

Unaccustomed to this amount of protesting from a new member the short man folded his hands carefully on the desk. "Yes, that's right. We just might send you to Luke Airfield."

Kent's arms fell to his sides and he told the clerk in an elevated voice, "I don't want that! I've already got me a job not five miles from home. Why would I come all the way here just to be sent all over tarnation if I've got a job so close to home? It just doesn't make any sense."

The clerk forced himself to stay calm. "Can't help you with that. If you belong to the union, the union will send you where it needs you."

"Hogwash," Kent swore. "We'll just see what Chuck Andrews has to say about this. He was the one who told me to come here in the first place!"

The young man left the union hall without so much as a backwards glance. All 30 miles back to the east side of town, he mulled over the situation. "I'll just have to tell Chuck what happened," he reasoned to himself. "Maybe he'll give me a job without being part of that union."

Instead of turning down the dirt road that would take him back to the ranch, Kent continued on to the airfield, intent on explaining what happened at the union hall. He just hoped that he could somehow keep that job without driving all the way to Phoenix every day.

Chuck was overseeing men on tractors at the farthest outreach of the airfield. Kent approached him and had to shout over the machines to be heard.

"Mr. Andrews! Mr. Andrews, sir! Can I talk to you for a moment, please?"

The large man's ever present cigar bobbed up and down in answer. Roughly, he motioned for Kent to follow him and together they walked away from the machines to an area that would allow more of a conversation than a shouting match.

"What do you want, kid? You aren't supposed to be here until tomorrow."

"I know. It's just that I did what you said; I went to the labor union in Phoenix. Did you know they want me to go back tomorrow so they can send me out on a different job? I told them that you had a job for me right here. But the man said that's not how the union works. Mr. Andrews, I can't drive 30 miles just to be sent wherever in tarnation they feel like sending me."

Chuck frowned around his cigar. "Those sons of bitches. Let me make a few calls and see what in the hell they're trying to pull. Wait here, Kent." He left the boy standing at the edge of a field as he waddled off to make his calls.

Kent waited. He was about to give up and go home when Chuck came back.

"I think they are all sorted out," he told Kent when he was near enough. "Don't bother going all the way to Phoenix tomorrow. Just come here and we'll put you to work." He stuck out his hand.

Kent took it and said earnestly, "Thank you, Mr. Andrews. I appreciate it. I will be here first thing in the morning."

Chuck grunted and nodded before heading back to his men.

True to his word, Kent arrived at Williams Field at six o'clock as instructed.

He met Chuck and his new team where all of the heavy machinery was parked. The group of men huddled in the center, surrounded by hulking yellow metal and larger than life tires.

"Good morning," Kent greeted everyone cheerfully.

"Morning," Chuck replied. "Fellas, this is our new Dandy Hander, Kent. Tommy, you ought to show him the ropes today."

A thin man of about 45 years gave a nod as he sized up the new guy.

"Alright then. You all have your assignments. Let's get to it."

The group of men dispersed into teams, chatting amicably with each other. Tommy approached Kent and adjusted his dirt smeared, crumpled, straw cowboy hat on the way.

"Hi Tommy. It's nice to meet you," Kent said and stuck out his hand.

Tommy gave a lopsided grin and shook Kent's proffered hand with a tight grip. "Good to meet you too. C'mon. I'll give you a ride over to runway two. That's where you and I are starting."

He climbed into the small cab of a machine with an elongated spider-like front supported by two offset wheels. On the bottom front of the cab was a long metal scraper that reminded Kent of a straight edge razor. The young man hoisted himself up onto the machine as Tommy started the engine. The ride was loud and smelled of exhaust. With the crawling pace of the machine, it took a good 10 minutes to get to the starting point of runway two.

Tommy parked the machine and killed the ignition. Gesturing for Kent's attention, he pointed to the uneven field of dirt piles in front of them.

"That is what we have to tame. They just finished pulling out all of the shrubs and mesquite trees and clearing all the rocks. Now there's nothing but good, wholesome dirt. Our job is to smooth all of this out and compact it so the concrete guys can come in here and pour. You follow?"

"Sure do," Kent nodded.

Pleased, Tommy continued. "Now, you see all those little flags waving in the breeze? Under those flags are blue pegs. Those are the markers that tell us where to level. Your job is to run ahead of me and pull the flags out of the pegs and make sure they aren't covered in dirt. I gotta go over them, see. You make sure I go over them pegs. When this thing is clear, put the flags back in where the pegs are. When you are done with that, you gotta run ahead of me and start the process all over again." He paused and eyed the young man. "You sure you're quick enough? I ain't gonna stop this machine and wait for you."

Kent assured Tommy as only an 18 year old could in the face of someone doubting his abilities. "Don't you worry about that. I'll be quick enough. You just tell me when to get started."

Tommy chuckled at the young man's bravado. "Alright then. Let's go. We'll do the ones on the right first." He turned the key and the engine roared to life. Recognizing his cue, Kent jumped off and ran to the first flag.

Over the next six months Kent certainly earned his dollar twenty-five an hour. It took him a few weeks to get used to running so much; he estimated he ran about twenty five miles a day with all the back and forth on the mile and a quarter runway. He and Tommy became good friends.

Kent only saw Johnny every so often. He was on the concrete crew so he and Kent didn't have a lot of time together. One bright morning, Johnny approached Kent as he headed into work.

"Did you hear?" Johnny asked.

"Hear what?" Kent asked a he sipped his morning coffee.

Johnny's excitement showed in the bounce of his walk. "Right now they're recruiting mechanics into the Army. They need fellas to work on those planes they're training their flyboys on. Word is that if you sign up then you don't have to be shipped out to war; you can stay right here in Arizona."

"Is that right?" Kent asked. The more he thought about it, the better the idea sounded. Besides, he'd done a fair amount of mechanic work on the farm. When the tractors broke down, it was he and his dad that had fixed them up again. Kent knew his way around an engine because of it.

"If you go to the front office of the airfield, they are signing people up."

"I'll think about it," Kent hedged. The thought of flying those planes excited him. He'd been fascinated with flying ever since he was a kid. Being so close to the planes as they worked on the runways had only rekindled that fascination. Now he might have a chance to fly one? It was mighty tempting.

"Well don't take too long. They might be full up by the time you decide." Johnny laughed and went along his way, leaving Kent deep in thought.

By the time he reached the spot where Tommy ran the grader, he had made up his mind to at least see what the Army was about.

"Hey there," Tommy called from the cab of the machine. He turned it off and gestured for Kent to come up with him. "You ain't gotta run today so why don't you sit up here with me."

Giving a distracted smile, Kent climbed up.

"What's with the long face?"

"Just thinking. Did you know they are signing people up for the Army? If you sign on you can stay right here and not go overseas to war."

Tommy grunted. "I think your friend is trying to rattle your cage. You aren't thinking of signing up, are you?"

Kent shrugged. "What if I am?"

"You don't want to do that," Tommy said, shaking his head.

"Why not? It's better than being drafted. This way I'd have a say in what branch I'd go into. Plus, if I stay right here in Arizona, all the better. I'd still be close enough to help my folks out with the ranch if they needed it."

"If it's the draft you're worried about, that's easy to get out of. You know we are almost done here. After this, we are due to go down and work on that Pan American Highway starting in Venezuela. We could go all the way down to Argentina. Why don't you come with us? I'll teach you how to run a grader and you can make a decent amount of money. It would be a lot more lucrative than joining the military anyway."

Kent thought about that for a moment. "Weren't Bill and Luis saying something the other day about being in South America? Didn't they say the natives hide in the jungle and shoot poison darts at the construction crews?"

Tommy coughed, but couldn't deny it. "I suppose the natives get restless, but it's a question of poison darts or bombs. Doesn't matter where you go; this whole world is dangerous right now."

"That's true, but I can say for sure I don't want nothing to do with poison darts in some jungle. Thanks anyway, Tommy, but I am going to sign up for the Army. I'll let Chuck know I'm quitting today."

Tommy sighed. "I wish you the best of luck then. If you change your mind, you know how to get ahold of me."

True to his word, after his shift ended, Kent went straight to the administration office to sign up for the Army Air Corps.

"Yes," the man assured him. "If you're mechanically inclined we will put you in the Air Corps and you'll be trained on production line maintenance to keep these training planes going for the new cadets."

"That's just fine for me," Kent agreed and signed the forms.

"Be back here in two days for the swearing in ceremony."

"Yes, sir." Kent took his copies of the forms and went home. He was elated and he couldn't wait to tell his family. This was the life. He was going to help his country without even leaving home.

That night, he told his family his decision over dinner. "Dad, Mother, I quit my job at Ashland Construction," he proclaimed as his mother placed the roast upon the table.

Albert and Eva exchanged surprised glances before Albert asked, "What do you mean you quit?"

"Just what I said. I told Mr. Andrews I won't be showing up tomorrow."

Eva took her seat at the table as Albert folded

his hands in front of him.

"Why on earth would you give up a perfectly good job like that?" His voice was deep with confusion. "You were getting paid damn good money."

Kent couldn't keep the grin from his face. "Yes, I was, but I thought you'd be more proud of me if I served my country so I joined the Army."

Whatever reaction Kent expected, it wasn't the prolonged silence that overtook the dining room.

His younger brother, Klove, was the first to voice the question that hung in the air. "Why did you do that?"

Kent gave a shrug of his shoulders, the wind taken out of his sails by his family's chilly reaction. "Well, they were accepting mechanically inclined men to join up to work at the airfield. They need people to keep those training airplanes in working order. Everyone knows that a draft is coming and I didn't want the government to decide which branch of the military I was going to. No sir, I wanted to make that decision myself. It was that or go down to South America with the construction company and work on building roads. I thought serving my country was the nobler choice."

Albert rose to his feet, his tall frame angling out of his chair. As he approached his oldest son, his expression was blank. Unsure of what was happening, Kent also got out of his seat. He'd just set his napkin on the table when his father extended his hand. Kent took it. Albert's grip was firm.

Solemnly, Albert looked Kent in the eye and said, "I am proud of you, Son."

Eva stood as well and went to embrace him. "I'm proud of you too. Will they really keep you here in town?"

"As far as I know. They need mechanics pretty bad at the airfield. I'll get more information after they swear me in."

Klove remained in his seat. "When I go into the military, I'm going into the Navy. None of this Army business."

Kent laughed at his brother. "That's if the Navy would even take you. You're too scrawny."

When Kent returned to Williams Airfield, the flagpole had just been erected on the front lawn. A flag filled with stars and stripes fluttered in the breeze as Kent and a handful of other men from around town gathered to be sworn into the Army by Colonel Martin.

The Colonel stood calmly in front of the flagpole, facing the line of new recruits standing at attention. His uniform was neatly pressed and the medals on his chest reflected the morning sun. Colonel Martin eyed the new recruits. He thought, *best to get straight to business before it started heating up.*

"Gentlemen, you are all here to swear an oath that will bind you to the United States Army. Raise your right hand and repeat after me. I, state your full name, do solemnly affirm," he paused, waiting for the recruits to echo back his words. When they had, he continued, waiting every few words or so for them to repeat back. "That I will support the constitution of the United States. I, swear to bear true allegiance to the United States of America, and to serve them honestly and faithfully, against all their enemies or opposers whatsoever, and to observe and obey the orders of the President of the United States of America, and the orders of the officers appointed over me, so help me God."

When the ringing of voices faded into the morning, the colonel allowed a brief smile. "Congratulations, gentlemen. You are now part of the United States Army. You'll be put on a train to Ft. MacArthur for your physical examinations, shots, and your uniforms. Please go on inside and sign your papers."

Together, the men trooped into the tan brick building. Kent felt a thrill of excitement mingled with dread. He wasn't expecting to go to Ft. MacArthur. He thought he would stay at Williams and work on the planes.

When he reached the office to sign the papers, the dread inside at the prospect of leaving Arizona overrode the excitement. What would he do if they shipped him off to Britain from Ft. MacArthur? He didn't know the first thing about being a soldier. He'd signed on to maintain the training planes!

"What have I gotten myself into?" he muttered under his breath.

"Excuse me?" the man collecting the paperwork asked. "Did you say something?"

Blinking, Kent fumbled for how to respond. "Say, do you know where Ft. MacArthur is? I don't think I am familiar."

"It's in California, near San Pedro." As if seeing the apprehension in the young man's eyes, the man added, "Don't worry. You'll come straight back after you've finished your checkup. You won't be shipped off quite yet. Here's your ticket. Be at the train station at two o'clock tomorrow afternoon."

Kent spent a week at Ft. MacArthur just to do his physical and get properly immunized. By the time the week was up, he was eager to leave behind the ocean air and tall chain link fences that made him feel like he was in prison. The Army did indeed send him back to Williams Airfield in Mesa. There wasn't any basic training or boot camp. After getting assigned to the barracks on the field, he started working on the AT-9s and the AT-11s that the advanced class of cadets trained on. Kent learned how to repair the wing coverings that were called skins, and maintain and fix the cables that controlled the ailerons and ruddervators.

He loved the military life. Though he was only a few miles away from home, he returned to the ranch only a few times in a month, choosing instead to go see the Clark Gable movies with his newfound friends.

The only part he hated about his new life was that every so often he would have to do kitchen patrol, or KP duty. He detested old Sergeant Walton who oversaw the men in KP. Nothing Kent did was ever good enough for the old coot. He had to scrub the floors and then wash them over again with vinegar. Old Walton said it was to keep the germs away but Kent thought it was a load of hogwash. Even after vigorously washing his hands after KP duty, he couldn't quite get the smell of vinegar out of his fingertips.

One of the trainers had an idea to take some of the mechanics down to the range for a gunnery lesson and target practice.

"Come on, you nut busters!" A lieutenant shouted at the production line. "Let's get you out to the range and see what you can do with a gun!"

The voice sounded familiar to Kent. He peered over to get a good look at the officer. In surprised recognition, Kent croaked out, "Coach Trenton?"

The man turned. When he saw who called him, a smile spread upon his broad face. "Kent Tone? Is that you? Why, I didn't know you enlisted."

Grinning, Kent jumped down from the wing of an AT-6 where he'd been perched and approached his high school football coach. "I didn't know you had either." The two shook hands amicably.

"Come on then, Tone. Let's see what you've got down at the range. You can't spend your whole military career without shooting a gun. It's un-American!"

Laughing, Kent and his fellow mechanics trooped down to the range with Lieutenant Trenton.

At the range, Kent stood in line for his first chance at a Thompson submachine gun. A sharp rapport echoed and the acrid smell of gun powder filled the air from the other enlisted men practicing their aim. At last, it was his turn.

Lieutenant Trenton waved him forward. "Alright, Tone. You're up." He handed Kent the machine gun, careful to keep the barrel downrange. "She's got a bit of a kick, so don't be discouraged" he warned as he stepped back.

Hoisting the gun up, Kent squinted down the sight, exhaled and squeezed the trigger. A spray of shells peppered the air around him. Bullets ripped through the paper target midway down the range. After what seemed like ages, Kent's finger released the trigger and he lowered the weapon.

It was a few more minutes before they could enter the range and get the target for inspection. When they did, the lieutenant couldn't believe what he saw. Almost all of the bullet holes were clustered around the center. Only one or two had strayed outside of the target area.

Trying to mask his amazement, Lieutenant Trenton asked the young mechanic, "Tone, you ever fire a submachine gun before?"

"No, sir. Just a pellet gun on the ranch. Once or twice I had a go with Dad's rifle."

Handing the paper to Kent, the lieutenant said, "You've got one hell of an aim. You've even beat my score — and I'm the instructor!"

Kent blushed. "Beginner's luck," he shrugged.

"Well, luck or not, it would be a shame to squander that talent just sitting here fixing planes. You should really consider becoming a cadet. Get a chance to make a difference in this war."

Kent shrugged again, but the idea turned over a few times in his mind. "Maybe."

After that, Kent watched the flyboys as they paraded around the base. The way they talked about being up in the air, seeing the earth sprawl out below them, made Kent recall all those days as a kid when he'd watch planes go over the ranch. He wanted to fly. Suddenly, repairing planes wasn't enough. He wanted to be a pilot.

One day, after a particularly unfair KP assignment, he decided to do something about being able to fly. He went down to the administration building to see about becoming a cadet.

"Excuse me, I want to take the cadet exam. What do I have to do?"

The man behind the desk raised his eyebrows, but kept his thoughts to himself. He handed Kent a slip of paper. "Here are the testing times. You can't get into the cadets without a passing grade."

Kent's eyes shone in anticipation. "Thank you very much." He ducked out of the building, clutching the piece of paper in his fist.

~ ~ ~

"Did you always want to fly?" I asked, interrupting a short silence where Grandpa had begun to stare off into space.

"What? Did I always want to fly?" He thought about the question. "I suppose I'd always been fascinated with it. When I was a boy, Dad raised Tamworth hogs. They're the type of hog where the really good bacon comes from. He had a 125 head at one time. When he took them to the market he could get 25 to 50 cents more for them because of the quality, you see?" He paused, waiting for me to nod my understanding.

"Well, anyway. One day, Dad asked me to help hold down one of the sows while he did something, I don't remember what. Probably gave her medicine or something of the like." Grandpa brought a gnarled, crooked finger up to his face and scratched at his prominent nose. "Well, there I was, hanging on to the legs of that sow as tight as I could, when a loud engine noise drew my attention away. It was one of those bi-planes with the big propeller in the front. Boy, I let go of that hog so fast and ran to watch that plane fly overhead. I remember thinking to myself how wonderful it would feel to be up there in that plane, as free as a bird."

"Wait, you just left your Dad there to deal with a sow all by himself? Did you get into trouble for that?"

Grandpa burst into a fit of chuckles. "Oh, I caught hell. Dad wasn't too pleased with me. I would have done it again, though. Those airplanes just fascinated me."

At that precise moment, Grandma fell into a coughing fit. The once open, eased expression on Grandpa's face disappeared. His brow furrowed and the smile fell from his lips. "Turn it off," he said roughly, dropping the mic. He turned his attention to Grandma, to see her through the violent cough.

I did as he said, glad that he was distracted for a little while at least. I'd try again later. Perhaps when Grandma took a nap.

PART THREE
GROWING UP

It was quickly apparent that the camera made Grandpa nervous. When he knew the record button was on, he wasn't as forthcoming with his tales. I or Grandma would have to prod and coax him into giving us the stories we knew he was capable of telling.

When the camera was off, however, we had difficulty keeping up with all of his stories and anecdotes.

On the last day of my week-long visit, I decided to try a new tactic. After breakfast, I said, "I've got to go into town. Grandpa, want to come with me?"

He glanced up at me from over his mug of tea. "What, you got some rat killing to do?"

"What?" The question caught me off guard. "No, I'm not going to kill anything. I just have some errands to run."

Grandpa chuckled. "You never heard that expression before? Rat killing?"

Confused, I shook my head.

"It means you've got some errands to do."

"Oh. Then yeah, I guess I do have some rat killing to do. Want to come with me?"

He cast a worried glance at Grandma.

She waved him off. "I'll be fine, Kent. Go on. You're driving me crazy."

At his doubtful expression, I promised, "We won't be gone long."

Begrudgingly, he agreed and together, we left the house.

"Why do you call errands rat killing?" I asked as we maneuvered through traffic.

"I still can't believe you've never heard that before," Grandpa laughed to himself. "It's an old saying I learned when I was a boy. You see, we had a lot of ranch hands who migrated west to escape the Dust Bowl. Those people taught me a lot of their phrases and they just stuck with me, I guess."

"That's why you have somewhat of an accent."

"Yes, that's right." He looked around at the passing landscape. "Where are we going?"

"You'll see. We are almost there."

He stared out the window. "Look, do you see that building there? That used to be a hospital. My children were born there." He paused, watching the buildings pass by. When he saw another landmark, he pointed. "That squat looking building was Goldwater's Department Store. My mother worked there in the basement making ladies hats with ostrich feathers. She used to watch Barry Goldwater when he was a toddler. They used to let him run about while she worked. You know who Barry Goldwater was, don't you?"

I frowned, wondering why the name sounded so familiar. "Wasn't he a senator?"

"Yes, he was a senator and he ran for president in the 60's."

We drove another 15 minutes before my original destination came into view. "Alright, here we are." I pulled into a fairly new middle class subdivision. The brick sign at the entrance proclaimed the houses within to be part of the Tone Estates.

"Well I'll be damned," Grandpa muttered.

"Do you know where we are?"

"This is where the ranch used to be. A lot has changed." He peered around at the stately new homes.

I parked the truck and asked, "What was it like growing up here in the 20's?"

"About as you would expect, I guess. None of this was here; all of this was farm land. My family owned 160 acres. I loved the ranch. There was always something new and interesting going on.

"Oh? Like what?"

Grandpa settled more into the passenger seat and I recognized the coming of a story. "In the fall and the winter, a lot of relatives would come down to visit from the Midwest. My aunts and uncles, mostly. One time, we had Uncle Donald and his friend Ed visit from Ohio and Aunt Oie and her husband Harry in from California. Mother was excited to have both of her siblings visit at once. I'll never forget that fall for as long as I live."

"Why is that?"

He glanced over at me, a mischievous glint

in his eye. "You wouldn't believe it, but I used to be somewhat of a trouble maker in my youth. That fall I got into a whole lot of trouble."

~ ~ ~

The family home was a large stone affair with a wooden shingle roof. A couple of lone mesquite trees lent sparse shade over the parked black 1929 Buick. Around the back of the house were the showers — some stalls made from corrugated steel on a flat of concrete — and the outhouse. The chicken coops rested on the left side of the house near the clotheslines full of linens flapping in the slight breeze. Dozens of chickens pecked at the dirt and squawked as Kent approached.

The smell of fried eggs wafted through the open windows of the home.

Kent opened the front door only to be greeted by a sharp rebuke from his mother. "Boots off! I don't need you tracking dirt in here when I just cleaned these floors."

Knowing better than to argue, Kent took off his boots and left them by the door. His brother Klove already sat at the breakfast table, scarfing down his fried egg and toast with gusto.

"Did you finish your chores?" His mother asked as she swept strands of her graying red hair behind her ear. Eva was in her mid-40's and of Welsh descent. Though life on an Arizona farm had left an indelible mark upon her, she remained a proud and resourceful woman. That morning, she stood by the sink with a basket of fresh eggs. One by one, she held each of them up to the window, scrutinizing it against the early morning light for any cracks. If there were any defects, she wouldn't be able to get her asking price from the local grocer.

"Yes, Mother" Kent said as he took his place at the table. He helped himself to an egg and a piece of toast. From a metal pitcher, he poured a glass of fresh milk to wash it all down with.

"Oie and Harry should be here by the time you are back from school."

Both of the boys nodded, their big, blue eyes earnest. She couldn't help but smile at them. "Finish your breakfast and go get washed up. The bus will be here soon and I've got to get these eggs down to the market."

After washing their faces, the boys gathered their school books before heading out the door. The bus stop was about an eighth of a mile away from the ranch house. To get to the stop, the two boys followed the weathered and uneven mesquite fence posts that bordered their property.

"I can't wait until Uncle Donald gets here," Klove said, making conversation during the short walk. "He's supposed to bring his friend Ed with him. Mother says, Ed's never been to Arizona before."

"Is that right? That should be some fun," Kent grinned.

Just then an old 1920's motor coach that served as the school bus rumbled down the dirt road and came to a halt a few feet from where the brothers stood. Kent and Klove climbed on and found their way to an empty wooden bench in the middle of the bus. A few of the other kids said hello as they passed by. The bus shuddered into motion, creaking as though it would fall apart at any moment. Kent watched the passing fields on the way to school, dreading the hours that lay ahead.

The school day passed with agonizing slowness. It seemed that the end of class couldn't come quick enough. At last, he was on the bus back home. Almost before the bus stopped, he jumped out of his seat and climbed out. Hitting the dusty road, he broke into a run, leaving his brother behind in his excitement to see what had happened while he'd been gone.

He spotted Andersen, the resident farmhand in the cotton field along with half a dozen hired men from all over the country plucking the sticky blossoms by hand.

"Hello, Andersen!" he shouted, coming up the row at the older man.

Andersen was tall, like Kent's father. However, instead of blonde and blue eyed, he had thick, dark curly hair with a matching beard. When he smiled, his light brown eyes were lost behind the apples of his cheeks. He had a thin build, but years of farm work had earned him strong muscles. Andersen had been living on the ranch for the last few years in his own little shack between the cotton field and the alfalfa field, not far from the guest houses and the cow pasture.

"Hello, Kent. Back from school already? Golly! The time just flies by, don't it?"

"Anything happen today?" Kent asked, grinning at the farmhand.

The man put his hand to his chin as if in deep

thought. "Now let me see. Something did happen, as a matter of fact. Your Aunt Oie and Uncle Harry arrived around mid-day. They got situated in one of the guest houses. I think they are at the ranch house with your Ma right now. Your Pa is waiting on you to come back so you'll go with him to do some rat killin' in town."

"Thanks, Andersen. I'll see you later." The boy ran towards the house, eager to see what sort of business his dad was up to.

As he approached his home, he saw a brand new 1934 Oldsmobile parked next to his father's dinged up Buick. He took a moment to appreciate the sleek lines, the shiny paint, and the sheer newness of the vehicle. What it would be like to ride in it?

"Hello, Mother," Kent said when he came in the door. He took a step inside and then remembered to take off his dust coated boots. After depositing them on the porch he entered the house in only his socks.

"Come in and say hello," Eva called from the kitchen.

Kent turned the corner to find Aunt Oie and Uncle Harry sitting at the kitchen table. A plate of sandwiches and cakes as well as hot coffee in delicate china cups had been laid out before them. Eva pulled out all the stops when family came to town. It was as if she wanted to prove that Gilbert, Arizona had as much class and sophistication as the big cites did.

"Where's your brother?" Eva inquired.

"He's coming. I ran ahead of him when we got off the bus." He made his way around the table. "Hello, Aunt Oie," he said as he gave the woman a hug. Aunt Oie was a large woman— maybe a good 300 or 350 pounds.

"Look at how much you have grown! Eva, he is going to be tall, like his father and just as handsome!" Oie enveloped Kent in a warm embrace.

Though her long, black hair was pinned up, Kent saw the telltale white hand prints that Aunt Oie invariably had after she visited the outhouse. Somehow she tended to get the lye powder that would be sprinkled into the outhouse hole all over her hands. As there was no mirror anywhere near the outhouse, when she primped her hair she left streaks of the powder all over her person. The sight of it always made Kent giggle and he fought to keep it in. His mother wouldn't approve of him making fun of their guests.

When Oie finally let him go, he turned to Harry. He was a thin man with an impressive salt and pepper moustache that matched the hair on his head. Harry was a lawyer, and a fairly successful one at that.

"Whose Oldsmobile is outside?" Kent asked.

Harry said, "That's ours. We just got her a few months ago. We didn't want to intrude so much on Albert's hospitality."

"It wouldn't have been an intrusion at all," Eva said, though Kent noticed the relief in her eyes. If they were without a car for a day or even two, it could prove to be disastrous; she had to get her eggs to market as smoothly as possible to minimize any breaks. While the car wasn't the smoothest ride, it was compared to horseback or wagon. Without the car, they would lose money in a time when money was very tight.

"Kent, are you in here?" Albert's deep voice called from the front door.

"In the kitchen," Eva answered.

Kent's father strode into the kitchen and greeted the women sitting around the table. Both Kent and his mother noticed that he hadn't bothered to take off his boots. Eva frowned, but didn't say anything.

"C'mon, Kent. We are going into town."

"To do some rat killing?" the boy asked.

This earned him a wry smile from his father. "Something like that." Looking at his wife, Albert said, "We will be home in time for supper. Klove is out feeding the horses."

Nodding, Eva stood to give him a kiss on the cheek. She did the same to Kent and told him, "Mind your father."

Kent followed his dad out to the car, grabbing his boots along the way.

"Did you see the car Uncle Harry bought?" He asked as he stared at the Oldsmobile with envy. "It's mighty neat."

Albert nodded, "It does look nice." The two of them got into the old car. Kent stared at the Oldsmobile with longing even as the Buick roared to life and a gust of smoke blew out of the tail pipe. The tires crunched the gravel of the drive way until they tuned onto the old dirt path that led out of the ranch and towards Baseline Road which would take them into town.

"Think we could get a car like that?"

"What for? We have a perfectly good car," Albert replied, patting the dash of the Buick affectionately.

Kent made a face. "It's ugly. I hate this car."

Albert shook his head. "Hate it all you want, boy. This is the car we have and it is a damn good one. Bought it new in '29. It's done a fine job for us."

The ride to downtown Mesa took about 30 minutes. The afternoon sunlight warmed Kent's face. The large, puffy white clouds from that morning had blown away, leaving a clear and bright blue sky.

Before long, they arrived in what Kent considered to be one of the biggest cities he had ever seen, rivaled only by the nearby Phoenix. They parked in an empty spot in the middle of Center Street. The parking spaces separated the north and south bound traffic. Buildings lined the road on either side, tall grand brick affairs with thickly painted signs and inviting shop displays in windows close to the sidewalks.

As Albert turned off the car, he looked at his son. "Here," he said and handed him a nickel. "Why don't you get some hard candy for you and your brother at the general store? Afterwards, come back here and wait for me. I won't be long."

Kent accepted the shiny nickel with excitement. It wasn't often his dad gave him money for candy.

The two parted ways; Albert headed towards OS Stapley and Kent towards the general store. Passing by the Nile Theater, Kent paused to see what pictures were playing. *Wild Boys of the Road* looked interesting, but that was about it. Besides, he didn't have nearly enough to see a picture; one ticket cost 15 cents and he only had a nickel. He doubted his father would give him another 10 cents, so Kent continued on his mission.

It didn't take long to get to the general store, only a few minutes of walking. There, Kent had his choice of hard candies, caramels, or peppermint sticks at a penny a piece. He got two peppermint sticks and two caramels, deciding to save the last penny for a rainy day. Once his purchase had been made, he walked back to where his father had parked.

Kent waited in the car. It felt like hours since his dad had left to run those errands. Out of boredom, he searched through the car for something to do. In the side of one of the doors was a lump of chalk. An idea blossomed in his head. With a wide grin and chalk in hand, he exited the car. In his messy 11 year old handwriting, he scrawled on the side of the passenger door "For Sale $10".

Satisfied with his work, Kent settled down on the foot board and waited. He imagined what he would do with all that money. He could almost taste the candy he could buy and see the picture shows he could go to. Even, he dared to dream, get an Oldsmobile, like the one Aunt Alice had rented.

So wrapped up in his daydreams, Kent didn't notice a man appraising the car until he spoke.

"Excuse me," said the short fellow in a business suit and a straw hat. He carried a briefcase, the kind Kent always imagined his lawyer uncles would carry — richly oiled leather and accented with shiny brass clasps. "Is this car for sale?"

Kent eyed the man speculatively before answering, "Why, yes sir it is. Ten dollars and she's yours."

The man was tempted, but wasn't quite

convinced. "Where's your father?"

"He's running errands. He'll be back soon."

The older man thought about it for a moment, scratching his bald head under the straw hat. "Alright then, I will wait for him. This is really quite a deal."

Kent shrugged nonchalantly, but inside he was panicking. What had he been thinking? His father would not be too keen on the idea of selling the car. Even if they did get a whopping 10 dollars, Kent wouldn't see any of it.

The man settled down next to Kent to wait, perching his briefcase on his knees.

Before the boy could figure out an excuse to get the man to go away, Albert came striding out from one of the buildings, a large paper bag in his arm.

Kent leapt up and stood to hide his chalk sign with his body. The man noticed Kent's sudden movement and looked over to see what had startled the boy.

"Is that your father?" he asked, nodding at Albert.

"Yes," Kent said. Then, a little louder, he called out, "Hey, Dad."

The man stood up and smiled, "Hello, sir. Is this car for sale for 10 dollars?"

Albert approached in confusion. "What?"

Gesturing to the Buick, the man said, "This car. The sign said it was for sale for 10 dollars."

"What sign?"

Sheepishly, Kent stepped to the side so his father could see what he had done.

The confusion left Albert's face when he saw

what had been written on the car door. His pale face flushed red and his voice turned low and harsh. "No, the car is certainly not for sale for 10 dollars. I'm sorry my son mislead you," Albert said, not once taking his eyes off of Kent. The boy squirmed under the scrutiny.

The man chuckled a bit, trying to ease the tension. "Well, no harm done. Thank you for your time, sir." He went about his way, giving a little wave at Kent as he left.

"What is this?" Albert demanded.

"I thought if I sold the car, we could get an Oldsmobile."

"Not for 10 dollars, we can't!" After tossing the paper bag in the back of the car, Albert told his son, "Wipe those chicken scratches off of my car and get in. We are going home."

The ride was tense and quiet. Kent knew better than to say anything while his father was mad at him. They pulled up to the ranch only to notice a commotion around the outhouse. Several of the hired men along with Eva, and Klove stood by. Even over the rumble of the Buick, they could hear shouts of distress came from inside the clapboard structure.

"Oh hell," Albert muttered as he parked. "What now?"

Hastily, he and Kent got out of the car and rushed over to see what happened. Albert went directly to the outhouse where Andersen stood halfway inside.

Kent trotted up to his brother who laughed uncontrollably a little ways away from the rest of the group.

"What happened?"

Klove could barely get the news out around peals of laughter. "Aunt Oie — ha ha ha! She. . . She fell through the floor in the —ha ha! The outhouse! They're trying — ha ha — to figure out how . . . how to get her out of all the crap!"

The laughter was contagious and, once the situation sunk in, Kent couldn't help but giggle as well. "That must be a sight!" He craned his neck to see, but his view was blocked by about five men — Andersen, Harry, and Albert among them — who advanced on the outhouse.

It took those five men a good 20 minutes to haul Oie out of the hole. When she was out, Harry escorted Oie back to the guest house where they were staying.

They boys rushed over to look at the damage. Squirming through the crowd of men, they gaped at the hole which was easily bigger than the two of them combined.

Albert took charge of the situation. "We've got to get this fixed and fast. There's some extra boards in the barn. Boys, go fetch us some nails and a couple of hammers. We haven't got a lot of time before sunset."

The outhouse was fixed just as the last dregs of light in the vibrant orange sky faded into a dark blue. Stars overtook the night, competing with the few kerosene lanterns that had been lit.

Dinner that evening was a quiet affair, with Oie and Harry taking their meal in the guest house. Eva remained steadfastly silent about the events that afternoon, though Kent noticed her stern glances over the pot roast. His dad must have told her what he did while they were in town. After the meal, Albert pulled his son aside.

"Do you understand what you did wrong today?"

Gulping, Kent answered softly, "Yes, sir."

With a solemn expression, Albert asked, "What do you think should be your punishment?"

Kent hated this question. It was one he got often because of his mischievous nature. "I should be sent to bed early?"

Albert tsked and shook his head. "No, not this time." He opened his hand. "Today was the last time you'll go to town with me for a long while. Now, give me the sweets you bought today."

"What? Why?" Kent's hand instantly went into his pocket to clutch at the candy protectively.

"Why should you get treats for how you acted today? Hand them over."

Reluctantly, Kent pulled out two of the four candies and handed them over.

Albert knew better. "All of them, Son."

Heaving a large sigh, Kent surrendered the rest of the sweets.

"Go on to bed."

The boy obeyed, regretting his bright idea to sell the old junker of a car.

The next day was steeped in routine. The boys got up, and had a breakfast of oatmeal after feeding the animals. The big news of the day was that Eva's brother, Donald, and his friend, Ed Woodland, were due to arrive. The two men had decided to make a road trip down from Canfield, Ohio to Arizona for a visit. Ed had never been to the Southwest and they thought it would be an adventure.

Eva was anxious to see her brother; it had been years since he had been down for a visit. That translated into making sure the house was cleaner than it had been for Aunt Oie's arrival, which Kent didn't think could happen. Eva was so intent on everything being perfect, that the boys were relieved when the bus came to take them to school. Their mother couldn't make them clean if they weren't there.

It was just after lunch time. Kent struggled through his history lesson, wishing the hours would slip quickly by so he could go home; his uncle had have arrived by now. A knock came at the classroom door, breaking the silence. The teacher, a woman a little older than Kent's mother, went to answer.

The person knocking was the secretary from the principal's office. "We need to see Kent Tone, please," she requested in a soft voice. The hushed cadence of her voice did nothing to mask the request; the entire class listened intently. Kent, hearing his name, began to worry. Why would he be called to the principal's office? He hadn't done anything wrong as far as he could tell. At least not that morning.

At his teacher's nod, he stood and moved towards the door.

The secretary added, "Please bring your books."

This request caused more worry for Kent as he tried to figure out what he had done. The rest of the class began whispering, their own imaginations carrying out the worst possible scenario awaiting their classmate.

With his books in hand, Kent followed the secretary to the front office. Waiting on a bench next to the office door was Klove. An equally confused expression on his face.

"You're in trouble too?" Kent asked.

His brother shrugged in response.

The secretary assured them, "Neither of you are in trouble. Someone is here to fetch you."

She opened the door to the school office. Sitting in the stiff wooden chairs on the other side of her desk were two young men. Both were dressed casually in gray slacks and button down shirts, their sleeves rolled up to their elbows.

The shorter one had a black vest and a matching hat that rested in his lap. His wavy auburn hair had been recently combed and slicked back and his chin was clean shaven.

Kent recognized him immediately. "Uncle Donald!" he cried and ran over to give him a big hug.

"Kiddo!" Donald exclaimed. He rose out of his seat and hugged him. "It's mighty fine to see you."

Klove, taking his cues from his older brother ran over to say hello as well.

"Boys, this here is my friend Ed. We were on our way out to the Superstition Mountains. Ed's never seen them before. We thought you two would like to come with us. That is, if you're not missing out on an important lesson." Donald gave a sly wink to the secretary who smiled politely back through thinly veiled annoyance.

At once, the boys responded with loud, "Yes! We want to go with you."

Ed chuckled while Donald held up his hands in surrender. "Alright. Let's go!" He waved at the secretary and followed the young boys out to the small parking lot.

The four piled into Ed's hard top convertible Hudson that sat low to the ground. Kent eyed the monstrosity of a vehicle and pursed his lips tight. This one was almost as bad as his dad's Buick. Ed started the engine and with a deep rumble they were on their way.

"What do you do for a living, Mr. Woodland?" Klove asked when they were clear of the school. His mother taught him to take an interest in people. You could learn a lot by listening to what they had to say.

"I'm a sheet metal man by trade," Ed answered. "My company fashions rain gutters, roofs, automobile parts, and street signs. Anything that's made out of metal, really."

"Is that right?" Kent asked. "Sounds like awful hard work."

"It's not so bad."

"What made you want to come all the way out here? It's a long way from Ohio," Klove inquired.

Ed smiled to himself. "Well, one day I went into Donald's hardware store and he received a letter from his sister, your mother, inviting him out for a visit. He asked if I'd ever been out to the wild country. I hadn't been outside of the state before. So, we decided to have ourselves an adventure. By the looks of this place, it does seem like wild country to me. There's hardly any trees! It's a wonder that you folks can get anything to grow. How do you boys manage out here?"

Sensing the opportunity to get into some mischief, Kent gave a sidelong glance at his brother who grinned in return.

"It's rough alright," Kent said, setting up to spin a yarn. "It gets awful hot in the summer. When it rains, it floods out all the roads. Coyotes come and steal the chickens. They get big too, those coyotes. But the worst, the absolute worst is at night when those Indians come. They ride down from the mountain. If they catch you outside when it gets dark, they'll scalp you right where you stand. They are so quiet and quick, you won't even see them coming."

"Like ghosts," Klove piped up, wanting in on the joke.

Donald and Ed gave each other a nervous glance. "Is that so?"

"Yes, sir. Why just the other week they took off with Billy Ackerson. He's one of the kids from school. All they found was his boot in a patch of jumping cactus."

The group approached the south end of the mountain. Turning off to a rocky dirt road, they started a slow ascent on a trail situated across from the Goldfield Mine. Mesquite trees and dry scrub dotted the pale dirt and rocks leading up to the cliffs. Saguaro cacti, easily taller than Donald and Ed combined, sporadically dotted the countryside. In such a foreign landscape, it was easy to imagine any number of things happening out here in the quiet desert, even Indian attacks.

"Of course, you know those Indians live on this mountain," Kent continued, putting an air of nonchalance into his words.

Donald's head whipped around to look at the boys, barely concealed panic in his eyes. "This mountain? The Superstitions?"

The brothers did their best to look solemn and honest as they nodded.

Turning back around, Donald took a careful look at their surroundings. "Hey, Ed. We might not want to get too close here. Those Indians might get us."

His friend scoffed. "It's fine. I don't think we are in any danger. It's broad daylight. Let's keep going a bit further. Where's your sense of adventure?"

Donald settled into a discomfited silence. After a few moments of traversing very rough road, a mighty thud and a snap startled everyone in the car. Ed hit the brakes and the Hudson skidded to a halt.

"What was that?" Donald asked as he clutched at the dash. "What happened?"

"The oil pressure dropped all of a sudden." Ed said as he opened his door. "Let me check it out."

Donald and the boys got out of the car while Ed crawled underneath.

To keep themselves busy as they waited, Kent and Klove picked up some rocks and started tossing them into the distance.

"Hey, you boys be careful. Stay close now. Your mother would kill me if you got taken by those Indians," Donald called out. He scanned the cliffs anxiously.

"That's true," Kent said. "Those Indians will get us for sure. Our scalps are as good as theirs."

Klove added, "As long as we are off the mountain by sunset, we should be fine."

Uncle Donald cast a horrified look at the horizon where the sun was heading. "Ed, what's wrong with the car?" The urgency in his voice made the two boys grin.

Ed scooted out from underneath the vehicle, his hands blackened with grease and oil. "Looks like a rock punctured an oil line."

"Well, can you fix it?"

Ed shrugged. "I don't know. I don't have any of my tools with me."

"What do we have?" Each of the men turned out their pockets. Ed had some change and Donald had a nail file. Looking in the car, Ed managed to find a pair of pliers. He took those and Donald's nail file and crawled under the car once more.

"Hurry, Ed! That sun is going down a lot faster than we want it to!"

The boys did their best to keep from snickering. They had a couple of hours before the sun completely set. Kent pointed to a small pile of rocks on the side of the trail. "Uncle Donald! I think I saw one of those Apaches! Right there, behind that rock!"

His uncle whirled around only to see nothing.

"They're watching us for sure," Kent added for good measure.

It was a good 20 minutes before Ed finally emerged from underneath the car. Donald spent the entire time peering at their surroundings and jumping at the slightest of sounds. The boys encouraged it by taking turns every so often making noises that would make their uncle twitch.

"That's the best I can do," Ed announced and dusted off his trousers. "Let's put some of that extra oil from the can in the back seat. In a minute or two we will see if I fixed it."

Donald and the boys watched as Ed poured the oil into the tank. He then sat in the driver's seat and turned the ignition. The car roared to life, but Ed wasn't satisfied. Getting out, he laid down on the dirt trail and peered underneath the car for any leaks.

"Well?" Donald asked, anxious to leave the mountain far behind him.

"There's a little bit of a leak, but she should get us back to your sisters. I can get her patched up fully at the house."

"Then let's go. I don't want those Indians to get my scalp."

Everyone piled into the car. The boys barely held their laughter in as Ed sped away from the mountains.

~ ~ ~

"I can't believe that horrible trick you played on Donald and Ed!" I exclaimed. "They really believed that Apaches were going to come down from the mountain and scalp them?"

Grandpa wiped tears of merriment from his eyes. "I still remember how they jumped at the slightest sounds."

I started the truck up again and turned out of the Tone Estates.

Grandpa asked, "Are you hungry?"

"I could eat, why?"

"I've got somewhere I want to show you. Turn left at the light."

After following Grandpa's instructions, we arrived in downtown Gilbert. Grandpa directed me to a red brick building on the right side of the road. The large neon sign attached to the side of the building proclaimed "Joe's BBQ".

"What's this?"

"My father was in a partnership with another fella named Charles. They owned this here shop. Back then it was a garage. Dad did the books and, later on, bought Charles' share. A while ago, Klove and I sold this to the fella that opened this barbeque restaurant. If you look next to the door, there's a little plaque that says the Tone building."

"Really? Let's get some barbeque and you can tell me about this place. It sounds like you have a story or two about it."

Grandpa had already unclasped his seat belt. "You know I broke my hip here when I was six years old."

~ ~ ~

Business had been rough since the market crash of 1929. Albert and Charles often met to discuss the fate of the garage as well as the attached store and restaurant.

Albert parked the Buick in the back of the building. "Don't you pester those mechanics. They've got enough to worry about without you being underfoot."

"Sure, Dad." Kent slid out of the car.

Charles met them at the door. Solemnly, he shook Albert's hand. "Hello there, Albert. Why don't we chat in the office?"

Together the two men went into the back room, talking quietly. On the whole, Kent didn't pay too much attention to grownups when they spoke like that. As the two men closed the door to the office, he looked around. There weren't any mechanics in sight; it must have been lunch time, Kent thought.

He wandered around the large room, eyeing the cars whose motors were halfway torn apart. Spaced equally apart in the concrete floor were four open service pits. Those were where the mechanics could stand underneath a parked car to access things on the undercarriage. The pits were small, but many tools and parts littered the bottoms of them. On a bench along the side of the room he spotted a newspaper. Kent didn't like to read much, but he did like to look at the funnies. He grabbed the paper and flipped through the pages until he came to the page with the comics.

Absorbed in the drawings, he didn't pay attention to where he was going. Suddenly, his left foot missed the concrete floor and he toppled into one of the open service pits. He twisted in midair and landed painfully on a few parts that had been left in the hole.

The landing knocked the air out of the boy and the sudden, intense pain was all he could think about. Later, he had dim memories of his father and Charles along with a few of the mechanics back from lunch fishing him out of the pit. Mostly, though, he remembered the pain.

Albert borrowed one of the Model T's from the shop and gingerly set his son in the back seat. He then drove as fast as he could to the Mesa hospital.

The bouncing Model T along the dirt roads proved too much; Kent passed out from the pain.

When he woke, his mother was next to him. An unfamiliar room surrounded him and he had the most peculiar sensation of being wrapped tight from the waist down.

His first instinct was to move, to break free of whatever confined him, but when he did, sharp pain shot through his leg and up his side.

"Stay still," his mother told him. "You've broken your hip. The doctor says you have to stay in this cast for a while.

In horror, Kent lifted his head to look down at his right leg. Sure enough, a bulky, itchy white cast encased his leg all the way to his hip. To prevent too much pressure on the break, his leg was suspended on a sling attached to a pulley on the ceiling.

"How long do I have to stay like this?" He asked, dreading the answer.

Eva sighed. "Doctor says about six weeks in the hospital. Then you'll have to learn how to walk again, but you should be completely healed. Thankfully it was a clean break."

Devastated, Kent let his head fall back against the pillow. Six weeks away from the ranch. It was too harsh a punishment for such a silly accident.

"What happened?" she asked. "Your father said you fell into one of those mechanic pits?"

Still silently bemoaning his fate, Kent replied tersely. "Yes."

"How did that happen?"

With his eyes closed, he answered, "I was reading a comic strip from the newspaper and not paying attention to where I was going."

Sensing that it wasn't the time to lecture Kent on paying attention to his surroundings, Eva patted his arm instead. "It'll be alright. I'm going to stay here with you until your leg is all healed up."

"What about the ranch? I've got to help Dad with the heifer that's calving. I can't stay in this place when we've got so much to do back home."

Eva sighed and kissed her son's forehead. "The ranch will always be there, Kent. It's important that you put your focus into getting your hip better. Otherwise, there's not much use for a crippled boy on the ranch, now is there?"

"No," Kent agreed, sulking.

The door opened and Albert, Klove, and Andersen piled into the small room.

"He's awake," Klove said happily. He'd been worried about his older brother ever since he heard what happened. Taking in the sight of the full on leg cast and the pulley system holding up his brother's foot, his smiled faded. That didn't look like too much fun. He stood by his mother as Andersen approached the hospital bed.

"Well I'll be," Andersen shook his head in amazement. "You did all that just by falling?"

Morosely, Kent nodded.

The farmhand tsked. "That ought to be the first rule of being anywhere; always pay attention to where you're at. Still, it's some rotten luck." He pulled a small paper sack out of his trouser pocket and handed it to Eva. "Here, ma'am. I bought this little invalid some hard candy to take his mind off the pain. I hope that's alright."

Eva smiled. "Of course, Andersen. Thank you. Kent, what do you say to Andersen?"

Kent gave a half-hearted smile. "Thank you for the candy."

The farmhand shrugged. "Heck, it's the least I could do. Well, I best let you folks be." He gave a nod to Eva and Klove and shook Albert's hand. On his way out the door, Andersen gave a final wave to Kent. "Feel better, kid."

Eva stayed with her son in the hospital for the entirety of the six weeks. Albert and Klove came to visit as often as they could, but life on a ranch demands constant work. With two people out for the count, the workload doubled.

~ ~ ~

Grandpa showed me around the restaurant as though he owned it. Really, he had for a long time. With pride, he pointed out the framed newspaper clipping of him and Uncle Klove when they had sold the place. The mechanic pits had been filled in with concrete long ago. Picnic style benches sat above where Grandpa had fallen as a child.

When we finished with his tour, Grandpa and I got some food to take back to Grandma. The excursion was a huge success; the specter of worry no longer creased Grandpa's brow and he looked happier than I'd seen him in a long time.

PART FOUR
THE FUNERAL

On a bright and unseasonably warm Saturday three weeks after the visit with my grandparents, the family gathered to lay Grandma to rest.

Everyone reacts to death differently. Some are quiet in their mourning. Others are loud and angry. Some are in complete denial.

Grandpa? Well, he mostly slept.

That day, with Grandma's casket open and her waxy figure laying serenely inside, Grandpa sat resolutely in the front pew of the church. He was dressed in a well-fitting grey suit and white shirt. His bolo tie had been polished and a new grey cowboy hat was in his lap.

As people filed past to take a final look at the deceased, I sat next to him in the pew and listened as people gave their condolences. He thanked them for coming, thanked them for their well-wishes, and inquired politely about their family or what they'd been up to since the last time he'd seen them. He dealt with the crowd as though his heart was not broken, as though he hadn't lost the love of his life. It would have been a convincing lie, except everyone saw through it.

How are you doing?' I asked when there was a break in the stream of visitors.

He glanced at me, tears making his blue eyes shine. "Oh, I'm fair to middling."

I was his standard answer, but I saw the pain and sorrow behind the words.

Before I could respond, he leaned back in the pew and asked, "Have I ever told you about how your grandma and I met?" It was obvious that he needed to tell the story; he had to get the pent up memories out in the open.

"No, how did you meet her?"

He toyed with his hat, shifting itself back and forth between his hands. "My mother and her grandmother, Blanche, you remember me telling you about Blanche, don't you?"

"Yes."

"Well, she and my mother were good friends. They played bridge when Blanche lived over at the Bixby Ranch."

~ ~ ~

It was during one of those rare evenings during the winter of 1942 that Kent had come home from the airfield for supper that Eva made a request of her oldest son.

"Blanche's granddaughters are visiting from California. She's worried they'll get bored and wanted to make sure they got out to have some fun."

Kent was suspicious. "Well what does that have to do with me?"

"I told her that you would get one of your friends to take these girls out for an evening," Eva said casually as she spooned some green beans onto her plate. "I'd ask Klove to go, but he's going on that trip with his friends and won't be back until Christmas Eve."

Kent groaned. "Mother, these girls won't want to go out with a couple of mechanics. Plus, I'm not even sure we will be able to get a pass. Lots of fellas will be asking for those if they can't get a furlough to go home. They'd be better off playing bridge with you ladies than relying on me and my friends."

Eva frowned at him. "Why, I am disappointed in you, Kent. Blanche is a dear friend of the family. I expect you to go down to whichever officer you need to and request a pass to take these ladies out. I also expect you to find a friend to bring with you. See if Ron can come with you. He's such a nice boy."

"But Mother —"

Eva held up her hand, cutting off her son's protests. "Enough. It's only for one evening. It is not going to kill you."

Kent sighed in defeat. "Alright. I'll ask Ron and try to get a pass."

Somehow, Kent did convince his friend to take the girls out the following Saturday evening. All they had to do was get a pass to leave the base. So, Kent and Ron breezed into Lieutenant Adams' office one afternoon after KP duty.

"Good afternoon, Lieutenant Adams," Kent said with what he hoped was a charming smile. "We need a pass to leave base tomorrow night."

The Lieutenant was a short fella with balding brown hair. He hung up his phone and stared at the two privates in disbelief.

"What are you idiots doing?" he demanded roughly. "Don't you know you're supposed to salute an officer when you see him?"

Kent glanced at Ron who shrugged. Returning his focus to Lieutenant Adams, Kent asked, "Is that a fact?"

"Yes, that is a fact," Lieutenant Adams said as he got to his feet. He crossed his arms and waited.

It took a moment before the young men to get the hint. Hurriedly, they brought their right hands up to their heads in a sloppy salute.

By the sour expression on Lieutenant Adams' face, Kent knew they hadn't done very well.

With his mouth in a grim line, the lieutenant asked, "Where did you boys learn to salute? I can't believe you got out of basic training with salutes like those."

"No sir, we never went to basic. We joined up and went right to work on the planes," Ron piped up.

His answer earned them a stern glare. "Well then, I can't exactly blame you boys for not knowing." He launched into a lecture on how to properly salute an officer. In the end Lieutenant Adams agreed to give them a pass for the following evening.

At the appointed time, the two servicemen arrived at the Bixby Ranch and politely knocked on Blanche Thompson's door.

"How old are these girls, anyway?" Ron asked

under his breath.

"I don't know. A year or two younger than us, I think," Kent replied.

The door opened and the two immediately straightened their backs. Blanche stood tall on the other side of the entrance. "Ah, Kent. It's good to see you." She stepped forward and wrapped her arms around the lanky boy.

Kent coughed, a bit embarrassed by the exuberant greeting. "Hi Blanche. This here is my buddy Ron."

Blanche let go of Kent and stepped back. Giving a nod to Ron, she opened the door further. "Please, come in. The girls will be down in a moment. Thank you so much for taking them out this evening. They've been looking forward to it all day."

The two servicemen shuffled into the house timidly, their caps in their hands.

Blanche said, "Eva said you plan to go to a show in town, is that right?"

Ron stayed uncharacteristically silent, so Kent cleared his throat and replied, "Yes, ma'am, that is what we intend to do."

"How wonderful. Just be sure not to keep them out too late."

Before either of the young men could respond, footsteps sounded on the wooden stairs just to the left of the door. Kent and Ron glanced up to see two teenaged girls coming down from the second floor.

In that instant, the world fell away for Kent. All he saw was her. She wore a red dress and her brown hair was curled and pinned in a way that framed her face perfectly. As far as Kent was concerned, she was an angel.

Quietly, he nudged Ron, "Oh, man. She's the one I want. The one in red."

"Ah, girls. These gentlemen are here to take you out to a show."

Kent nodded and made eye contact with the beauty in red. "How do you do?"

Ron stepped forward and offered his hand to the older girl. Finding his voice, he said, "I'm Ron."

"I'm Betty," she replied, her mouth turned in a half smile. She took his arm with a cool confidence that would have suited a much older woman. Gesturing to the girl in red, she said, "This is my sister, Loretta."

Ron raised an eyebrow. "Nice to meet you, Betty. We should probably get going. We don't want to be late, do we Kent?"

The sound of his name shook him out of his stupor. "What? No. We certainly don't." he held his arm out to Loretta. "Are you ready?"

She nodded, her brown curls bouncing ever so slightly with the movement. She accepted his arm with a feather light touch. Together they walked out of the house into the cool evening air.

Kent didn't remember much about the show they went to see, nor about much else that night other than talking with Loretta. She was intelligent and funny. Kent was smitten, it was simple as that.

~ ~ ~

"That is so sweet," I said. "How old was she?"

Grandpa answered with a grin, "I didn't know it

at the time, but she was only 14."

"What? 14? That's not right," I exclaimed, scandalized.

Grandpa shrugged. "It was a different time. Things like that weren't out of the ordinary back then. Heck, her mother, your great grandma, married Brownie when she was only 16." He fell silent for a prolonged moment. "I knew on first sight that Loretta was the one for me. We were married for over 60 years."

I conceded his point. "You kept in touch while you were in the war?"

"Yes, we wrote to each other quite a bit. She was always a good artist. She'd draw little characters like the seven dwarves on the envelopes."

"That's so sweet."

He nodded and a stray tear found its way down his pale cheek.

"When did you get married? Before or after you got shipped out to war?"

His calloused hand brushed the tear off of his cheek. "After. I was stationed in Southern California when I came back from overseas."

~ ~ ~

When Kent returned from Italy, he was stationed at Ft. MacArthur, which was pretty lucky since Loretta and her family lived in Hollywood. As was their custom, when Kent finished his shift, he picked up Loretta from school and drive her home. On one particular autumn day, there was a slight change in their routine. He pulled to a stop in front of her parents' house. As Loretta went to open the passenger door, Kent asked her to wait.

"I've got something I want to ask you," he explained with a slight tremor in his voice.

Curious, Loretta set her books down on the seat next to her and waited. He looked so nervous that she was compelled to ask, "Is everything alright?"

"What? Yes. Everything's fine." He couldn't even bring his eyes up to meet hers.

Her curiosity turned to concern. "What is it?"

He took in a deep breath and dug into his trouser pocket. His fist closed around the small circlet of gold. "Loretta," he gulped, willing the words to get past his teeth. "Would you do me the honor of being my wife?"

Opening his hand to reveal a small golden ring with a modest diamond, he held his breath, waiting for her answer.

Loretta stared at the ring for a full minute before issuing a high pitched squeal of excitement. "Yes! Yes, I will!" She encircled her arms around his neck.

Kent let out the breath he'd been holding. "We've got to get permission from your parents though. You're still only 17."

Loretta waved off his worry. "Mother married Dad when she was 16. Besides, they adore you. I don't see why we wouldn't be able to get married before I even finish school."

"There's one more thing I want to ask you," Kent continued, buoyed by her acceptance. "Would you move back to Arizona with me? I'm making arrangements to move back to the ranch. My folks helped me buy a little trailer to get out of the apartment I'm in now. Ranching is hard, but it's a good, satisfying life. We could be happy."

Loretta was quiet for a long moment as she considered what he wanted. It would mean uprooting and leaving everything she'd known. It would mean a completely different life than she ever imagined for herself. But along with the doubts and uncertainty was a spark of excitement. It was the prospect of something completely new.

Having made up her mind, she met Kent's clear blue eyes. "Yes. I'll go with you to Arizona."

Kent couldn't believe his ears. "Really? You truly mean it?"

"Of course I mean it," she laughed. "I love you. I'll go anywhere with you."

The feel of her lips against his made Kent's heart flutter. He truly was the luckiest man alive.

Loretta and Kent announced their engagement that very evening at supper.

Dorothy's fork clattered against the china. "Excuse me? Don't you think you're both a little young?"

Loretta was not to be dissuaded. "I'm older than you were when you got married."

Dorothy didn't like being sassed by her daughter and was about to say so when Brownie put his hand on hers.

He let out a deep, rumbling laugh. "She's got you there, dear. Tell me, Kent. How do you intend on taking care of my daughter?"

Now was the moment of truth. Kent fidgeted in his seat. "Well, sir, once I've saved up a bit of money,

I intend on moving us back to Arizona. We are going to be ranchers, like my parents."

It was Brownie's turn to turn somber. "Loretta, is that what you want?"

She held her chin up high as she answered, "Yes. I love him."

Dorothy rose from her chair, flustered. She glared at the couple, struggling to convey the anger and disappointment she felt inside. Finally, she sputtered, "You both think you're so smart, don't you?" She threw her napkin on the table before stomping to the refuge of her kitchen.

Kent was taken aback by such a display from Dorothy. She'd always been so kind to him.

Brownie coughed and also stood. "It seems you two know what you want. I do, however, have a request."

"Yes, sir," Kent said, wondering if Dorothy would be alright with him after this. He'd heard horror stories in the military about mother-in-law's that were complete nightmares. He certainly didn't want that.

"Loretta needs to finish high school before you move to Arizona."

Kent fully agreed. "Of course."

Brownie gave a nod. "Then may I be the first to offer you two congratulations?"

Loretta somberly inclined her head in thanks. She hadn't been expecting her mother to be so upset.

Brownie's expression remained pensive. "I wish you both many years of happiness. Now, if you'll please excuse me. I've got to make sure your mother is alright." He removed himself from the room, leaving Kent and Loretta sitting at the table.

The next few months were a whirlwind of activity. Dorothy did eventually came around to Kent marrying her daughter. Together, the two ladies threw themselves into planning the wedding.

On Sunday, April 14, 1946, at two in the afternoon, Loretta and Kent were married in the Wayside Chapel in Los Angeles.

Two months later, Loretta graduated from University High School.

At last, Kent and Loretta began their life together.

~ ~ ~

"Where is Grandpa?" my sister Becca asked. The funeral had ended two hour previous and everyone had gathered at my aunt's house for the reception. People milled around with plates of half-eaten food, quietly talking.

"I don't know. Isaac was supposed to drive him back."

"It's been almost two hours," she pointed out.

There wasn't much I could say to that.

The sound of a car door slamming brought us both to the front window. Through the gauzy curtains, we saw Isaac as he helped Grandpa out of the truck. Becca and I ran out to the drive way to meet them and to see where they had been.

"Hello, girls," Grandpa said, his expression somber. "I better get in there. People are probably wondering where I am." As he scooted his walker over the threshold of the house, Becca and I rounded on our cousin.

"Isaac, what took you so long? We left the church hours ago!"

He looked sheepish. "I got lost. I don't know my way around town. Grandpa said he'd be able to tell me how to get here, but then he fell asleep."

"Why didn't you just wake him up then?" my sister asked.

Isaac shrugged. "I didn't know he was asleep. He kept telling me to make turns. I thought he knew what he was saying. Then, he woke up and demanded to know where we were. That's when we got back on track."

Becca and I exchanged worried glances. "You mean he was dreaming that he was giving you directions? Where was he telling you to go?"

Isaac shrugged again, his face long with sorrow. "I don't know. He kept calling me Loretta and telling me that we gotta get home. He misses her very much."

PART FIVE
LEARNING TO FLY

The sky threatened to snow on me as I approached Grandpa's small modular home in Southern Colorado. The late autumn air was crisp and nipped at the fingers that held onto my bag. Grandma had been gone nine months. During the hot Arizona summer, Grandpa picked up and moved to his property up north. He intended to stay the winter, but I had my doubts about that. As much as he hated to admit it, he was frail and wouldn't do well in the ice and snow.

During the nine months since we'd buried Grandma, I'd spoken with him every day after work. We had more or less the same conversation each time I called. I'd ask how he was doing, he'd say "oh, fair to middling" and then launch into the latest doings of the family. He would grouse about stock prices and try to impart some of his business acumen. I didn't doubt he knew what he was talking about, but none of it made a lick of sense to me. After a while, I'd say that I had to go and that I'd call him again tomorrow. He always thanked me for calling.

The idea to visit him up at the ranch came from the realization of how lonely Grandpa was; sometimes he'd call me multiple times just to have someone to talk to. So, I packed my warmest clothes and made my way north.

The night I arrived, he and I sat down to a late dinner of goulash; a concoction of potatoes, tomato soup, onions, corn and sausage. It was a recipe from my childhood and it tasted wonderful.

As we ate, Grandpa told me, "I found something the other day that I thought you'd like to see. It might help you with those stories you are collecting."

My interest was piqued. "What is it?"

After wiping his mouth with a napkin, Grandpa reached over to the chair next to him and brought a half full plastic shopping bag onto the table. He shoved it towards me.

"These are some of the letters I wrote home during the war."

"Really?" I put my fork down and reach for the plastic bag. Inside were stacks of weathered envelopes.

"I wasn't much of a writer, but it might help with that story we're doing."

"It definitely will! I don't want to get them messed up, so I'll read through them when we are finished eating."

Grandpa smiled, "Good idea."

Unable to resist the chance for more stories, I said, "Last time we left off, you had just taken the exam to be a cadet. Did you pass?"

Grandpa finished chewing the bite he'd taken. "Not the first time. It took me three tries to pass that dadgum test. I started to think I'd never be a cadet."

"But you eventually made it, didn't you?"

"I did. They sent me to Manhattan, Kansas for college detachment training. I was there during the winter time."

"That must have been hard for you."

He settled back in his chair, his plate clear. "I suppose it was. I'd never seen snow before. They'd make us practice our drills outside. Because of how tall I was, I was at the front and the instructor hated me. I never went to boot camp, so I never learned how to march and drill like the others. Also, I didn't know how to walk on ice, so I kept slipping and falling. If that ice got the better of me, I'd take the whole row down with me. I couldn't help it. I grew up in the desert."

"Was college easy for you?" I asked as I picked up our empty plates.

Grandpa watched me clear the table. He played with his napkin, warming up to the tale he was about to tell. "No, it was nothing like high school. I really had to apply myself at college or I was out of the military. I can tell you that I learned more in six months of college detachment training than all of my years at school before that."

"Where did you go after college training?"

Grandpa paused for a minute, thinking about it. "I went to Santa Ana, California. That's where they would see if we had what it took to become flyboys. That's when I really started writing home." He patted the bag of letters. "My mother kept them all for me for when I got back."

I finished rinsing off the dishes and dried my hands. Returning to the table, I picked the letters out of the plastic bag and stacked them on the table. Careful not to rip the aged envelope, I opened the first one.

***

March 6, 1944
Santa Ana, Calif.

Dear Folks:
Today was the first real day of classification but no tests until tomorrow. They told us today that it is not an IQ test but an aptitude test to tell whether or not we are adapted to air crew training. I don't think I have much of a chance and don't feel surprised if I wash out. I did make good grades at CTD that's true but from what I hear that is not needed for these tests. Either you have what they want or you haven't.

The weather here is just like Arizona and I like it fine. There is snow on the high mountains to the North. The ocean is not over four miles from here.

I'll call you over the phone if I find out I'm made a cadet. That will be exactly 13 days from today. Is that OK? If I wash out I'm getting a furlough some way if possible. No it makes no matter how hard a fellow works around here he can never get a long enough pass to go that far. Everyone here is on the ball all the time. Every Sunday we have a dress parade from 3:30 pm until about 6 pm. Yesterday was my first one to be in. I bet there was near 50 squadrons on the field at once and 200 or more men in each squadron. We were the last squadron to pass by the reviewing stand so that caused us to stand at parade rest for damn near two hours before we could start marching.

Yes, I know all about them meeting the Evans. Loretta told me all about it just after it happened. I guess she was scared to death when they asked her that. You can't make me blush anymore, ha!

Tinsley said to tell you that if he could tell you what he thought about that sour orange, it wouldn't be very gentleman like.

The other day I called Loretta over the phone and talked for 19 minutes. I didn't think we were talking for that long, but we did. It just cost $2.50 and I had to hunt up change in the barracks so I could pay the phone. I'll remember next time not to talk so long or else have a handful of coins.

We had two lectures today one by a Major and another by a Captain. They all told us the danger we would be in while flying in combat. The Captain was a bombardier and has seen action in Europe. In fact he said he was the first American to drop the first American bomb in Germany. He was wounded and sent back here to teach new air crew members. He said from now on each of us would have to be trained to meet the enemy in combat. The going is going to be tough and hard going because they have to train us in the shortest time possible and the best trained air-crew member in the world. He said we would be taught the expression "kill or be killed" a thousand times before we are thorough. He told us the importance of each member of the crew on a combat mission. Everyone has his job to do just like on a *football team and we have to train to work together.*

The food here is good but most of the time it all don't go around to all of us. If we happen to be the last one on the table, well we have to do without food that meal. They told us today that we each are allowed 55 cents a day for food. That don't give us much to eat but after a guy gets to cadet you get more to eat. I've just got to make the grade. Tomorrow's the day for the mental.

I'll have to close for this time.
Love, Kent

* * *

March 8, 1944
Santa Ana, Calif.

Dear Folks:
I have a little time off so I'll write you a line to let you know how I'm getting along. I finished all of my written tests this morning and then this afternoon I went to take some kind of coordination test but they wouldn't let me take them today. The other night I hurt my finger while playing catch so they said it would hinder me. I have to go take the test on Friday. Oh! Well, I don't give a darn anymore because after taking the written tests, I'm sure I'm a washout. I am going to try like heck to get back to my squadron at Williams Field. If not, I'm going to apply for Aircraft Mechanic School some place.

The weather here is still good but I'm afraid there's some more rain coming. The wind is blowing just like it does in March. I like the climate here because it reminds me of Arizona.

I guess tomorrow I go in front of an officer which will ask us all kinds of questions and try like heck to make us nervous so he can wash us out. It's a heck of a fight to keep from washing out. They keep us sweating all the time.

I got a letter from Ron and he is in basic training now. He said he is having a hard time making the grade but he is trying like heck to make the grade. When he went through Santa Ana, they only had to make a rating of three to pass but now it has raised up to seven so you see what I have to put up with.

Did I tell you I got my diploma from Kansas and it is signed by the President, Eisenhower, and Captain Craemer? We had a graduation exercise in which we were presented our diplomas by Captain Craemer. He wished us all the luck in the world.

One week from today I can go to the PX show or anything here on the post after duty hours. Being restricted to the barracks would drive a guy nuts in a months' time.

My bunk's got to be made yet and I've got to shave before 10 o'clock so I'd better close.

Love, Kent
P.S. We got paid the 15th.

* * *

March 12, 1944
Santa Ana, Calif.

Dear Folks:
I have a little time now before we have to go to

chow so I'll write you a line. It sure was good to hear your voices again.

It is starting to rain now so we won't have to stand parade this afternoon (I hope). This will be the last Sunday in restriction for me if I wash out. I think I can have a pass on the weekend after washing out. Maybe I won't wash out but I'm sure I will be though. I have passed all my other tests except the interview with the psychiatrist, he said I was too nervous for combat flying. The reason was because I couldn't hold my hands out in front of me without having them shake. I get one more chance with him, tomorrow. I guess I was lucky because the other fellows washed out right then and there for nervousness. I get scared when I go in there, he is a Major. I am going to talk like heck to get him to let me go on.

Monday afternoon —

I never got to finish last night so I'll try this afternoon. I went to see the psychiatrist today and they haven't got my grade yet so I have to wait. They are going to call me when they get my grades.

It is trying to rain today so we don't have to parade tonight. Tomorrow our whole flight gets mess management (KP). I hate to start that stuff again but it won't hurt any of us. We will get plenty to eat any way.

If I'm still here when you come over, I'd like you to come. But I don't think I will stay here very long after washing out. And if I do happen to make what I applied for, I'll be here for at least three months. That is pilot pre-flight school. I don't care if they give me bombardier just anything to stay in cadet.

I'd better close for this time, I'll write more on

Wednesday.
    Love, Kent
    P.S. I've got to get rid of these air mail stamps.

* * *

March 16, 1944
Santa Ana, Calif.

Dear Folks:
    Well, I'm still on AV/S and there has been three lists out so far. About 10 of the old flight 52 has washed out so far. Vassar is still in my barracks and I'm sure he will come through OK. Papson, the big shot here and back at Kansas State College washed out today. Most of the fellows washed out on mental. I'm sure I passed the mental OK because I'd have been washed out the first bunch. I can't tell you the number but there's plenty of us washed out.
    Tell Klove not to enlist into anything yet. He might stand a chance to stay out for some time. He should get all the schooling he can before he is taken in the service. That's the only way the Army, Navy, or any other branch has in telling what job you are suited for. As for cadets, no civilian can come into cadets anymore. Not even enlisted men here in the states. You have to be overseas before you can apply for cadet training.
    I've got to hurry and finish this letter and shine my shoes for inspection tomorrow morning. Tonight I pull guard duty from 10 pm until two am. All of us pull guard duty at once.
    I didn't care for that kind of hair oil because it

looks like it will make your hair grey. And besides they keep our heads clipped so short we do need anything to comb it with.

I don't think I can make it over there in three days and still get back on time. If I wash out, I'll go to some mechanics school and before I start to school I get a furlough. So that will be better than a three day pass.

I'm getting sun burned from this sunshine. My face is red tonight from being out in the sun this afternoon. I guess I got plenty white while I was in Kansas. Now I'll get sun tanned again.

I'll close for this time. Next time I write I'll tell you whether or not I'm washed out.

Love, Kent

* * *

March 20, 1944
Santa Ana, Calif.

Dear Mother:
I am going before the faculty board this morning and that means I'm going to wash out. All the fellows that haven't washed are going to be classified today.

Loretta came to see me yesterday but this place is no good for entertaining visitors. She got to see the parade and I never marched so I could see it too.

I don't know what they are going to do with me but I'll find out this morning. I think I'll be grounded and sent to Texas, someplace. I never dreamed I was nervous.

I won't be able to get a three day pass but when I get to another field I will try to get a furlough.

*I've got to go now, I'll write a letter tonight to you
and let you know more about what they tell me.*
Love, Kent

* * *

March 20, 1944
Santa Ana, Calif.

Dear Folks:
*I wrote this morning that I was going before the
faculty board. Well, I did and they washed me out for
nervousness. They told me that I made pilot OK and
all that held me back was that they thought I was a
little too tense. They kept another boy and myself
after they dismissed the others. Both of us was washed
for the same reason and the other boy had over 200
hours of flying time. They told us that our assignment
was Las Vegas, Nevada gunnery school. He (I mean
the Captain in charge of the board) told us that we
had had experience on the line so they figure that we
will make Ariel Engineer without going to AM school.
He said that our job was just as important as a pilot,
navigator, or bombardier but it didn't take as much
strain. They were very nice to us and made us feel
much better. I was glad to hear that I was classified as
a pilot and had passed all the written tests. The only
thing that was wrong was my damn nervous tension.
One thing I did wrong was, when I made out a folder
for them, I put down that my parents didn't want me
to fly. I think that had a lot to do with it. I guess I was
too damn honest. I put down "they prefer me not to
fly."*

I hope I can get a pass before I leave here. I won't get a furlough for some time to come. Gunners don't get passes while they are in training nor do they get paid. When they graduate they will get paid their back pay and get a pass. Oh well. If I get on a good ship I might fly all over the U.S. before going across.

I'm sure glad they never grounded me because I thought maybe they would because of my nervousness. I'll make a good gunner, I think. Come out with Sgt ratings. Then before long you make TSgt. so what do I care. TSgt with flying pay is almost as good as a commission. Maybe I can get on a B-29 and all the crew on them are commissioned or have flight officer ratings.

The weather here is swell but it still looks like rain. I sure hope it doesn't rain next week end. If I'm here I'm getting a pass.

The rest of the fellows have been classified and about 60 of them made pilot. Vassar made bombardier. Tinsley made navigator. I never thought Vassar would make the grade but he did. He sure didn't have much as far as a student. His grades were poor at CTD. They can't say I was too dumb because I passed all the tests OK.

Gunners School lasts about eight weeks and then I go to a replacement wing and from there to an outfit.

I've got to close now. Write soon.

Love, Kent

P.S. I feel like a free man now. No more gigs and plenty of time to myself.

* * *

"Wait." I put down the aged paper. "You classified as a pilot, but they wouldn't let you fly because of nervous tension?"

Grandpa nodded "You see, part of the test was to go in front of a Flight Commander and answer questions. I was so dadgum nervous. My hands kept shaking. That's why they washed me out."

"Were you devastated?"

He shrugged and fiddled more with his paper napkin. "It all turned out alright. I still got to go up in the plane, I just didn't have the strain of being a pilot. I was glad they didn't wash me out of the military altogether."

I couldn't argue with that logic. Eager to learn more, I returned to the letters.

* * *

March 24, 1944
Santa Ana, Calif.

Dear Folks:
I'm in another squadron now, waiting for the shipment to another squadron. After I go to another squadron, I'll be shipped out to Las Vegas from there. I'm getting a pass this weekend but there's not a chance of getting a three day pass.

How are things getting along at home? I'd like to be there on furlough right now. In about three months or less I'll get a 10 day delay in route to Salt Lake City. That means I can take 10 days' time getting there from Las Vegas. When I get there, I'll be assigned to a combat crew.

I'm sending a picture of our quarters at K.S.C. and some pictures of our old flight 52. The little dog we called GI is one of the pictures but I'll send it later. I've only got one of it. The picture of us in flying boots and jackets was taken just before we went up. That is the plane I always flew. I got my log book back the other day. The one that my instructor kept for us. He has all of our grades in it. My grades were all between 80 and 85 and some of the reports he wrote were pretty good. When I go to Las Vegas I'll send my log books home and you can keep them for me.

I haven't had any letters from you in darn near two weeks. I think maybe the mailman — I take it all back. A guy just gave me a letter from you. It took days to get here.

Yes, I got three papers since I've been here and there is always lots of news in them. I knew about the Cumming boy it was in the paper. He is a radio operator and gunner. That's the ones they train at Yuma. All the airplane mechanic gunners go to Las Vegas. All the poor fellows in college now are going back to the ground forces. Around 36,000 of them and all the classification here at Santa Ana is frozen. They don't need any more air-crew members. Tell Klove not to get into the Army until they make him. But still the Navy deal is a good place to be. That's the only chance to get any schooling out of the services. I think maybe I'll go and see Donald if I get a pass and find time.

Love, Kent
Write soon.

* * *

March 29, 1944
Santa Ana, Calif.

Dear Mother:
I'm still in this Squad One yet. I think maybe the gunnery school is full or something. Before I leave this post I have to move to Squad 414 for shipment out. I'll stay there at least five days so I should get at least two more weekends off. Unless I'm on KP over Saturday or Sunday.

I sure hate that about Aunt Oie and Uncle Harry coming to see me and I wasn't there. Darn it, I came through that gate two times that afternoon and I'm sure they were in the crowd there.

Some of my pals from K.S.C. that washed out are shipping out today and tomorrow. Some go to Denver, Colo. some to Texas and some to South Do.

Thanks for sending me that clipping. I was already informed about the air-crew trainees.

Things have come to almost a stand still around here as far as classification is concerned. More and more are washing out and some are not being classified. Even the fellows that are classified are going to have it plenty tough to stay a cadet.

I sure had a swell time last weekend. The Browns were sure nice to me. Tell Blanche that I experienced Brownie's driving while coming back to the base. I thought we were going to start flying any time. He drove from Knots Berry place to here in about 10 minutes. My pass was up at three pm and I just made it. They wanted to bring me back so they could take me to Knots Berry place.

I hope you have found a helper by now. That's too

much work for Klove and Dad to do. I think he should get rid of those darn cows. It don't pay to work so hard. Why not take life easy.

I've got myself a new pen. My other one is just no good anymore. When I get to Las Vegas I'll send it back. I may get a new one for it. I like this one just as good.

I'll have to close for this time.
Love, Kent

* * *

April 4, 1944
Santa Ana, Calif.

Dear Mother:
I moved to this squadron yesterday and they put us in tents. Tents aren't so bad in fact, I like them because there isn't any cleaning to do much. We have no foot lockers so we have to live out of our barrack bags. All we do here is wait for shipment and pull a little work once in a while. We have to work on KP once or twice while we are here, but it's not bad. This afternoon our commanding officers took about half of us to the theater to see a show. This field is full of wash outs now. There was more than 4,000 cadets pushed out to be sent back to their old outfits. I sure feel sorry for them because there isn't anything wrong with them. They are getting a dirty deal.

I sent you an Easter card with some money in it. I want you to get whatever you want with it to make a happy Easter for you. Maybe you need a new hat to wear to church Easter Sunday. Klove and Dad, I wish *you too a happy Easter and don't work too hard.*

I think I'll be here for another weekend in LA unless some more gunners ship out before Saturday.

We have more time off at night for the first time in about seven months. It sure feels good to be a regular GI again. We can wear our flight jackets at night without being gigged for it.

I got paid today after waiting four days after regular pay day. I didn't need it, but I always like to have my pay on time.

When I get to my next field I'll have you send some of my things back. My O.D. pants and the small work jacket.

I'll have to close for this time, I can't think of anything else to say right now.

Love, Kent

* * *

April 12, 1944
Las Vegas, Nevada

Dear Mother, Dad and Klove:
I'm now stationed at Las Vegas, Nevada. We got here about 5:30 this morning after leaving LA about 6:30 last night. The field is not bad at all, there are mountains all around us. My barracks are near the flying line, so I feel right at home listening to the planes roar. Reminds me of Williams Field.

There will be no 10 day delay in route for gunners leaving this field. I found out this morning. They stopped it last month. So the only furlough I'll get is just before I go across.

Our stay here will be seven and a half weeks and the last two weeks will be flying time. We will fire from B-17s and try to hit P-40s and P-39s with camera guns. They will attack us with camera guns too.

The 18th replacement wing has changed to Lincoln, Neb. so that's where we go from here. And from there I don't know. But I do know I'll either be on a B-17 or a B-29 bomber. We start school Saturday.

I had another weekend pass in LA last week. I was on KP all day Saturday and when I got to LA I was plenty tired. Three of us hitched hiked in together and we stayed at a hotel in Hollywood. Then Sunday I went with the Brown's on a picnic. I had a very nice time. I hitchhiked back to the base about 12 that night. I never got back until four am and my pass was up at six am I still haven't caught up on my sleep.

I'll have to close for now.
Love, Kent

* * *

April 18, 1944
Las Vegas, Nevada

Dear Mother, Dad and Klove:
I haven't anything to do for about 45 minutes this morning so I'll try and write you a letter. The sky is cloudy this morning and looks like rain. But I doubt it if it does rain here.

I went up in the pressure chamber yesterday and my ears are still feeling stopped up from it.

We went up to 20,000 feet without oxygen and

stayed there for 12 minutes then put on our masks and went up to 30,000 feet. Tomorrow we go up to 38,000 feet or higher to see if we can stand the low pressure because most of our real flying will be above 38,000 feet.

Today we take a night vision test which I've already taken once before at Santa Ana. I passed it there so I guess I'll pass it here.

There are a lot of new army men in my squad and most of them are just kids. They went into cadet training and got about two months college and now they are kicked out and made plain gunners. None of them have been in the Army longer than two months. There are a lot that didn't get as far as college. A big bunch came in from A.S.T.C. at Tempe, Arizona.

Will you tell the (Mesa Tribune) where my new address is and take it off of this letter? The mail must be plenty slow around here. I haven't got any yet from you.

April 19 — Wednesday Night

I didn't have time to finish yesterday so I'll finish tonight. Your letter came today and I was glad to hear from you. I went up in the pressure chamber today to 38,000 feet. It didn't hurt me any except at 38,000 feet I had a slight case of the bends in my right knee. Everybody gets them sometimes at that altitude. My ears were OK too. One poor boy just couldn't relieve the pressure in his ears coming down and his ear drums broke. Both ear drums. I sure felt sorry for him because he was suffering something terrible. 38,000 feet is plenty high and it means certain death if you don't have oxygen. Most of our flying will be less than 30,000 feet.

If you do drive up here, I doubt if I'd have much time off to have any time with you. You see we are only here six weeks or more and part of that time we are 50 miles up in the mountains at a place called Indian Springs. We are up there for most of our flying. I don't know when we are to go up there so you might miss me. This town is a heck of a place to stay in from what they tell me, too.

Now that I've gotten this far I'm going to finish this training out. I figure that it's better to fight up in the air rather than on the ground. I'm going to get all I can out of this gunnery school so I can shoot damn good when ready for combat. The ground crew doesn't have it so nice and have to work so darn hard. We get flying pay and good ratings and also good training. The pilot and co-pilot are just as dangerous or more than a gunner because he hasn't anything to shoot back with.

I'm glad you got your kitchen floor fixed the way you want it. You must have had a big crowd at the party the way you talked. You must have worked plenty hard.

Well, I've got to clean up before going to bed. I done all my laundry yesterday and it was some job. Damn this Army. It takes so darn long to do anything. They had better not try and charge me for laundry this month.

Love, Kent
P.S. Don't worry about me. I'll be OK.

* * *

May 20, 1944
Las Vegas, Nevada

Dear Mother, Dad and Klove:
I'm sorry I haven't answered your letters sooner. Tomorrow we go to Indian Springs to fly. I have a graduation present for Klove but I'm sorry, I can't send it until we get back from the springs. The mail has gone out today and the post office is closed. I'm glad you liked the card and candy.

We were issued flying clothes and oxygen masks today. We finished taking the written exams yesterday. I passed them all as far as I know. I made 40% hits on the range shooting .50s and .30s. I hit 800 rounds out of 2,000. None of the fellows got over 50% so that's not bad for me. I couldn't hit the broad side of a barn with the shot guns. We had to shoot them from pick-up trucks going 35 miles per hour

I saw Lutz this afternoon at the mess hall. I talked to him for a while. He knew me the minute he saw me. He said he might be in charge of a troop train when we leave. He says he tries to get one troop train a month. It will be OK if he goes with us.

That card I sent you had air mail stamps on it by mistake. I first put one air mail on it before taking it to the post office. The clerk had me put on more to make it go airmail. It cost more to send than the package.

I'm on fire guard tonight from nine pm until eleven pm and it's almost time to start.

Darn it, I just can't think of anything to write. I probably will be flying over Bolder Dam and Grand Canyon while up at the springs. Also Death Valley.

Well, I've got to close for this time. Write to the same address. I'll get it at the springs anyway.
Love, Kent

* * *

May 29, 1944
Las Vegas, Nevada

Dear Folks:
Well, I'm back here in Las Vegas again. I fly again this morning and all this week. No, I don't care much for flying in a B-17. They're the roughest plane I've ever flown in. I got sick every time I went up last week. And I mean sick too. There was plenty of the guys that got sick. The reason was there was hot weather, rough country, and long missions. We had to stay up anywhere from four to six hours at one time. I got to shoot the chin guns, waist guns and top turret. It's fun shooting the chin guns at a target on the ground. I could shoot it straight too. It's the guns that the bombardier uses. You sit up in the glass nose in the bombardier's seat. The ground was plenty close to that nose too. We were about 50 feet off the ground and flying about 150 miles per hour. This morning I go up for high altitude to 20,000 feet. We have to use oxygen for any altitude over 10,000 feet.
All your letters came while I was up at the springs but I never took any writing paper with me. So I couldn't write back. I didn't have much time anyway.
Klove, I'm sending your present today if I can get to the post office.
Next Saturday we graduate.

Well, I've got to go now and get ready for the flight line. I'll write more soon.
Love, Kent

* * *

May 30, 1944
Las Vegas, Nevada

Dear Mother, Dad and Klove:
How is everything at home these days? Is the weather getting hotter yet? The weather here is hot and the last two days it has rained. Today was the first mission this week because of the rain. I never got sick this time. This time we had lots of fun up there shooting at real planes. They were AT-6s and they came in just like the real thing. We were shooting at them with cameras instead of bullets. Did I ever tell you that each student shoots about $1,700.00 worth of ammunition? Think of all the money this Army has spent on me already.

I'm listening to Eddie Rickenbacker over the radio. He sure is laying it on thick.

It won't be long before I get out of this hell hole. I think as soon as I get to my new field they'll give me a furlough. I hate to start out for Fla. and then come right back on that same train.

I'll have to close for this time so I can get this off in the mail.
Love, Kent

* * *

June 3, 1944
Las Vegas, Nevada

Dear Mother, Dad and Klove:
Well, today is the day we graduate and get our wings. We finished up flying yesterday and turned in all our flying clothes. We get passes tonight and also get paid flying pay this morning.

I got by this place just getting sick one time. That was yesterday. The pilot was flying through the mountains. We were so close to the cliffs that the wings almost touched the sides of them. The mountains were so high that snow was on them. The clouds were all around us and we were dodging them and the mountains too. Boy it sure was rough in those mountains. The air pockets in the canyons caused the roughness.

I guess we are going to Tampa as far as I know. They don't tell us where until we are on our way.
June 5th
I never got to finish this letter the other day so I'll do it now. Well, we leave tonight and we go to Lincoln, Nebr. They gave us passes over the week end. I never had enough time to go home but if I did, I sure would have come. Three of us fellows went to Boulder Dam and on over into Arizona. It isn't as big as I thought it would be. We hitch hiked up there from Vegas. We stopped at Boulder City for a while. That is the best little town I've seen yet. It is clean as it can be and all kinds of green lawns and trees. It doesn't seem possible to see that kind of place out in the rocks like it is.

We got our silver wings but we had to pay for

them out of our flying pay. I made Corporal. After a
hell of a long time. Well, I'd better sign off for now. I'll
write as soon as I get to my next place.

Love, Kent

* * *

June 24, 1944
Lincoln, Nebr.

Dear Folks:

I'm almost done with most of the classifying here.
Tomorrow I have to take some kind of a trade test to
see what I know about airplanes. Then I'll be sent to
another squad to wait for shipping. I think I'll be here
from 5 to 10 days. We work on Sundays just the same
as any other day. I got a lot of new clothes today and
had to turn in all my wool pants and shirts. They
made us send our non GI shirts home. When I get to
my next field I'll send home for them.

I got to see Todd again but now he is in another
squad. He got in three hours late on his furlough but
they never said anything to him. The train was late.

The weather here has been OK but tonight the
over cast is coming in and it might be raining
tomorrow. I sure hope I will be sent out west some
place. I hate this Middle West. Tomorrow night we get
passes to town. We have to be off the streets by 11:30
at night on week nights and 1:30 am on Saturday
nights. Lincoln is a swell town I think.

We aren't going overseas now. It will be from
three to four months yet. Lots of times the gunners get
a five day pass. I might even get home in five days
from where I get stationed.

I'll have to close for now.
Love, Kent

* * *

June 26, 1944
Lincoln, Nebr.

Dear Mother and Dad and Klove:
Well, I'm still here in this hell hole waiting to be shipped out. I haven't been assigned to a crew yet but it won't be over four days yet. I think I will be shipped out next week some time. The first part of the week. I haven't had a pass yet and I doubt if I ever get one in Lincoln.

We are kept busy most of the time doing detail work around the post. I figure I might get some KP duty before I leave this place. Oh! Well, it all comes in a day's work.

There is plenty to do on our off time. They have three service clubs and four PXs on the field. Also three theaters and a library too.

Did I tell you I have moved three times since I've been here? Three different squadrons. Now I've ended up in squad F and I'm living in a tent. They aren't bad but the bath water isn't hot half the time. Today the wind is blowing and this darn tent feels like it's going to blow away any minute now.

I got the Mesa paper today and my name was in there bigger than heck. Too much bull.

I'm anxious to find out what kind of pilot, co-pilot, bombardier, and navigator I'll get. I hope they know their stuff, and also the gunners too.

I sent some socks and undershirts home today. I don't need them anymore. They're too much to carry around with me. Some of them need mending, but I'm sure you could use them to work in. They took away one of my barracks bags so I have to cram everything in one bag. I can't carry too much extra junk anymore.

This second Air Force is sure a big training command. It supplies all the heavy bombardment groups for all theaters of combat. So you see they put through a good many men here. I will go into another Air Force when I'm done with my combat training, depending on which theater of war I go to.

Well, I'm about out of ink and no more around so I'd better close for this time. Write soon.

Love, Kent

* * *

July 4, 1944
Lincoln, Nebr.

Dear Mother, Dad and Klove:
I'm here in the service club this afternoon trying to rest a little bit. This field keeps us busy every day of the week if we don't manage to get out of it somehow. I pulled KP Saturday and worked all day Sunday. The way it looks I won't ship out until sometime next week sometime.

Your letter came Friday. Sorry I haven't gotten around to answering it but I've been pretty busy.

I went on KP Saturday morning at three am and got off at seven pm. Then I went to town with some of the boys and we never got back until 1:30 in the morning. I've been tired the last two days. The weather here has been hot but today it cooled up a little bit and looks like rain.

I don't have any idea where I will be sent from here. I found out that the second Air Force has two fields east of the Mississippi river. There is a chance I'll be sent down to Tenn. or LA. What a place to be sent to, another hot and clammy state.

I was glad to hear that Dick is still in England. He must be in a pretty safe place.

I got paid the other day and now I have some extra money. I bought a $100.00 bond yesterday and sent it home. I hope you get it OK. Keep it for me, will you? Our squad alone bought 3,000 bucks worth of war bonds this pay day. That's pretty good, don't you think? The payroll was worth about 50,000 bucks just this squad.

Have you got the grain in yet? I say, there was a fellow in another squad that received a telegram from his folks that they needed some help on the farm and asked him if he couldn't get a few days off to go home and help. He took the wire to the CO and they are giving him a three month furlough. So if you get too bad off for help, you know what to do. The Red Cross has to check up and see if he is really needed at home.

Today being the 4ᵗʰ of July, the guns saluted with a bunch of loud rapports at noon time. Then tonight they sounded retreat as usual.

Well, the war news seems to be getting better every day. But I don't like the way people are acting about getting a new president. Sometimes that will be the biggest headline on the paper. These Republicans are sure strong on that Dewey. I wish they would wake up and realize that there is a war on. We get good news broadcasts here and all kinds of maps describing the advances made.

Well, I guess I've wound down for this time so I better close. Write soon.

Love, Kent

P.S. I have KP again Thursday.

* * *

July 16, 1944
Lincoln, Nebr.

Dear Mother:

I'm on a shipping list now and will go out of here sometime in the middle of the week. They read it off this morning. It's for B-17s and we think we will go to Alexandria, LA. Away down south almost to New Orleans where there's nothing but swamps and rain.

I was glad to hear that the grain turned out so good. That was a lot of money at one time for grain, wasn't it.

Those pictures came the other day and the guy sent them out yesterday. Be sure and save one or two of them, will you? I don't care what you do with the rest. That is, if you think they are worth a darn. I saw the big one but not the small ones. Tell me what you think of them will you? I don't think they are worth a darn. My gold tooth shows up too much. I've changed my mind. I want you to save me three little ones. You can have the rest.

Did you get a $100.00 bond I sent home? I sure hope it got home OK I had it insured.

I'm at the service club now and it is raining like heck outside now. This is the darndest country around here. It will rain down near an inch of rain in about three hours and in six hours all the water is gone to the ground. Arizona would be flooded off the maps if it got as much rain.

I was put on KP again Saturday but I got out of it. I went over early in the morning and they needed a fellow to help wake up the KPs so I helped. They took me off KP for helping and I managed to get a sleeping pass out of the deal. So instead of KP I slept all morning until noon.

OK I'll be careful what I write to the gal. Thanks for telling me. I hope it isn't too bad. Excuse this ink because beggars can't be choosers you know. I had to get it from my bunk neighbor. I'm back at the tent now and just got back from the show.

Well, I think I'll have to close for now. I can't think of anything more to say. Write soon.

Love, Kent

~ ~ ~

The day before I was supposed to leave Colorado, Grandpa insisted on taking me to the new Ute casino the next town over.

"They built it only a few months ago. It's a very nice place," he assured me.

He parked the big truck and we slowly walked in through the large double doors into a sea of blinking lights and slot machines.

"Do you want to try one of them machines?" He asked, pointing at the colorful diplay.

112

"Not really, but you can."

He looked a touch disappointed in my answer. "I'm not lucky enough. You do it for me. Here." He reached into his pocket and drew out a crisp five dollar bill. "Pick out a machine and let's see if we can win some money."

We headed over to the penny slots and I selected a machine at random. "This one looks good." I put the five dollar bill in the machine and press the button. It took a few tries, but in the end, we won a couple hundred dollars.

As I cashed in our ticket, Grandpa patted me on the back. "See? I knew you had better luck than me!"

PART SIX
THE CREW

My uncle dropped Grandpa off at my apartment early one Saturday afternoon. I'd invited him and my neighbor over for a dinner of chili and fry bread. It was the first time that Grandpa visited my home.

I was in the kitchen kneading out the dough for the bread when a knock sounded at the door. "Come on in!" I called out. Grandpa opened the door with a big smile. His straw cowboy hat perched rakishly atop his head.

"Make yourself comfortable. Brad will be here in a while. Do you want something to drink?"

"Some iced tea would be nice," Grandpa said as he steered his walker over to the couch. Once he sat, he took off his cowboy hat and looked around. "You sure have a nice place here."

"Thank you, Grandpa." I handed him his drink. "I've got to finish up the fry bread, but we can still talk if you want."

Just then a knock sounded at the door. It opened and in came my friend and neighbor, Brad.

"I brought beer," Brad announced, brandishing a couple of growlers. "My newest concoction. Lemon mint."

"Well that sounds interesting," I said. "But first, I want you to meet someone. Brad, this is my Grandpa, Kent. Grandpa this is my neighbor, Brad."

A chorus of pleasantries followed the introductions. Brad handed me the beer to put into the fridge and went to sit on the couch next to Grandpa. They sat quietly, neither wanting to be the first person to talk. Finally, Grandpa asked, "You ever been to Louisiana?"

"Can't say that I have," Brad responded. "Were you born there or something?"

Grandpa shook his head. "No, I was stationed there for a while during the war. That's where I met my crew."

~ ~ ~

Louisiana was so much more humid than Kent ever thought it would be. The air was thick and, to his desert acclimated lungs, it was akin to breathing water. This was the first time Kent had been so far south or so far east.

As far as he was concerned, the only good thing about being stationed in Alexandria, Louisiana was that his buddy Todd from gunnery school was with him. The two men had bonded over target practice and KP duty in Vegas.

Within a week, the fresh shipment of airmen were divided up into new crews for B-17s. Over the next month or so, these teams would learn how to work together in combat.

As soon as he got the name of his pilot, Kent went to compare with Todd. Wouldn't it be something if they were on the same team? On his way to see his friend, someone stepped in front of him, blocking his path. It was a big guy, not necessarily fat, just big. His face familiar though.

"Kent! It's great to see you!" The big man stuck out his hand.

It took Kent a heartbeat longer for him to recognize the man shaking his hand. "Gary Johnson! How the hell are you?"

"I'm doing just fine. What did you end up getting trained for?"

"I'm a gunner. What about you?"

"I was a pilot but I got demoted to co-pilot not too long ago."

Kent's jaw dropped. "Demoted? Now why in the world would they go and do that?"

"These higher ups don't have a sense of humor. I just showed them how those bombers could be flown if they had a pilot with any kind of talent."

With a groan, Kent ran his hand over his face. "Do I want to know what you did?" he asked, a horrified curiosity building inside of him.

Gary's broad features split into a prideful grin. "Ever see one of those B-17s do a chandelle?"

The horrified curiosity morphed into a begrudging admiration. "You didn't."

With a wide grin on his face, Gary nodded. "I did. I was down in Texas. Flew that baby under a couple of bridges too. Scared the piss out of my crew, but she landed without a scratch on her."

Kent couldn't keep the wonder from his voice. "And they demoted you for that?"

"It's all politics. Had I crashed her, then I would have been kicked out of the military altogether. Since it was successful, they couldn't say I didn't have the chops to fly. So now they have me flying co-pilot with this Lieutenant Fletcher fella."

The name brought Kent out of his amazement. "Fletcher is your pilot? He's my pilot too!"

"Well ain't that something!" Gary clapped Kent on the back. "Looks like we'll be flying together!"

At once Kent was struck with how this could be a bad thing. Did he really want a co-pilot who was willing to flip a plane upside down just to prove a point? A move like that would send him and whomever else wasn't strapped in straight for the top of the plane, if not out altogether.

To cover up his growing unease, Kent asked, "Have you met Lieutenant Fletcher? Do you know if he's any good?"

Gary shrugged. "I haven't met him yet. All I know is that Greer, the radio operator, met him yesterday. Apparently, Lieutenant Fletcher has been flying for a while now, doing patrols over South America or something like that."

"Well that's a good thing, don't you think?"

Gary shrugged. "We'll see, I suppose. Hey, I've got to get going, but I'll see you at practice!" He pounded Kent's back once more and strode confidently towards the mess hall. Kent watched him go with a growing sense of unrest.

"Doing a chandelle in a B-17," he muttered to himself. He couldn't even picture a B-17 doing a backwards loop like those smaller agile fighter planes. "What in the world possessed him to even try that?"

* * *

July 23, 1944
Alexandria, Louisiana

Dear Mother and Dad and Klove:
I got here Friday morning after a long train ride of three days. They made us busy right away going to school. This is the first chance I've had to write. I'm OK and this place is not very bad. I'll be here around 10 weeks.

Your letter came the day I got here. You never did say if you got that $100.00 bond or not. I'd like to know if it got home.

I haven't met my pilot but one fellow saw him yesterday and he is a first Lieutenant and has been flying sub-patrol over the coast of South America for a good many months.

Our radio operator is a Staff Sgt. and has been overseas before on a B-17. So now we have to get two more on our crew for gunners besides the bombardier, navigator, and co-pilot.

This place is sure hot and I mean hot too. It is a real wet heat. The town of Alex is crowded with infantry soldiers from three large camps around there. They say there are about 300,000 soldiers here in a town of 30,000 civilians before the war.

We will fly over the Gulf of Mexico most of the time and will have to wear May-West life jackets.

I'll have to close for now, but I'll write more later. I haven't much time now.

Love, Kent

P.S. May get a furlough when I leave here.

* * *

July 25, 1944
Alexandria, Louisiana

Dear Mother:

Your letter came today, the one you sent out the 21st. That's too bad about the well, don't you think you can get a driller some place? That will mean you'll have to haul water for the livestock. I sure hope you can find a well driller.

It rained real hard yesterday afternoon and now it's raining again this afternoon. But this time it's coming down twice as hard. A cloud blows up in five minutes time and by that time you had better look for cover.

I have been going to ground school for five days now and two of them were 10 hour days. I don't think I will get to fly this month but I might get a chance to. We have to take a 64 physical exam sometime next week. Also we get some of our overseas shots. Only seven shots and one long needle in the back for Yellow Fever. I hate to think of it.

Todd and I went to the town of Alexandria last Saturday night. You should see the soldiers in town on Saturday nights. You can hardly walk down the street they're so thick. We took our laundry in town to have cleaned. We have class "A" passes and can go to town any time we're off work. Our food is sure good here, we get three big meals a day with everything we want. Sometimes we get four meals a day. And there's no limit to the amount we take either.

So you like my pictures, do you? I can't help it if I'm thin. How about sending me three of them will you? I've got a certain place to put each one of them, maybe. Be sure and pack them solid.

I'm glad to hear that my bond got home OK. I was afraid it might have gotten lost or something. I can't do that anymore because I was a little short on cash this month.

That's swell about the knife. I'll get a lot of use out of it. I'll be glad to get it.

I've got some more things to send home before long. I won't be able to take any letters with me overseas. And a lot of other things too.

My pilot's name is Cavendish or something like that. I haven't seen him yet. He has been over here at our barracks two or three times trying to catch me here in the barracks. But every time he comes, I've gone some place.

I've got to stop for now and go to another class. I'll write some more a little later.

July 26 — Wednesday Morning:

I'm off school from 10 am until one this afternoon. Then I go from one to three and I'm off the rest of the day. We went out to the pistol range this morning and this afternoon we will go to the machine gun range.

This morning was a funny morning for summer time. The fog was clear down to the ground and it didn't lift until 9:30. It sure looked funny with all the fog settled in through thick swamps. They have some real big swamps here.

I met my pilot this morning out on the range. He went around asking for Tone until he found me. He is fairly tall with reddish black hair. He reminds me of John of Williams Field. I seem to like him OK.

I've got to go to town tonight to pick up my laundry.

I can't think of anything else to say now so I'll close for this time. Write soon.

Love, Kent

* * *

The rain pounded on the roof of the barracks, waking Kent up from a fitful sleep. His whole body ached and it felt as though a heavy weight pressed against his chest. A violent sneeze made his already stuffed head explode with pain.

"Tone, is that you moaning?" Todd hissed.

"Who else would it be?" Kent mumbled, his own words echoing in his head.

"Man, you've been sick for a couple of days now. You better get yourself to the infirmary. You can't fly if you're sick. It's already cost you your first crew."

"They have me on another one," Kent argued.

"For how long? The crews go when they have to. If you're not ready, you're just gonna get left behind like you were for Fletcher's crew. If you haven't gone to the infirmary by tonight. I'll drag you there myself." Todd turned over in his bunk, a clear indication that the conversation was over.

"I'm not that sick," Kent whispered to himself.

Even the whisper caused his temples to throb and his throat to sting. He shut his eyes and listened to the patter of rain, wishing for all the world that he felt better than he did.

When sleep refused to come, Kent sat up, determined to take his mind off of his ailments. He started a letter home.

* * *

July 27, 1944
Alexandria, Louisiana

Dear Mother:
Well, for the first time of my time in the Army, I'm in the hospital. It's nothing serious but a head cold. I'm almost over my cold but my head kept aching so I went on sick call. The Doc took my temperature and its 100 so he said I had to go in the hospital for three or four days to rest up. The Doc up here thinks I'm coming down with the measles but he's not sure. My head is still aching but I think I'll be OK in a few days. They sure feed you good here at the hospital. If I hang around here very long I'll get fat. I asked them here when I'd be getting out and they said "Oh, maybe three days or two weeks". They didn't know. I hear it's hard to get out of the hospital after getting in.
They told me I won't lose my crew, I sure hope I don't. I forgot to tell you where my pilot is from. He's from Saint Paul, Minn.
It sure is hot here. I'm just wet with sweat. I was talking with my pilot last night and he said for sure that we would get at least seven days leave after

graduating from this field. He said we could get a
class four priority on the civilian transport plane. So I
might be home about the first or middle of October.
Maybe if the war is going much better by then and
they don't need gunners too bad we will get a few
more days leave.

Well, I'd better close for now. Don't worry about
me because I'm OK. I'll be out in three or four days, I
hope.

Love, Kent

* * *

July 29, 1944
Alexandria, Louisiana

Dear Mother:
I'm getting out of this darn hospital in the
morning and I'm sure glad to get out too. I just got
back from a checkup by a Major and a Captain. I'm
still on flying status and I'll fly tomorrow or Monday.

How is everything at home? Is the well back to
normal yet? I sure hope it is.

I can't think of anything else to say right now.
Only it's plenty hot here. I wanted to let you know I'm
getting out in the morning.

Write soon.
Love, Kent

* * *

Kent walked out of the base hospital feeling like
a new man. They kept him longer than he thought

was necessary, but with the additional shots he had to get for his overseas missions, he knew it was better to be a hundred percent better.

The base teemed with soldiers, all heading off to their different duties. Kent was to report to his new crew later on that afternoon for flight practice. Until then, he thought he'd go on a walk around the base to take advantage of the rare sunshine of the day. First, he had to drop off his paperwork at the barracks.

He was just putting away his foot locker when someone called out, "Tone? You here?"

Curious, Kent stood. "Yes, sir."

The man who had called his name was Captain Cavendish, his pilot.

He was a tall fella with dark brown hair and a moustache that covered his upper lip. He reached out to shake Kent's hand. "I'm glad to see you up and about. You're fully recovered, then?"

"Yes sir. They wouldn't have let me go if I weren't. I feel good as new."

The Captain returned the smile and clapped the boy on the arm. "That's good to hear. Listen, I'm headed over to meet the rest of the crew. Care to join me?

Kent nodded. "Sure." Together the two left the barracks and made their way to the flight line.

"What made you want to join up?" Cavendish asked. He was curious about this gunner of his.

Kent shrugged. "The draft would have gotten me anyway. I wanted to have a choice in where I went. And I've always wanted to fly. It's the best feeling in the world being up in those clouds."

Kira Shay

Cavendish gave a soft chuckle. "I feel the same way. There's a lot of us flyboys. That's why I became a flight instructor for the new pilots coming up the ranks. I wanted to be sure those boys knew what they were doing up in the sky."

Shifting on his feet, Kent asked, "I thought you said you were a pilot?"

"I am," Captain Cavendish assured him. "See, one night one of the other instructors — a navigator by the name of Lyndon — he and I went out to the bar. Well, we got to talking and came to the conclusion that we'd like to see some action ourselves instead of sending off all these youngsters off to fight in the war. The next day, we went to our COs and told them our decision. Well, here I am."

Despite himself, Kent was impressed. "What about Lyndon? Is he on our crew too?"

"No, Lyndon is on a different crew. Our navigator is a fella called Greer. He's standing near the wall." He pointed at a group of men standing around a B-17.

As they came closer, Cavendish called out, "Fellas, I want you to meet Kent Tone. He's our new waist gunner. Tone, meet your crew." Captain Cavendish approached a square-jawed man with soot black hair that grayed at the temples. His chin had a healthy amount of stubble and his brown eyes were shaded by thick eyebrows. He chewed on the end of a cigar as he regarded Kent.

Patting the man on the shoulder, Cavendish said, "This surly looking son of a bitch is Fred Grey. He's your co-pilot. Nate Greer, our navigator." The short guy with a nervous smile standing next to Grey gave a small wave. "Next to him is Andrew Warrens, our radio operator." An average looking guy with a lot of freckles gave Kent a nod at his introduction. "Then we have Frank Barrett, our flight engineer." A skinny Italian man with a big nose nodded at the sound of his name. "George Wollard, Tony Bayer, and Larry Arnolds. They are your fellow gunners." The remaining three men each waved as their names came out. All of them looked friendly enough to Kent. "Our bombardier, Alex Smith, isn't here yet, but I expect him to arrive any day now."

Captain Cavendish gave everyone a long, hard look. A hush fell over the group as they waited. "Alright, men. Let's get up in the air and show 'em what we got!"

The team broke apart and made their way to the B-17 G they would be training in. Wollard trotted up to Kent. "Hey, Tone. Looks like you and me got the waist guns. I call dibs on the left." He had a thick southern accent that reminded Kent of some of the farmhands on the ranch when he was growing up. Wollard was a skinny guy. Privately, Kent wondered if he could handle those machine guns on the plane.

Kent shrugged. "Fine with me. I don't much care which one I get as long as I can shoot it."

Wollard laughed appreciatively. "You'll fit in just fine, Tone. Just fine indeed. Hey, you got any gum? My mouth is awful dry."

"Sure." Kent reached into his pocket and pulled out a few pieces of gum.

Wollard took what he'd been offered. "Thank you, sir. Come on. We don't want to be the last ones on board."

* * *

August 1, 1944
Alexandria, Louisiana

Dear Mother:
Your letter came Sunday. I got out of the hospital Sunday morning. This afternoon I flew from 1:30 until 8:00 tonight. Boy, did we get tired up there. We were flying in an 18 plane formation and was it rough flying. I thought the darn plane was going to shake to pieces. You see, the slip stream from the other planes caused us to fly through rough air. I got a little sick. They said they wanted to show the state of Louisiana what kind of Air Force they have here at Alexandria Airfield.

I like my co-pilot, he reminds me of Jack. He don't give a darn for anything. He slept most of the time up there today. We have a bombardier now, I met him today too. He never flew with us today.

I thought we were going to get paid yesterday but we never did. I guess we will have to wait until the 10th to get paid. I doubt if I can make it until then. I have exactly 20 cents left. I've even borrowed $6.00 already this month. I'll never send any money home anymore unless I'm real sure I have enough.

Mother, please send me three pictures and don't say anything to anyone about them. I'll send Loretta one from here. One more thing, be careful what you say about Loretta over the phone, will you. I've got two on the string and their pretty close together. I don't want Loretta to get mad or I don't want to hurt her in any way. Keep this under your hat, will you.

Monday, I got my flying clothes and also my 64 physical exam. They gave me three shots in the arm. I've got to go back in a week for some more. I've got the Cholera, Typhus, and Yellow Fever.

I like this field OK except for the hot weather. Last night it rained plenty hard, and Todd and myself was caught in it on our way to town. We were waiting on the bus when it started to pour. We got plenty wet before the bus came. I had to take some laundry into town. I only had a dollar in my pocketbook. Todd loaned me $6.00 already this month.

Tell Neil hello for me, will you. Tell him not to get over heated out there in Arizona. I wish I could be there to see him.

Sure send me those gloves, sweater and socks. I can use them very nicely. It gets cold up there about 25,000 feet.

I sure missed out on another furlough when I left Lincoln. All the gunners that were still there the 20th got furloughs and no set time to report back. Darn it anyway I could have gone on sick call and got off of this shipment. I heard about them but I didn't believe that it could be true. Now, some guys have heard from the fellows that got the furloughs. Darn the luck.

Tomorrow is our day off and am I glad. I'll be able to get some good old sack time.

The war doesn't looks good, does it? I wish the reds would hurry up and get to Berlin.

You asked me about those fellows from Mesa. I never got acquainted with them. When we got on the train we spread out all through the cars. I slept all the way to Tucson and then some more out of Tucson.

They're not here on this field.

Well, I'll have to sign off for now and hit the sack. I'm plenty tired.

Love, Kent

* * *

August 5, 1944
Alexandria, LA

Dear Mother, Dad and Klove:

Your letter came the other day, also the knife. Thanks a lot, Klove. It's just what I wanted. It will come in handy many times while in combat.

I flew almost all morning this morning and yesterday morning too. Today we went on a bombing mission, bombed the target from 8,000 feet. Our bombardier is a darn good one, he put nine bombs out of 10 smack in the center of the targets. Our ball turret gunner took moving pictures of the hits from the radio room. It's fun to watch the bombs fall. It wouldn't be much fun to ride one of them down, though. I walked across the open bomb-bay on the narrow cat walk. The strong wind coming through took my hat straight up to the top of the bomb-bay. It was a new cap I just got through buying. I thought for sure it was a gone cap. But when I got to the radio room door, I stopped and looked back and there it was resting on top of a bomb. I was lucky it never went right on down 8,000 feet.

OK you can give Jane Meyers a picture if you will. No, don't invite anybody over when i come home on furlough.

Sunday afternoon — I couldn't finish this last night so I'll do it now. I've been to ground school all day today. This morning we went to the machine gun range about 12 miles from here. I fired about 400 rounds of .50 cal.

The weather has been hot with cloudy skies and rain once in a while. That's one thing it really does here and plenty too. Seems like the ground here is always wet. There's even moss under all of the buildings. When flying around here you can see many swamps with muddy water in them. When we fly low enough, we can see the crocodiles sunning themselves on the banks.

If you will give Jane a picture that will save me a lot of trouble. If you haven't already sent them, will you give Jane one? She knows that I sent for three pictures. Tell Klove to use some common horse sense. Please.

Boy, you know it's no fun to be broke flat. I have borrowed 12 bucks since I got to this place. Still we haven't been paid. I have hopes we will get paid tomorrow. I can't even buy a coke or a candy bar. I have exactly one penny left. Boy, what a life!

We fly again tomorrow afternoon and I guess it will be a gunnery mission over the Gulf. It's no fun to go on those missions with guns all around you. I'm sorry I never finished this yesterday but I guess I'm kept too busy. Now it's 10:30 pm Monday night. We just got back from our gunnery mission over the Gulf. We flew out 38 miles from the coast and the range was 60 miles long and 10 miles wide. We could see fishing boats out there and had to watch out and not sink any of them. We flew real low over the water and shot at the white caps on the water. It was a lot of fun. The water was real pretty blue with a lot of white caps on it. I shot out of the nose and the waist of the ship. That's the only guns we can use on air to water. Once the waist gun ran away and before we could stop it about 40 rounds went wild out into the water. After we fixed it, it was OK.

Tuesday morning — they are paying us this morning. We fly again this afternoon and won't come in until 10 pm.

I'll close for now and mail this. Write soon.
Love, Kent
Hello Neil! Hope the heat isn't getting you down.

* * *

"Alright, men. This is Lieutenant Whitmore. He's going to accompany us on our drills today," Captain Cavendish announced one afternoon. "He is a good friend of mine visiting from Texas. Grey was good enough to sit out this practice round so we can take him up with us."

"Good enough to sit out," Wollard scoffed under his breath. "More like he was too hung over to fly."

Kent fought hard not to laugh at that. Grey was a good guy, but he did love his whiskey. A couple of times, he'd seen a fifth of the stuff poking out of Grey's pocket.

"Wollard, you got something to say?" Cavendish glared at the young gunner.

The man tried to wipe the smile off of his face. "No, sir. Just happy to have Lieutenant Whitmore with us today."

Captain Cavendish didn't believe any of it, but chose to let the matter drop. Addressing the whole crew, he said, "Today, we are focusing on target practice. Some of our AT-6s will be towing targets for you. For the love of God and country, don't shoot down the planes! Once we are done with the in air targets, we will move to some that are fixed about 500 feet off of the water. We are going pretty far out, so don't expect this to be a quick trip. Gunners, each of you will pick up different colored rounds so we can tell who hit what. The one that scores the highest amount of hits will earn a drink on me. Let's get a move on, gentlemen."

Wollard and Kent started towards the plane. In what had become a customary question before each practice run, Wollard asked, "Hey, Tone? You got a piece of gum?"

Wordlessly, Kent handed over a piece.

"May the best gunner win," Wollard grinned.

Arnolds piped up from behind them. "Yeah, that will be me."

"That'll be the day," Kent laughed.

As soon as they were safely off the ground, the Captain called out over their headsets, "Alright you gunners. It's time to show us what you got. Man your stations. The first AT-6s are coming our way."

"Loaded and ready," Arnolds confirmed from his place in the tail.

"Show off," Bayer retorted.

"All you bums had the same amount of time I did as we were taking off."

Cavendish's voice cut through their banter. "That's enough, fellas. Keep your focus."

In the wake of the warning, a tense silence descended. Kent scanned the skies just beyond his bay window.

Suddenly, the radio crackled to life. "We've got a bogie at three o'clock." It was the voice of Barrett, the flight engineer from the top turret.

That was Kent's side. He shifted the machine gun around and peered through the sites, searching for his target. A sudden burst of gunfire caused Kent to let out a curse. Barrett got the first shots off.

Just as he was sure he'd missed it, a flash of color through the clouds revealed the AT-6.

"I got eyes on him!" Kent exclaimed.

"Easy, Tone," Arnolds chided. "Don't get too excited. You're liable to shoot the plane down."

"Negative, do not, I repeat, do NOT shoot that plane down," Cavendish interjected.

Kent ignored the gibes and followed the cable trailing out of the AT-6 in his sites. About 180 feet behind the AT-6 was a flag with a bullseye painted on it. Kent aimed his machine gun and let rip a spray of .50 caliber bullets straight at the flag. More gunfire erupted from the tail and the turret guns.

"Damnit," Wolf cursed into his throat mic. "Just my luck I'm stuck on the wrong side of the damn plane."

Kent opened his mouth to give a smart retort when Barrett announced with excitement, "Bogie at 10 o'clock. Stop yapping and start shooting, Wollard."

For the next half hour, the steady rata-tat of machine guns firing against the droning noise of the bomber's engines filled the crew's ears. Kent lost himself in the noise and the smoke. The smell of gunpowder invaded his senses.

At last, Captain Cavendish's voice broke through the din. "Cease fire, cease fire! We are heading out to our next set of targets."

The cacophony stopped, leaving a ringing in the gunners' ears despite their ear protection. An exhilaration pumped through Kent from all the shooting. He'd made some pretty good hits and wanted to go again. Out of all the things he did in the military, this was by far his favorite. The plane shifted into a turn as they made their way to the water targets. Kent took the opportunity to reload his weapon.

In no time at all they were over the Gulf, the white targets bobbing innocently in the water. This time, the colored bullets didn't matter since they had joined up in formation with other B-17s. One by one, the bombers would dip close enough to the water so that the gunners could take aim. The targets formed a sort of run way that the planes followed. At the end of it, they would pull up, return to formation and wait their turn once more.

After 10 rotations of this, it was time to get ready and head back to base. Since the crew had to wait for the other bombers in the formation to complete their final runs, there was time to spare. Armed with a pack of cookies, Kent headed back to the tail of the plane where Arnolds sat. The tail gunner had already broken out his thermos of coffee by the time Kent settled in a makeshift seat of empty ammunition cans.

"Some damn good shooting today," Arnolds

commented as he offered a paper cup filled with black coffee to Kent.

"You too." Kent opened the cookies, selected two and exchanged the rest of the pack for the cup. He removed his earpiece and let out a breath. "Now we just wait to get back to the base."

The two gunners chewed quietly, each lost in their own thoughts. Eventually, Arnolds noticed something was off.

"Tone. You seeing this?" He gestured out the small window.

Kent peered out, not quite understanding what Arnolds was pointing to. Then it hit him. "The water! Those waves — are they from the propellers? We're way too close to the Gulf. What the hell is going on?"

Arnolds scrambled to put on his earpiece. "Warrens, we're mighty close to that ocean. What's happening? Are we gonna ditch?"

Kent waited in terrified anticipation for any sign of what was going on in Arnolds' face. The tail gunner listened for a moment, then his eyes got wide as he looked back up at Kent.

"We're ditching. We've gotta get to the radio room now!"

That was all Kent needed to hear. In a flash, he was up and running as fast as he could towards the radio room which was between the waist gun turrets and the bomb bay. Arnolds cut in front of him. There was no sign of Wollard at the waist gun turret. He must have already gotten to the radio room. Kent just passed Arnolds again when he realized he forgot something.

"Damnit!" he shouted. "I forgot my chest pack!"

Arnolds didn't pay any attention. Kent turned back for the flotation device he was supposed to wear on his chest. It laid benignly next to his gun. Quick as he could, he snatched it up, and slung it over his shoulder. Without missing a beat, he turned and took huge strides to catch up to his crewmate. Kent actually beat him to the radio room. Together, along with Wollard and Warrens, they crammed into the small compartment and waited for the violent crash into the Gulf. Warrens called over the radio several times, waiting to hear from Cavendish or even Whitmore.

With still no word from the cockpit and fearing the worst, Warrens started sending out the SOS or Save Our Souls transmission.

After what felt like an eternity, each of the crew members could feel the plane swing upward. Daring to let out a breath, Warrens, tried again for the cockpit.

"Captain, what in the blazes is going?"

Muffled laughter broke the radio silence. "Apologies, Warrens. I was just showing Whitmore here the fish we get in the Gulf. We didn't scare you men too badly, did we?"

The crew cast each other amazed and irritated glances. Finally, Warrens got back on the radio. "No, sir. We're all just fine jammed into this radio room."

There was more laughter before the mic cut off.

Wollard spoke first. "All that just to look at some damned fish?"

~ ~ ~

"Dinner's ready," I announced as I set the last plate of fry bread on the table. Brad helped Grandpa off the couch. Both of them approached the kitchen table.

"Grandpa, did I hear something about you having two girls on the line at once while you were in the military?"

Grandpa had the decency to appear sheepish, though a sly smile tugged at the corners of his mouth. "Yes, you heard right. Jane and Loretta."

"What happened?" I asked as I poured myself some of the beer Brad made. The two men sat down.

"Well, I had to decide which one would make me the happiest. When it came right down to it, I couldn't bear the thought of hurting Loretta. So, I said good-bye to Jane. Oh boy! Was her mother angry with me! She unleashed some spitfire on me, that woman did."

I snorted into my drink at his cavalier attitude. "You deserved a little spitfire," I told him.

Grandpa gave an amused chuckle. "Yes, I suppose I did."

Brad offered Grandpa a nondescript brown bottle. "Would you like to try some of the beer I made?"

"I would," Grandpa nodded. "Just a little bit though. I don't usually drink."

When they came to sit at the table, Brad poured him a small amount in a glass and handed it over. Grandpa took a sip and sat back. "It's not too bad. It reminds me of a night out with the crew in Louisiana."

~ ~ ~

A hurricane had blown through Louisiana, leaving the crew grounded. When the worst of the storm was over, more rain poured down on the small town than Kent had ever seen in his whole life. It rained for a solid week. At first, it was a novelty, the constant patter of the water on the roof, the sloshing wet whenever they left their bunks. After a couple of days, though, it all became tedious.

Sensing that some of the crew were becoming anxious, Grey decided it was time for a much needed reprieve. He burst into the barracks to find Kent, Arnolds, Warrens, and Barrett.

"Alright, men. We may be grounded, but we can still have some fun. Who wants to go out on the town tonight?"

"No thanks, Lieutenant," Barrett said. "I hear this rain is gonna let up. We should be back in the air tomorrow."

Grey threw up his hands. "All the more reason to celebrate!"

Barrett shook his head. He'd been out with Grey before and he knew it was better to stay in one more night than to get tangled up in all that.

"I'll go," Arnolds piped up. "I could stand to look at something other than these barracks."

"Tone and I will come too," Warrens said.

Grey nodded in approval. "Great. Barrett, last chance. Are you sure you want to stay here?"

Barrett was more than sure. "Absolutely. I'm due to write my wife anyway."

"Alright then. Arnolds, Warrens, Tone, come on

with me."

The four left the barracks, eager for the night ahead. Barrett waved to them as they left. When the door closed behind them, he settled back with his magazine and muttered, "Good luck, you bastards."

Grey led the young airmen to his car, a sleek black Cadillac coupe.

As Grey held the door open to his coupe, Arnolds balked at getting in, a thought crossing his mind.

Grey barked out, "Arnolds, what's the hold up? You look like you're about to get into a whale's stomach."

"Sorry, sir. It's just . . ." he hesitated, trying to find the right words. "Should we change, sir? Into our dress uniforms?"

Grey let out a deep belly laugh while keeping his cigar tightly in the corner of his mouth. "Son, where we are going, the ladies won't care a whit about dress uniforms. What you've got on is just fine. Now get in, Princess."

Arnolds blushed at the nickname and clambered into the back seat with Kent. Warrens had gotten the front passenger spot. Grey took his place at the wheel and the engine roared to life. "Alright, men! Let's have ourselves a grand evening, shall we?"

With a loud squeal of the tires and a hearty exhalation of smoke, the car lurched forward into the night.

The evening began at one of Grey' favorite establishments; a dimly lit club called the Lion's Den. It was a small place crammed in between two other bars that were no less noisy or busy. It took Kent a long moment for his eyes to adjust to the dark colored lights and the smoke. He trailed behind the others as Grey led them to a table at the back of the club.

"Wait here," Grey shouted before grabbing Warrens and heading back over to the bar.

A band played a slow, melodic jazz number as a woman dressed in what seemed to Kent as nothing but sparkles crooned along with the music. It was quite different than his preferred country western music, but he found his toes tapping along despite himself.

Grey and Warrens returned with drinks in each hand. When each of them held what smelled like scotch, Grey raised his glass and shouted, "To you, Arnolds, Warrens, and Tone. We're gonna give those bastards in Europe what's coming to them!" At that pronouncement, Grey brought the glass to his lips and tilted his head back, allowing the amber hued liquor to slide down his throat. The airmen did the same. Kent choked a bit on the acrid taste and burn of the liquid.

A young, pretty waitress sauntered over to the table. "Celebrating, I see," she said with a smile. "Did you boys just get back state-side?"

"No, ma'am," Arnolds said. He was about to go on, but Grey kicked him under the table.

To distract from Arnolds' sudden yelp of pain, Grey took hold of the waitress's hand. "Yes, miss. We just got back and we are wanting to celebrate! Would you get us a bottle of your finest whiskey and let your girlfriends know that we've got some soldiers here that have been waiting a long time to see a pretty face?"

The waitress nodded knowingly. "Of course I will, darlin'. That whiskey will be right up."

Since he wasn't used to drinking, the shot of whiskey had already gone to Kent's head. The next shot was accompanied by two women sitting themselves at the booth. The third arrived as one of the ladies took Arnolds out to the dance floor. The fourth came just after Warrens and the lady hanging on his arm wandered into a dark corner of the bar.

The room started to swim. He smiled and laughed at the way his crewmates were awkwardly dancing with the more experienced women. Grey clapped him on the shoulder and laughed, his cigar smoke adding to the hazy atmosphere. He said something, but Kent couldn't quite make it out. Something about pie-eyed and light weight.

What happened that night was a dim memory; he'd been drunk, that much he knew, but specifically what happened, he would never remember.

When he woke up in what looked like a jail cell, his head hurt so badly that he thought he was going to die. The room spun maliciously, as though it were trying to make him vomit all over the cot he was stretched out on. Casting his gaze to the left, he caught sight of Warrens. He looked as bad as Kent felt. Groaning, Kent shut his eyes against the light coming through a small window on the other side of the bars.

Suddenly the sweet aroma of a cigar brought back jumbled memories of the night before and an undeniable urge to vomit. He barely made it to the small garbage can left next to his cot by a considerate MP before the contents of his stomach evacuated.

The sound and the smell of him retching were enough to set Warrens off as well.

When they could vomit no more and were gasping for air, they heard Lieutenant Grey' deep chuckle. "You boys look like you've been through Hell."

The loud, chipper quality to the Lieutenant's voice grated on the young man. All he could do was grimace.

"Well, come on then. We are due on the flight line in an hour and you boys need to get yourselves cleaned up."

"Flight line?" Warrens moaned. "Aren't we grounded?"

"No. Turns out Barrett was right. The rain stopped. Now we gotta do our jobs. Come on. I'll give you a lift back to your barracks."

It was through sheer will power that Kent got to his feet and walk out. As he and Warrens climbed into Grey' car in the blinding brightness of the sunny day, Kent gathered enough courage to ask, "Lieutenant Grey? What happened last night?"

"Yeah," Warrens added. "I can't remember any more than dancing with some woman in a club."

Grey smiled as he started up the car. "Believe me, boys, you had quite a night before you were picked up by those MPs for being out past curfew. Kent, you seemed determined to get one of their hats. You managed to get one too; but you couldn't run to save your life, so you just flopped onto the ground, clutching it like a football and didn't want to give it up. It's too bad you don't remember it."

Once the two of them were showered and more or less presentable, they made their way to the flight line, grimacing at the sheer amount of noise. Kent kept his sunglasses on as if to minimize the brightness of the day. Warrens nudged him and pointed at Arnolds. The tail gunner looked positively green and swayed a bit on his feet. "Wonder why he didn't get picked up by the MPs," Warrens whispered, half envious, half grateful.

Captain Cavendish started with an overview of what they would be doing that day. His voice seemed overly loud, each syllable making Kent's head pound even more.

"Today we are going to practice flying in formation over the Gulf and then up over Texas. There aren't any targets for you gunners, but be sure to keep an eye out. We are treating this like a real mission, not just a practice, alright?"

Kent was too nauseas to nod, so he added a soft "Yes, sir" before shuffling off with his crewmates to their stations.

It was the worst flight in Kent's life. A few bumps of turbulence had him hanging out of his gunner's window ready to hurl. One particularly nasty piece of air caused the whole plane to drop about 10 feet. Kent and Wollard both hit the ceiling before slamming onto the floor.

"What the hell was that?" Wollard bellowed into his throat mic. "We almost flew out of the damn plane!"

"Can't help turbulence," the Captain responded. "Just hang on and you'll be fine."

Muttering under his breath, Wollard picked himself up and gave Kent a hand in getting to his feet. "Hey, you notice something?" he asked Kent in his thick Arkansas drawl. "Weren't we supposed to be in formation?"

With one hand on his throbbing head, Kent asked, "Yeah, so?"

"Well, where are the other planes? I haven't seen any since we took off."

Squinting out into the bright blue sky, Kent realized that Wollard was right.

At Kent's sudden look of panic, Wollard got on his mic once more. "Captain, I don't like to complain, but ain't we supposed to be in formation? I don't see any other planes."

"Greer, confirm our heading to the rendezvous point," Cavendish requested with a deadly calm.

"Hang on. I am confirming coordinates."

The Captain had never sounded so irate. "What do you mean, 'hang on'? Greer, this is not some Sunday drive. Coordinates, now."

"I — I don't know. They aren't coming out right. I am not sure where we are."

"Are you saying that we are lost?" Grey injected incredulously.

"No!" Greer said. "No, I think I can do this. Based on the current trajectory, if we adjust 23 degrees south we should be on track for the Gulf and the rendezvous."

"Negative," Cavendish replied. "I know exactly where we are. If we adjust 23 degrees south, we will be in Mexico."

Wollard and Tone looked at each other with

concern. Their navigator didn't know where they were? If they'd been overseas, they could have gone into enemy territory alone. The radio silence didn't bode well.

Using his own memory of the layout of the land, Captain Cavendish returned the B-17 to Alexandria, touching her down before the rest of the formation finished their run. As soon as they landed, Cavendish was out of the cockpit and stalking down the flight line, leaving his crew behind in wonderment.

Kent felt bad for Greer. It must be tough luck having screwed up so bad that a practice mission had to be abandoned.

* * *

September 25, 1944
Alexandria, Louisiana

Dear Mother, Dad and Klove:
Your letter came the other day and I'm sorry I haven't written sooner. But I guess I'm just too lazy or something. There isn't much to write about around here.

Well, the CO of the field told us the bad news yesterday. He said that we will get no furloughs from here or anywhere else. So that's that. He said that we are headed overseas soon and fast. Of course he said he felt sorry for us but there wasn't anything he could do. We leave here around the 6th. I can't tell you any details. Only that we are headed for Lincoln. There we will stay about four to eight days and then we pick up a new B-17 and fly it over. We will get all new clothes and all the combat equipment we need. So I guess I won't see you until I get back. I'll get my 35 missions (only 35 now) in and come home. I've got a good pilot and he takes no chances at all.

I didn't take out any allotments at all. I've decided to send home what money I get over there. They tried to make me take out a will but there isn't any sense in doing that. Because I haven't got anything.

You can still write to me through my address here. Then I'll send you my APO number as soon as I can. After I leave Lincoln, you won't hear from me for a long while. You know how it is.

I'll be glad to get the cookies because it's hard to stay on the post. Oh. I forgot to tell you that I'm restricted. You see that fellow second from the left in our crew picture? Well, he and I went to town Friday night. The MPs pick up all the GIs that stay on the streets after 11:30 at night. Well, we were picked up and brought back. I guess we are restricted for a week. Anyway, our passes have been taken and I don't know when we will get them back. Some life.

They had another crack up here on the post. All of the crew bailed out OK but the plane cracked up. That's two in one week.

I'm going to send another box of things home. Please keep it for me, will you.

That's too bad Klove never passed the test. Maybe he can find something in my old Army tests I took in college. Physics is the most important. Look over them. That's about all they ask you about engines. Hope you pass it OK next time.

Gee, I hope you get that well drilled pretty soon. That's too much work hauling water.

Well, I guess I'd better sign off for now. I can't think of anything else to write. Write soon.
Love, Kent

* * *

The next day found the entire crew back on the flight line with the notable absence of their navigator, Greer. Standing next to Captain Cavendish and Lieutenant Grey was a tall gentleman with blondish-red hair streaked with grey.

"Crew, I want to introduce Lieutenant Lyndon. He will be our new navigator."

Lieutenant Lyndon nodded and said, "Hello."

"Lyndon," Kent whispered to Wollard. "Why does that name sound familiar?"

"Probably because he used to be an instructor, like Cavendish," Wollard replied. "They were buddies who decided not to teach anymore. They wanted to see some action."

"That's right. Wow, we sure are lucky. Both pilot and navigator used to be instructors. Most crews would kill for the amount of knowledge we have on our side."

Wollard grinned, "Damn straight, Tone."

They returned their attention to Captain Cavendish. "In addition to losing Greer, our own bombardier Smith is going on a different crew. Since we are mostly going to attack in formation, we will follow the lead plane. When they drop their payload, we will drop ours. Barrett will be acting as bombardier while we are overseas.

"Speaking of which," Cavendish paused to let all

of the new information sink in. "Gentlemen, we have our orders. We leave for Lincoln, Nebraska in two weeks. Then we will get orders for overseas."

A sudden thrill ran through the crew in the form of excited murmurs. Orders! That meant they'd see some action sooner than they thought. The odd mix of thrill and dread made it hard to concentrate on what else the Captain had to say.

"Now, since we didn't get to complete our practice mission yesterday, we are going to go through it at least twice today. Gunners, your targets will be set up in the Gulf. We will be in formation, so be careful not to shoot anyone down, alright?"

* * *

September 29, 1944
Alexandria, Louisiana

Dear Mother, Dad and Klove:
Your letter came yesterday and the cookies should arrive today. Don't you worry, I'll get rid of them without any trouble. I'll bet they are real good.

The weather has been bad yesterday and today. It kept us grounded both times. I'm glad because we have to fly every day we are here anyway.

We lost our bombardier and navigator the other day. Our navigator wasn't any good so they gave us another one. He is a 1st Lieutenant the same as our pilot. So that makes our crew the highest in rank. They took our bombardier off because we don't need one. Our armor gunner is acting bombardier in combat. All he has to do is push a button to release the bomb when the lead ship drops his. The lead ship does all the bomb sighting.

We got our passes back yesterday so now we can go to town again. We were restricted for five days. The radio operator and myself.

Well in about two weeks I guess I'll be over in England some place. Our pilot is sure that we are going to England. The way we will go will either be the northern or southern route. Northern route takes us up past Iceland and we will stay there about two weeks before going on. But the other route goes from Fla. to South America and that way looks like a better route. I'll see a lot of country and water too.

No, there is no chance of getting any kind of furlough or leave now. Not until I come back. They could give us leaves but they won't. That's the Air Corps for you.

Well, pay day comes again tomorrow, this time I think I'll send some money home. I've saved up quite a bit from last pay day. We won't need any money over there.

The other night our mess hall had some poor chicken salad. About 130 guys went to the hospital with ptomaine poison. The meat wagon was going back and forth to the hospital all night taking sick guys out. I was lucky I never ate supper that night. When I got over to the mess hall it was closed up tight. Even the Mess Sgt. got sick too. It was good for him.

I'll send you my new APO address as soon as I get it. But you still can write to me through this field. I won't be able to write until I get over there. And it will take a while to get over here.

Well, I can't think of anything else to say. I'd

better sign off for now. Write soon.
   Love, Kent

* * *

October 2, 1944
Alexandria, Louisiana

Monday Afternoon
Dear Mother:
   I want to thank you for the box of cookies. They
were very good. The boys on my crew liked them too.
Todd liked the date cookies as good as I do. Gee,
thanks a lot. I got another box of cookies and one fruit
cake from Aunt Oie and they were very good too. They
came today so I haven't gotten them eaten yet.
   I got my picture taken the other day in my blouse
but they turned out with too much light in them so
they had to be taken over. I had to have them taken
over in my sun tan shirt and cap. I saw the proofs this
afternoon and picked the one I liked. I won't be here
to pick them up but they are sending them home for
me. One large one and three small ones. I know what
you will say when you see them. You'll think I'm thin
but I don't think I'm very thin. If you think they are
very good pictures, will you give Jane one? Not unless
you think they are OK. Tell her I said for you to give
her one.
   We have been flying every day now for the last
week and so far no time off. We are to fly tomorrow
afternoon and then again the day before we leave.
Darn their hides anyway.
   I wired home $90.00 the other day. Did you get it?

I don't want to carry so much money around with me. I've got plenty to last over until next payday. Keep it for me, will you?

Well, it won't be long until we will be headed across the pond. Darn it I wish they would give me a furlough first. I think the second Air Force is mean as heck to do this to us. Other fellows are getting furloughs.

Well, I guess I better sign off for now but I'll write more before I leave here.

Love, Kent

* * *

The train to Lincoln left Alexandria before dawn. The cars were filled to the brim with airmen. Everyone sat with their crews, for the most part. Kent and his crew were near the back of the train, their gear stowed in open compartments overhead. Wollard sat next to Kent, a map in his hands.

"Look!" He shoved the map into Kent's hands. "We are going right through Cherry Valley, Arkansas! That's naught a mile away from my home town."

"Is that so?" Kent asked, not really interested. He was too polite not to be courteous in the face of so much excitement.

"I'm gonna get off this here train and hide in the woods. I know them like the back of my hand. Ain't no one in the military gonna find me until this war is over!"

Kent eyed his fellow waist gunner apprehensively. He'd been acting funny since they

151

got the news of their deployment.

"You don't mean that," Kent laughed off his worry. "Why, you'd miss out on all the fun. You know as soon as we go, we're gonna put an end to this war. We're gonna be heroes."

Wollard frowned at Kent, his expression serious. "Tone, heroes get shipped back in pine boxes." Having said that, he stared out of the window and didn't say any more.

The way Wollard acted unnerved Kent. He switched seats with Barrett, choosing to put himself near Arnolds and Warrens.

"Hey, fellas. Watch out for Wollard. He's liable to run if we stop for any reason. He's got himself the jitters."

Each of the airmen solemnly nodded. For the rest of the trip, one of them stayed with Wollard, though he never tried to run.

Compared to the sweltering heat of Alexandria, Lincoln was downright chilly. The crew checked in at the airbase and waited to hear what their next orders would be. They waited for three whole days without a word.

Because of the change in temperature and the higher altitude, Kent developed a head cold. On the fourth morning in Lincoln, he had a headache that wouldn't quit. Still, when Captain Cavendish ordered the crew to meet at 10 o'clock, he took a couple of aspirin and went to see what their orders were.

"I know you're all anxious to get news as to where we are headed." Captain Cavendish paused, more for dramatic effect than anything. What he had was good news and he wanted to savor it.

At last, he couldn't hold it back any more. "You will have a two-week furlough before we ship out."

As the crew erupted into sudden hoots and hollers, Cavendish held up a stack of envelopes. The men reluctantly quieted and waited for him to go on.

"I have here a train ticket home for each of you and one to come back. At the end of your two weeks, you are to report back here and we will be heading overseas."

He handed out the envelopes, watching as the men snatched them and then ran to find the nearest telephone to call home. Kent was the last to receive his. He waited anxiously, thinking only that he had to call Loretta. Maybe she'd be able to come for a visit while he was back.

Captain Cavendish handed him his envelope. "God speed, Tone. Don't get into too much trouble, you hear?"

Kent nodded, though he couldn't wipe the smile off of his face. "No, sir. I am just thankful I get to go home. I didn't think we were going to before we had to go overseas."

"I know. I had to pull a few strings, but you men deserve it. After all, we will be getting into one hell of a mess. Go on, then. Best call and make sure someone will come and get you from the train station."

"Yes, sir!" Kent walked as quickly as he could back towards the barracks. His head, though still stuffy, felt loads better than it had an hour ago. It was amazing what the thought of heading home could do to a soldier.

~ ~ ~

My uncle came to pick up Grandpa as I cleaned up dinner. Brad and I had been enraptured by Grandpa's stories. We didn't want him to leave so soon.

My uncle waited patiently as Grandpa wrapped up his tales. At last, he was maneuvered into the waiting truck and they drove away.

As I closed the door behind them, Brad said, "Your Grandpa is really cool."

I grinned. "I know."

PART SEVEN
GOING TO WAR

"We have to stop at a store," Grandpa told me when I picked him up one bright summer day.

"Why is that?"

"Because Mother always told me to bring a gift when you are visiting someone's home. It's the polite thing to do."

"Alright. What do you want to get?"

Grandpa bit his bottom lip, deep in thought. "How about a cake or something?"

"Sure, we can do that," I said. "We will stop at a store over in my mother-in-law's neighborhood though. I'm afraid whatever we get her from this side of town will melt on the drive over."

"That's fine," Grandpa said, and settled back into his seat. "You know, Aunt Oie was amazing at making cakes. She had one particular recipe that she was known for; her white cake."

"Really? I didn't know she baked."

"Oh yes. She was a wonderful baker. This one

time, when she was visiting, she made her signature dessert; a white cake with white frosting. Her and Mother were taking it to a bridge party."

~ ~ ~

While Kent was still healing from his broken hip as a child, he couldn't do all of his usual chores of feeding the cows and pigs. Instead, he had to do tasks around the house, which he hated. Being confined made him more than a little stir crazy. He couldn't wait to get better so he could go run in the fields.

He cleaned the windows on that bright, clear Saturday. His mother had gathered up her eggs and was going into town to sell them to the local markets. Kent wiped at the glass with a rag, frowning at the sunshine and the cloudless desert on the other side.

"Aunt Oie and I will be back in a while," Eva said as she donned her jacket and hat. "We are taking the eggs to Mr. Basha. I expect all of those windows to be done. And don't touch the cake in the kitchen. That's for the card party tonight, you hear me, Kent?"

"Yes, Mother," the boy said morosely.

Eva stopped to give him a kiss on the head before heading out. Oie waited for her in the car.

Kent watched the two of them drive off down the dirt road. When they were out of sight, he tossed the rag onto a nearby table and hobbled out to the porch. Filling his lungs with the crisp winter air, Kent decided that it was a good day to cause some trouble. He had been good since getting out of the hospital, but the restrictions were weighing on him. Even his favorite aunt and uncle couldn't brighten his mood. Yes, sir, it was about time to stir things up. The only question was how. After looking around at the desert and the cotton fields beyond, he remembered what his mother had said.

With a devilish grin, he hobbled back into the house and made his way in to the kitchen. Sitting enticingly on the table, was a beautiful three layer white cake with snow white frosting.

The implement of his destruction sat innocently enough next to Aunt Oie's gorgeous and delicious creation: the salt shaker. In a flurry of movement, before he could talk himself out of it, Kent seized the shaker and sprinkled as much salt as he could over the icing. When the light caught the crystals in just the right way, the cake glittered.

The sound of the front door opening made Kent jump. Slamming the salt shaker back onto the table, he took up his crutches and moved over to the kitchen sink.

Heavy footsteps preceded his father's deep voice. "Kent, what are you doing?"

Thinking quickly, Kent raised up a dirty glass from the sink.

"Are you finished with the windows like your mother asked you?" Albert knew his son was up to something; Kent had that smug smile on his face.

"Not yet. I was just getting back to those."

A moment of silence descended as Albert considered what to say next. "Well, when you are finished, come on out to the barn. I need you to mix the feed for the hogs. I reckon you can do that without putting too much pressure on your leg."

The smug expression on Kent's face morphed into a genuine smile. Finally, he got to stop this housework nonsense. "I'll be down in 15 minutes. I just have to finish the bedroom windows." He wasted no time in putting the glass back into the sink and hobbled off to complete his work.

Albert watched him go with a look of bemusement. For all the mischief his sons caused, he was really lucky that they had a strong work ethic and a love for the ranch.

After hours of measuring and grinding the feed for the pigs, Kent's arms ached but his spirits were high. Albert was meticulous about the feed, often times he would change up the ratios of the grain and alfalfa. Sometimes he would put store bought nutrients in it, but that was only on occasion. Kent soaked up all of that knowledge like it was water.

With the feed mixed and ready for morning, Albert and Kent made their way to the ranch house for supper. Oie had lit the kerosene lamps, making the house bright while Eva put the finishing touches on supper for the men. The women would have supper over at Blanche's as they played bridge. Sitting at the table, Kent caught sight of the three-tiered white cake and a pang of guilt coursed through him.

When Oie came into the kitchen to set one of the kerosene lamps on the table, Kent couldn't hold in his wicked secret any longer.

"Aunt Oie, I have to tell you something."

"What's that, dear?" she asked as she placed the

glass cylinder over the flame.

"I don't know what got into me, but I ruined your cake."

Oie stilled and glanced over to her cake sitting benignly on the kitchen counter. Nothing seemed amiss. "What on earth are you talking about?"

Taking in a deep breath, Kent confessed in a rush, "I poured salt all over the icing. I'm awful sorry I did it. I don't know what came over me."

Disbelievingly, Oie went over to her cake and squinted at it. One of the glinting salt crystals caught her eye and she scooped up some of the icing with her finger and tasted it.

She nearly spat it back out.

"Kent! How could you do such a thing?" Eva scolded, putting her hands on her hips. "Your aunt took a long time to make that. Now we won't be able to take anything to the bridge party!"

Oie donned an apron and grabbed a butter knife from the drawer. With quick, methodical movements she began scraping the salted icing off of the cake. "Eva, hand me that mixing bowl. I think I have just enough time to whip up some new frosting. Hopefully the salt didn't soak into the cake itself."

"I'm awful sorry, Aunt Oie," Kent said.

Oie shook the butter knife at her nephew. "You will be sorry if this doesn't work. I can't begin to think of what would have possessed you to do such a thing."

Kent hung his head. "I know. I was just so tired of being cooped up. . . Sorry, Aunt Oie."

Eva sighed, her fingers pressed against her

temple. "Go to your room. You won't have any supper tonight. With the way things are, we can't afford to be so wasteful."

With his gaze cast down to the floor, Kent slid off of the kitchen chair and took his crutches with him to his bedroom. He glanced back into the kitchen once to see his brother, father, and uncle digging into their supper. Eva finished scraping the remaining salted frosting off of the cake as Oie started to prepare the next batch.

In the morning, Kent emerged from his bedroom, his stomach growling. Music floated through the air, emanating from the large horn attached to his mother's victor in the living room. He smelled the eggs being fried and freshly baked bread being grilled into toast. Coming into the kitchen, he found Aunt Oie and his mother laughing as they finished making breakfast.

Kent sat himself at the table, more than eager for breakfast. Oie brought a freshly fried egg and toast on a plate and set it in front of him. Seeing as the women were in a good mood, Kent thought it only polite to ask, "How did the cake turn out last night?"

Casting knowing glances at each other, the women quieted their laughter. Kent began to wonder if everything had turned out so badly that they weren't going to talk to him at all.

At last Oie said, "I don't know how, but I got more compliments on my cake than ever before. Several of the ladies wanted the recipe. But so help me, Kent, if you ever do something like that again, I will tan your hide."

Kent tried unsuccessfully to hide his grin by stuffing a large bite of egg into his mouth.

~ ~ ~

"I am truly amazed that you survived your childhood," I told Grandpa as we pulled into the parking lot of a grocery store.

Grandpa laughed. "I was a little rascal, alright."

I parked the car at the local grocery store and regarded the smiling visage of my grandpa. "How about we get Carla some flowers instead of a cake?"

Grandpa dipped his head in a nod and replied, "Whatever you think is best."

Not long after we left the store, we sat around my mother-in-law's table. The bright and cheerful bouquet Grandpa had presented her with sat in the center.

"It was mighty nice of you to invite me for dinner," Grandpa said.

Carla returned, "It was mighty nice of you to come over. I love it when you visit. You always tell the best stories."

I served Grandpa a plate of Carla's lasagna and he dug in with gusto.

"He was telling me on the way over here how much trouble he got into as a kid," I said as I took my seat. "Were you as mischievous in the Army?"

"Oh, I don't know about that," Grandpa replied. "I like to think we all pranked each other. It wasn't just me."

I raised an eyebrow at that. "Is that so?"

Carla chimed in. "What did you do in the

military?"

Wiping his mouth, Grandpa cleared his throat. "I was a waist gunner on a B-17 during the Second World War."

"Really? Where were you stationed?"

"Italy, though we thought for sure we were going to Great Britain."

"Is that right?" my mother-in-law asked. "They didn't tell you where you were going?"

Grandpa shook his head. "Not at all. We had to wait until we were up in the air to open our coordinates."

~ ~ ~

"Where do you think they'll send us, Tone?" Wollard asked. The whole crew sat in the mess hall, having returned only three days previously from their furloughs. All of them were anxious about their upcoming orders.

"I suspect we will go to England like Captain Cavendish says," Kent replied, taking a big bite of his oatmeal.

"I hear we are getting a brand new plane to take with us," Arnolds piped up. "A shiny new bomber that will have to be outfitted with guns once we get wherever we are headed."

Kent's friend Todd swallowed his mouthful of orange juice and added, "So is our crew. Our pilot got our orders this morning. Don't know where we are going yet, but we leave later on this afternoon."

"Then the Captain probably already has our orders," Wollard said. "We're all in the same squadron. I don't think they'd send us to different places. That wouldn't make sense."

Kent addressed Todd, "Do you know where you fellas are going?"

Todd nodded his head. "We're headed to Goose Bay, Newfoundland. We'll fuel up and get the rest of our orders. They didn't tell us outright where we were being sent."

Kent shrugged, "Well, what do you expect? If the wrong people got wind of our deployments, we'd be sitting ducks."

The men nodded and chewed the rest of their breakfasts thoughtfully. Before they were able to finish, Lieutenant Grey found them. "Tone, Arnolds, Wollard," He called in a deep, commanding tone. "Meet me on the flight line. It's time."

The men glanced at each other. Without a word, they got up and followed in Grey' wake.

"Good luck," Todd called.

The rest of the crew had already assembled. Captain Cavendish waited until he was sure he had their undivided attention. "I hope you all had a good time with your loved ones. It's good to see you all back here refreshed and ready for action." He held a small white envelope above his head. "Gentlemen, in my hands, I have our orders. Tonight we go to war."

A cheer erupted from the assembled crew. Finally, some action! A thrill of excitement and a bit of fear thickened the air around them.

"Where are we going?" Barrett called out. "England?"

"Algeria?" Wollard guessed.

"Hawaii?" asked the ever hopeful Arnolds.

Cavendish let out a chuckle and brought the envelope down. He ran his fingers along the edges. "It's not that simple. Today, we head for Goose Bay, Newfoundland. After we leave Goose Bay, we will receive the coordinates to where we will be stationed. Until we are up in the air, we won't know where we are headed. I don't even know, so don't bother asking. Be ready, we leave at 1600."

"It's just like Todd said," Kent whispered to Arnolds.

"Of course it is. We're going with him," Arnolds replied. "Bet you anything we are going to England and we'll go the Great Circle Route."

"I don't want to take that bet," Kent laughed. You're probably right."

Newfoundland was dreary and bitterly cold. The squadron of brand new B-17 bombers landed in St. Johns under the cover of a cloudy night. What was supposed to be a quick refueling turned into three days of agonized waiting for the weather to clear. There wasn't much for the men to do except keep close by in case the haze cleared enough to take off. The waiting played hell on their nerves, all of them anxious about where they might be headed.

* * *

October 17, 1944

Dear Mother, Dad and Klove:
I'm writing this letter to let you know that I'm OK and feeling fine. I have an APO number now and it's

on the envelope. It's just a temporary APO until the Army gives me another number.

I can't tell you where I am now but it's not a bad country. I'm a long way from home but so far I haven't gotten home sick. I'd like to be home, sure, but I'm not home sick. I guess I've been in the Army too long for that.

I bought a lot of things today. Shoes, gloves, scarf, watch band, billfold, and lots of other things. Boy, I really blew myself today.

I've got to go now. I'm OK. Don't worry I'll be OK. All my love, Kent

* * *

At last, on the fourth morning, Captain Cavendish gathered his crew and announced they couldn't wait any longer and would be taking off.

"Alright men, let's get this bird in the air. It's soupy, so be extra vigilant."

Within a half an hour, everyone and their one bag was on board and ready for take-off. The fog was so thick, Kent could barely see a foot in front of his face.

"How in the hell is Cavendish gonna take off in this? He can't possibly see anything," he grumbled to Arnolds and Wollard who were perched with him in the belly of the plane.

"Don't worry. He's a good pilot. We are in safe hands," Arnolds assured Kent. A tremor of worry made his voice waver.

The roar of the engines covered the tense silence as the B-17 began to move down the runway, gaining speed with every foot it traveled. A shuddering lurch preceded their take off. Higher and higher they climbed, the air getting colder and colder.

In the distance, beyond the rumble and whir of the bomber's engines, were other quieter booms. Flashes of light could be seen below them, muted by the thick fog so it looked like distant lightning.

Arnolds pointed at the light. "What in blazes is that?"

No one had an answer for him.

As the bomber gained more altitude, the fog lessened. Kent could see more clearly than he had in days, though the cloud cover wouldn't go away. The tense silence in the plane evaporated as time marched on. After about an hour or so, the quiet contemplation of the crew was broken by Captain Cavendish's voice coming over the com. "You men may want to get out your oxygen masks. We are cruising at 17 hundred feet."

"Criminey," Wollard muttered and fumbled for his mask. "What's he trying to do, kill us? We're supposed to have these on at 10,000 feet!"

"Calm down, Wollard. We're perfectly fine," Kent assured him as he fastened on his own oxygen mask.

"Lyndon, have you opened our orders yet?" Arnolds asked over the com. "Where are we headed anyways?"

"Yeah," chimed in Barrett. "Where are we going?"

"Gentlemen, I am opening our orders now."

The coms were quiet as each of the men waited, holding their breath.

Lyndon's voice broke the silence. "We are headed to Foggia, Italy."

The men took in this information and turned it over in their minds. At last Wollard spoke up. "Where the hell is Foggia, Italy?"

"Hell if I know," Bayer replied.

Lyndon piped up again. "According to the map and coordinates, it's a small town in the heel of Italy near Bari."

"That's well and good, but right now we need to focus on getting over the Azores," Captain Cavendish chided. "I can't get over this cloud bank. Lyndon, do you know if we are on course?"

Muffled curses could be heard as Lyndon tried to get a reading. "Negative. The cloud cover is too thick. Can you get this plane under the clouds? Maybe I can get a reading using the white caps."

"Is he crazy?" Wollard asked Kent and Arnolds.

"How close do you need?" Cavendish asked calmly. He seemed genuinely unfazed by the request.

"Five hundred feet ought to do," Lyndon replied.

"Five hundred feet?" Echoed Bayer. "Sir, that puts us well within range of any German U-boats."

Lyndon didn't like Bayer's tone. He argued, "There may or may not be Germans, but I can tell you for sure we will go down somewhere in the Atlantic if I can't get us to the Azores. I don't know about you, but I'd risk the German attack to make sure we are going the right way."

No one said anything in the wake of Lieutenant Lyndon's reasoning.

At last, Captain Cavendish simply said, "Roger that."

The plane tilted downwards as the pilot aimed the nose of the plane towards the water. Kent, Arnolds, and Wollard held on tightly to whatever they could to keep themselves in place.

"You can thank me later," Lyndon assured the crew.

"Remember that time in training when we thought we were gonna ditch over the Gulf?" Arnolds asked Kent.

"You mean when our pilot decided to look at some fish? Yeah, I remember."

Arnolds forced a laugh. "Seems like old times."

Soon enough the plane leveled out. Kent peered out of the window at the riotous ocean below. For the life of him he couldn't fathom how Lyndon would be able to tell a thing from those conflicting waves of water.

Lyndon, for his part, sounded confident on the com as he advised to adjust course. They stayed low under the cloud cover. Hours passed without even the suggestion of a German U-boat. At long last, Kent spotted islands in the distance.

"Behold, gentlemen," Lieutenant Lyndon said over the coms. "Those would be the Azores."

They landed and refueled the plane as the others in the squadron touched down. Kent kept a look out for Todd, but he never showed up.

As they prepared to leave the next morning, Kent pulled Captain Cavendish aside. "Sir, did all of our squadron make it? I thought my friend Todd's plane was supposed to be with us, but he isn't here."

A somber expression came over the Captain. "Tone, I'm sorry to have to tell you this. A couple of our bombers were shot down as they were taking off by some U-boats. I just got the news."

The information hit Kent like a ton of bricks. "Are you sure, sir?"

Solemnly, Cavendish nodded. "I'm sure." By way of consolation, he patted Kent's shoulder twice before heading over to make his final checks.

Todd's face flashed through Kent's mind. Always smiling, always jovial. Suddenly the war seemed more real, more visceral. Todd's loss was a strange ache that made him somehow heavier. Kent boarded the bomber with the rest of the crew.

"Why the long face, Tone?" Wollard asked.

"Todd. His plane was shot down out of Goose Bay. U-boats." His voice sounded hollow even to his own ears. Speaking of Todd's loss made the ache inside of him bigger.

The other men bowed their heads in silence in a moment of respect. Wollard was the first to speak up. "I'm sorry, Tone. I know he was a good friend of yours. When we go on our first mission, we'll drop a bomb with his name on it over those damned Germans."

"Yeah," Arnolds chimed in. "Those bastards will get what's coming to them."

Kent gave a weary nod. "Let's just go."

The next stop on their journey was Marrakesh, French Morocco. They landed just as the sun set on the horizon. Stepping out into the Moroccan air was like being back home. The warmth soothed Kent's bones and, on the way to the barracks, he spotted more than a few familiar looking cactus plants.

Kent was too exhausted to follow the others out to the mess hall. He wasn't all that hungry anyways. All he wanted was some sleep and to stop his mind from playing Todd's face over and over again. His crewmates, understanding his mood all too well, left him alone that night and hoped he would be better in the morning.

Kent slept fitfully, his dreams were full of plane crashes and watery graves that startled him into consciousness. By the time morning came, he'd given up sleeping altogether and decided instead to take a walk around the small base. Only a handful of buildings dotted the small space, the biggest being the barracks he'd come from and the mess hall. With the borders of the enclosure marked in some spots by low chain link fencing, it was easy to see the city. Like in Arizona, the morning was chilly, but not at all compared to the iciness Kent experienced in Newfoundland or even Nebraska. As Kent walked he stared in open awe at the red buildings coming into focus with dawn's light above the walls.

"Tone, what are you doing out here?" A deep voice asked from behind him.

Startled, Kent nearly jumped out of his skin as he turned to see who addressed him.

Grey stood with his hands in his pockets and the end of his cigar burning a bright orange against the semi-darkness.

Sighing out his relief, Kent answered. "I couldn't sleep so I thought I'd take a walk. What are you doing?"

"The same," Lieutenant Grey' answer was

noncommittal. "It sure is a beautiful city, isn't it?" He asked, changing the subject.

"It is. It feels like home," Kent confided. "At least, the plants and the climate are like home."

Grey eyed the young man critically for a minute. "Cavendish told me about your friend," he said at last. "I know it must be hard on you, but you've got to understand something, son. This is war. More of us will end up dead the longer it drags out."

"I understand," Kent said, and he did. "It's just that I wasn't expecting it to happen so soon. I mean, Todd didn't even get a chance to be here."

"That's the thing about war. It doesn't give two shits about fairness. Moping about isn't going to bring your friend back. If anything, it will cause one of us to be hurt or killed if you're too much in your head."

Kent nodded. "You're right."

"Of course I'm right. I'm not saying don't mourn your friend. Just understand that you've got people living who depend on you to keep them safe."

Kent gave a wavering smile. "Yes, sir."

"Good man. Now, I seem to recall that today is your birthday, is that right? The ripe old age of 21?"

Blinking, Kent realized that it was. "I totally forgot," he admitted. "Yeah, I'm 21 today."

Grey gave a grunt. "Well alright then. Tonight we will celebrate properly. In the meantime, think about what I've said." He clapped Kent hard on the back and left him to his thoughts.

Kent took the Lieutenant's words to heart. He missed Todd, sure, but this was war. If his head wasn't in the game, a lot more of his friends could die. He could die. While that notion was hard to come to grips with, it settled things for Kent more than anything else.

He went about his day with a firm resolve to leave his grief in the cigar smoke-filled air. It wouldn't do any good to carry it around.

Grey must have told the whole crew that it was his birthday because each and every one of them wished him a happy one. That evening, as they paraded out of the mess hall, joking around, Kent noticed some of the locals laughing and drinking on the other side of the chain link fence. He stopped and listened to them speak in an oddly guttural, yet melodic language he'd never heard before.

"Not a bad idea, Tone," Warrens said when he noticed Kent stop. "Let's celebrate your birthday Arab style!" He went confidently over to the fence, calling out to the men on the other side. After a series of gestures and a fair amount of miming, Warrens exchanged a pack of cigarettes for a bottle of whatever the men had been drinking.

Triumphantly, Warrens returned to his crewmates. "Alright then. Let's celebrate!" He held the bottle aloft. "To Tone! Happy birthday, you son of a bitch!"

"And many more," chimed in Wollard. This was followed by several murmurs of agreement from all of the crew.

Warrens handed the dark glass bottle over to Kent who grinned from ear to ear.

"Go on, then," Warrens egged him on. "Drink it!"

Still grinning, Kent brought the bottle to his lips. Sweet liquid that burned like lava trickled down his throat. He sputtered and gasped, spilling some of the liquor in the process.

"Easy, Tone," Grey warned. He took the bottle from the young man. "It can't be as bad as all that." He threw back his head and took a big swig, grimacing when he pulled the bottle away.

And so the bottle was passed around, each of them taking a couple of swigs until finally, it stayed with Kent. He drank the rest of it, convinced by his crewmates that he had to finish it off lest they be discovered with it in the morning.

By the time dawn broke over the Atlas Mountains, Kent was thoroughly and utterly drunk. He lay in his cot completely sick. In his mind he cursed the Arab men outside of the fence and he cursed Warrens for getting the bottle.

As he stewed in his dark thoughts, Wollard came over to shake him awake.

"Come on, Tone. We've got to report."

Every syllable his fellow waist gunner spoke fell like anvils on his aching head. Kent groaned back at him with hope that he would go away. He wasn't so lucky. Instead, Wollard laughed and continued to torment Kent. "Drank a little too much, did you? Well that's alright. That stuff was something else. Who knows what those Arabs put in their wine. It's liable to be poison."

Kent moaned. It did feel like he was dying. What would they tell his poor mother? 'I'm sorry, Mrs. Tone, but your son died from poison before he even got to the fighting. He remained motionless, because if he moved he was surely going to vomit all over Wollard. While he may deserve it for being so damned smug, it wasn't something Kent was too keen on doing.

After a while, Wollard left Kent in relative peace.

Good, Kent thought. *I can die without him yammering at me.*

All too soon though, he returned with Grey in tow. "He won't get up," Wollard said. "I've tried everything."

Grey waved the young man back and sat on the cot next to Kent. He regarded the prone young man seriously, recognizing the hangover well enough. He couldn't blame Tone for overindulging a bit, but he wasn't about to let him get away with sleeping all day either. He'd have to learn to moderate himself better than this if he was going to last. No, Grey decided. The boy didn't need coddling. He needed some tough grit and with any luck some of it would stick.

"Tone!" he roared in his best Drill Sergeant impression. "Get your ass up now! You were to report for duty an hour ago."

Jolted by the sudden intense noise of the Lieutenant's command, Kent bolted upright in bed and immediately regretted it. The room swam around him and his head thundered with the quick movement. He brought his hands up to his head and closed his eyes as though to contain the pain. Nausea rolled through him and to prevent anything from coming out, he moved one of his hands up against his mouth.

The older man sighed. He hated to do this, but there was no help for it. "On your feet, Tone. We've got our orders and it's time to go."

Kent wasn't sure if he could get up, but if he moved his hand to say so he would vomit all over the place. In complete misery and in aching slowness, he swung his legs over the edge of the cot. The movement was too much. He made a strangled sound from behind his hand. Grey, understanding at once, quickly put a nearby waste basket into Kent's hands.

After a long bout of retching, Kent leaned over to set the waste basket down on the ground. Grey was ready with a canteen of fresh water.

"Feel better?" he asked gruffly as Kent swallowed the water.

Gasping for breath, Kent gave a weak nod.

"Good. Now clean up this mess and report to the Captain. We can't wait on you much longer, Tone." Grey left the barracks with Wollard in tow. If Kent wasn't out in 30 minutes, he'd go back in and drag him out by his ears, hangover or not.

Somehow, Kent managed to do it. He got ready to fly, though he looked a bit more green than normal.

Captain Cavendish took one look at him and said, "Tone, you don't look so good. You aren't getting sick on me, are you?"

Before Kent could even respond, Lieutenant Grey spoke up. "He's fine. Just a rough night is all. Isn't that right, Tone?"

Mutely, Kent nodded and wished everyone would stop yelling at him. His head couldn't take much more of it.

The flight to Italy was not the best flight Kent had ever been on. As he watched the rolling patches of clouds fly by, he swore to himself that he'd never drink again. Not a single drop.

~ ~ ~

"I remember getting that drunk a few times myself," Carla said. "Those hangovers are the worst. It feels as though you'd be better off dead."

"Yes, indeed," Grandpa agreed.

"I'm sorry about your friend, though. How terrible to be shot down like that, right out of the gate."

He nodded, with a vague, faraway look in his eyes. "Old Todd. I haven't thought about him in years."

"Kira, would you get us some of that peach pie? Kent, would you like some ice-cream to go along with that?" Trust Carla to know the best way to deflect sadness away from a perfectly good evening.

The mention of pie brought Grandpa back into the present. "You know, I'd love some pie á la mode."

Carla winked at me and I went to fetch dessert.

"So, did you ever drink again?"

One corner of Grandpa's mouth turned up in a smirk. "Not a drop."

Carla raised her eyebrow disbelievingly, "Uh-huh. I'm sure you didn't. What happened once you got to Italy?"

"We left our plane to be outfitted for war where we touched down in Bari. The crew and I were transported in those two-ton Army trucks to Foggia, where we were camped."

~ ~ ~

Kent wasn't sure what to expect when they were let out of the truck. He spotted rows and rows of tents with small sign posts pointing the way to things like the mess tent, the briefing tent, and infirmary. The trucks had let them out right in front of the orderly tent. Kent followed his crewmates into the tent to check in and to get their orders.

Once his name was checked off on the list, Kent was given a pillow, a sheet and two blankets by a bored looking man behind a desk.

"A crew went down yesterday so a tent just opened up," the man said in an oddly monotone voice. "You're lucky. Some crews have to sleep in the fields."

Kent couldn't tell if the man was joking or not.

"You'll want to stow your things and get some rest. Gunners are in high demand here. Your first mission is tomorrow morning. Be at the briefing tent at 0330."

Kent blinked at the swiftness of it all. His first mission tomorrow, were they sure? Before he could ask, his crewmates pulled him away to go get their uniforms and to put their newly acquired bedding into their tent.

Their assigned quarters was a small tent with four cots crammed inside. There was no floor, only hard packed dirt.

Arnolds grimaced at the sight of the floor. "Heaven help us if it rains. We'll have a snowball's chance in Hell to keep our boots clean here."

Kent, dazed at how fast things were moving,

asked his crewmates, "You fellas get the mission assignment for tomorrow too?"

Arnolds and Wollard glanced at each other. Arnolds answered, "No. Are you telling us you did?"

Kent nodded, feeling a little sick with anxiety.

"I don't believe you."

"Go look on the missions list back in the orderly tent. My name is on it for tomorrow morning."

Eager to prove that he was right, Kent led Arnolds and Wollard over to where the mission lists were posted in the orderly tent.

"Well I'll be damned," Wollard muttered.

Kent barely slept the whole night thinking about what his first real combat mission would be like. He was so anxious to get it over with that he rushed through getting dressed and getting his breakfast.

At the appointed time, he followed several others to the briefing tent. Inside was a raised stage where the officers stood in front of a large map.

Kent let out a nervous sigh. The man next to him noticed and nudged Kent. "I'm Tully, Andrew Tully."

Kent shook his hand. "Kent Tone."

"This your first mission, Tone?"

"Sure is. Seems a crew was short one waist gunner."

Tully smiled, "That would be my crew. Nice to meet you. I'm your other waist gunner."

Relief flooded Kent at finally meeting someone he'd be flying with. "Tell me, is it bad out there?"

Tully shrugged. "Sometimes it is. Sometimes it isn't. Depends on how thick the flak is and where the target is."

"Flak?"

"You don't know about flak? I'll tell you, it's the worst part of the gig over here. Its little bits of metal contained in the anti-artillery rounds that the Jerries shoot at us. At a certain altitude, those shells explode and the flak is shot out of it. Flak can take whole bombers down and kill a man in the blink of an eye. That's what we really have to watch out for."

Kent gulped back his fear. They both fell silent after that as the officers on the elevated stage area began talking. The group was to run a bombing over Lintz, Austria, specifically the munitions factory. It was a straightforward mission; not too many anti-aircraft guns had been detected over that stretch of land. However, with the railroad not too far away, it was only a matter of time before they were. Get in, drop the payload, and get out. All without getting themselves blown out of the sky.

When the briefing ended, Tully took a look at Kent and said, "Let's get you ready to fly. You'll need a chute and a heated suit."

Together, Tully and Kent made their way to the supply office where Kent was given all the gear he'd need. When all the people who were going with were similarly provisioned, they all loaded what they'd been given into another large truck with a canopy that would take them to their planes.

The B-17 Kent would be flying in had seen better days. Small sheets of bolted metal covered what Kent assumed were bullet holes in the siding. It was a far cry from the brand new plane he'd flown in on. There was, however, a fairly large painting of a pair of dice along the side of the plane, just under the cockpit window. Below that was in slightly curved letters "Ladies Delight".

"Come on. I'll help you into your suit. You'll be glad for the warmth when you're up in the air. It gets mighty chilly." Tully zipped Kent up and in return, Kent zipped him up. Automatically, Kent moved to the right waist gun and peered through the sight. A few scratches marked the outside of it, but nothing too bad that would impair his shot. With only slightly trembling hands, he loaded his machine gun as he'd been taught and had done a thousand times before. This time it was different, though. This time it was the real deal.

As the pilot made the final checks, time slowed and sped up all at once for Kent. He strapped in with the crew and waited for what felt like an eternity for takeoff.

"Don't look so worried," Tully chuckled as he strapped himself into the seat next to him. "It's a piece of cake. Just do your best to shoot the Jerries before they shoot us."

Kent gave a nervous laugh at that comment. "Sure," he said. "Sounds simple enough."

Finally the plane got clearance and taxied down the runway. Within moments they were in the air.

Once they were at a suitable altitude and in line with the rest of the formation, the pilot said over the coms, "Best get to your stations. Keep a sharp look out, gentlemen."

With only a little grumbling, the crew took their places, Kent manned the right waist gun. Sunrise was still at least an hour away. A few lights dotted the primarily dark landscape below them. Kent kept his eyes trained on the horizon, checking for any airplanes that weren't part of their formation.

"Put your oxygen on, fellas," the co-pilot announced. "We're at 10,000 feet."

Kent and Tully did as they were told and waited, peering out of their windows and squinting to see against the darkness. The others on the crew kept radio silence, and the tension in the air was palpable as each crew member waited for the inevitable sharp burst of gun fire from an attacking plane.

None came.

"What, did the Nazis oversleep this morning?" Tully asked Kent after a long, strained silence. "There's usually some action by now."

"I hope they're still asleep," Kent said earnestly. "That would make our lives easier."

The sun rose up over the horizon. Kent figured they'd been in the air about an hour and a half. Suddenly, the coms crackled to life with the pilot's voice. "Alright, fellas. We are getting into enemy territory here. Be on the lookout."

Just as he had issued the warning, a deafening boom made Kent jump. Small bits of metal flew at them from all sides. Tully was the first on the mic. "We've got flak, Captain!" In a quick, deft move, he grabbed a couple of heavily armored vests that hung from pegs on the interior wall of the plane. Tossing one to Kent, he barked out, "Put it on!"

Scared, he did as he was told and resumed his post, flinching every time he heard the deep bang of an anti-aircraft gun. What he saw out of his window terrified him; big plumes of smoke and violently flung shrapnel dotted the skies. It was hard to see the other planes in the formation through the debris.

"We are approaching the target. Prepare to drop those bombs," the pilot ordered in clipped tones.

Kent held his breath, waiting. He trained his gaze out the window, watching for when the other planes dropped their payloads.

Seconds crawled by. A minute. Two.

At last the order came. "Bomb's away!"

Moments after that static order, the B-17 across from Kent's window let loose all eight bombs in their bay. He watched in awe as the bombs fell amidst the black smoke and blue morning skies.

"Bombs away!" his own bombardier cried out over the coms, his long southern drawl sounding jubilant. "Gentlemen, we've sent our regards to the Nazis. Now, can we please get out of here before those big guns blow us out of the sky?"

The Captain laughed. "Alright, we're on our way back. Gunners, keep watching for Jerries. We're not out of harm's way yet."

It was smooth flying all the way back to their base in Italy. Kent never had to shoot once that mission.

"Are they all that easy?" Kent asked Tully once they'd landed safe and sound. They, along with the rest of the crew were headed to the traveling kitchen for a much needed cup of coffee and doughnut. It was the first stop in what would become a predictable "after mission" routine

"No, they are not," Tully said. "Usually there's a lot more flak and enemy fighters trying to shoot you out of the sky. Equipment can malfunction sometimes too. No, this mission was as perfect as you could ask for. It ran like clockwork. You got lucky on your first run."

With their coffee and doughnuts in hand, the crew made their way to the debriefing room. The officials demanded to know if they'd seen anything out of the ordinary, or if there was any intelligence the crew could give on the enemy; anything that would give the Allies an edge.

When they were through with the debriefing, all of the crews that made it back went to the Flight Surgeon's office for a shot of whiskey to calm their nerves. Kent, remembering all too well what happened the last time he'd drank alcohol, willingly gave his shot to Tully who poured it into a small canteen.

"What, aren't you going to drink that?" Kent wanted to know.

Tully gave him a lopsided grin. "Yeah, when there's occasion for it. I'm saving it up for when I finish my 35th mission. Once I do that, I intend on getting rip roaring drunk because that means I've done my duty in this damned war."

Kent nodded at Tully's wisdom. "Say, that's not a bad idea. Listen, it was great flying with you, Tully," Kent extended his hand for a shake.

"You too," Tully took his hand and pumped it a couple of times. "Good luck. Maybe we'll get teamed up again before the wars over."

"Maybe. I look forward to it."

The two went their separate ways; Kent headed back to his tent, fully intending on going back to sleep. Who knew flying actual missions would take so much out of you?

Before he could even reach his bed, Wollard, Arnolds, Bayer, and Warrens caught up to him.

"Tone! You made it!" Arnolds exclaimed. "How was it?"

Wollard demanded. "Was there a lot of flak?"

Warrens chimed in, "Did you shoot any of those sons of bitches down?"

Kent paused a moment, savoring the opportunity to psych his crew out. Taking in a deep breath, he did his best to wipe the knowing grin off of his face and appear concerned or even troubled. "You don't want to go up, boys," he told them seriously. "It was awful, just awful. There was so much flak! Then you have these fighter planes shooting at you. Why, it's pure chaos. All of that training they give us is for naught. It's a wonder that we made it back in one piece."

His crew stared at him in terrified wonder.

"It's really that bad?" Wollard asked.

Kent gave a solemn nod. "It is. I wouldn't ever go back up if I could help it."

"But you're supposed to go up again the day after tomorrow," Arnolds replied faintly. "I just saw it on the board."

This was news to Kent. "Really? So we're all going up tomorrow?"

The boys answered his question with silence. Finally, Wollard said, "No, it's just you."

Kent did his best not to smile. After the surprising ease of his first mission, Kent was confident that his in-flight time would be a breeze. Putting on his most solemn expression, he bowed his head and mumbled, "I better go write a letter home. If they're sending me up again, I might not get another chance."

Without another word, Kent shuffled off into the tent, leaving the rest of his stunned and worried crew to gape after him.

PART EIGHT
MISSIONS

One weekend in late March, my sister, Shannon returned to Arizona for a visit. Her husband, Wade was in the Air Force and they'd been stationed in Japan. When she heard about my mission to record all of Grandpa's stories, she immediately proposed an adventure.

"Why don't we take Grandpa to Commemorative Air Force Museum? It's in Mesa. That's where they keep Sentimental Journey."

"Sentimental what?"

"The Sentimental Journey. It's a B-17 that they keep in working order. They take people up in it for tours and such. When they aren't flying it, or when it's not on tour around the country, it stays at the museum. I bet Grandpa would love it there and you'd get a lot more stories out of him."

It took me all of two seconds to make up my mind. "Alright. Let's see if he wants to go tomorrow."

So it came to pass that Shannon and I took Grandpa to the Commemorative Air Force Museum down in Mesa.

It wasn't too far from our aunt's house, and along the way, Grandpa could hardly contain his excitement.

"How is Wade doing?" He asked Shannon. "Is he still doing well in the Air Force?"

"He is," Shannon nodded.

"Boy, I am sure proud of him. And you too."

"I know. Thank you. Hey, where's your cowboy hat, Grandpa?" Shannon asked. Instead of his trademark straw cowboy hat, Grandpa had on his navy blue World War II Veterans hat.

He gave a goofy grin. "This here's a conversation starter. More people are likely to talk to me when I have it on."

"People to talk to no matter what hat you have on," I said.

Grandpa winked at me in acknowledgement then completely changed the subject. "Do you think they will have it there? The Sentimental Journey?"

"Probably," Shannon answered from the back seat. "From what I understand, they keep it down here during the snowy months."

"What I wouldn't give to go up in one again," Grandpa sighed.

"We thought of that, but it's a little too expensive."

Grandpa sighed. "You're probably right. Plus I don't think I could get these old bones up inside one again. I am not as spry as I used to be." There was the barest hint of disappointment in his voice.

"Well, let's at least see what they have. There's probably a lot of really cool stories you could fill in for us."

There weren't that many people at the museum when we pulled into the parking lot. My sister and I helped Grandpa out of the car and into his motorized scooter. We hurried along after him to the entrance. When he was in that thing it was hard to tell him to go slow.

The exhibits in the museum were poignant; full of history about the local airfield and about the men who trained there. Grandpa gave each a moment of cursory attention before going on to the next. Every so often he would call one of us girls over to point out some fact and then wheel his way onto the next. Finally, he reached the doors that led to the hangar outside of the museum. That's where he really wanted to go.

Shannon went with him into the hangar while I continued reading through the displays. By the time I finally made it to the door, more people had shown up to the museum. In the hangar itself, Grandpa and Shannon stood next to a shining silver B-17. Grandpa gazed up at a small window in the side of the plane, his expression pensive.

"Grandpa?" I asked. "Are you alright?"

"Yes."

"This is what you flew in?"

Grandpa raised a gnarled finger towards the window. "There. That's where the waist guns were. I can just hear the engine roaring now."

~ ~ ~

The next mission Kent flew was the same as the

first; breakfast, then the briefing tent for their mission objectives. Kent wasn't flying with Tully this time around. Instead, he was placed with a tight-knit crew who had recently lost one of their waist gunners to an enemy fighter's bullets.

It was with some amusement that Kent noted the name of the plane painted just under the cockpit — (Ain't) Miss Behavin'.

Unlike the first crew Kent flew with, these guys were talkative. They didn't pay Kent much mind as they went through the system checks. The other waist gunner finally asked in a gruff manner, "How many kills you got?"

"How many what?"

"Kills. How many of the bastards have you shot down?"

Kent blinked at the man. "None."

"None? You ain't a rookie, are you? Its bad luck to be a rookie on a veteran crew."

Swelling with an indignation he wasn't aware of even having, Kent bristled. "No, I've been up before."

The other waist gunner wasn't buying it. "Yeah? How many missions have you flown to have no kills? Or are you just that bad of a shot?"

"I was in the air just the other day. There wasn't anyone to shoot. The Jerries weren't ready for us."

The man wasn't impressed. "So that's it? You were up in the air only the other day?"

Kent narrowed his eyes. "I'll shoot straight, don't you worry about me."

"Hey, lay off him, Mariano. You were worse off on your second time up," one of the guys said. Kent thought he was the radio operator, but couldn't be sure.

"Its bad luck, I tell you," Mariano muttered.

When the pilot gave the order to get to their stations, the radio operator who had stood up against Mariano held Kent back a moment. "Don't let him get under your skin. Our other waist gunner and he were best friends even before the war. Mariano's a nice guy, but he's not dealing with Chester's death very well."

Not sure what else to do, Kent nodded and made his way back to the waist gun position.

Almost as if to contrast how easy his first mission had been, his second shaped up to be a completely different story. They weren't in the air more than 30 minutes when the ball turret gunner shouted out that enemy planes were coming towards them. The fighter planes that usually escorted them right after rendezvous were late. A thrill of panic swept through Kent. Everything was drowned out by the sudden rapport of the machine guns firing into the morning. A cacophony of voices sounded over the coms from the ball turret and the tail gunner as they called out their targets.

Adrenaline pumped through Kent's veins as he caught sight of an enemy fighter. He swung his machine gun around and took aim. Before he could squeeze the trigger, one of their fighter escorts came between them and the enemy. The shots coming from that plane were deafening. They must have hit the mark because one of the fighter's engines sputtered and began spewing dark, thick smoke into the sky. It buzzed past the plane and then just out of Kent's sight.

"Where did they go?" Kent asked.

Mariano gave a short, humorless laugh. "Run off by those colored boys, I'd imagine. That or they left on their own accord. We must be getting close to those anti-aircraft guns the Germans like so much. Those fighters don't want to be caught in friendly fire."

Suddenly, music could be heard over the coms. Kent recognized the familiar melody of Glenn Miller's song "In the Mood".

Before Kent could ask what was happening, the Captain cursed over the coms. "Damnit, Garcia! Turn that American Forces Network off."

Garcia responded hotly to the order. "It isn't me! I think they patched into our signal somehow. If I turn it off, then we lose the coms."

The song came to an end and one of the sultriest voices Kent had ever heard began talking. "Hi, fellas. Are you still around? Well, you won't be for much longer, that's for sure. What would your death be for, hm? You're nothing but a sacrifice made by Franklin D. Roosevelt. Go home. Save yourselves. Go home to your girl who even now is in the arms of some F-4 because you aren't there. Doesn't seem fair, does it? You're risking your neck while some yokel idiot that couldn't even make it into the military cozies up with your girl? Turn back now. Nothing but death awaits you in Vienna."

Abruptly, the woman's voice stopped and was replaced by Jimmy Dorsey's song "Blue Champagne". Eventually, the signal faded into static and then silence once again.

The odd broadcast made Kent uneasy. He

glanced over at the other waist gunner. "What is going on? How does she know where we are going?"

Mariano scoffed. "That was Axis Sally. That dumb broad is always trying to get us to give up, to stop fighting. Sometimes she uses our names and tells us where we are going on our mission."

"How does she know all of that?" Kent breathed.

The older waist gunner shrugged. "I don't know. Don't pay her any attention. We've got a job to do and if she gets you distracted, well then, the Nazis have done their job, haven't they?"

Kent could only nod as he turned his attention back to the skies outside of the window. Inside, he couldn't help but tremble. If the enemy knew their missions, how could any of them survive?

Once they'd gotten back to the base in Foggia safely, Kent went right to the Flight Surgeon's tent. He downed his shot of whiskey in a quick gulp, not even feeling the burn of it down his throat. He did his best to avoid his crewmates, who, of course, wanted to hear all about it. He didn't answer any of their questions, just made his way back to his tent to think.

~ ~ ~

"Excuse me," a middle aged fellow in a windbreaker approached us. "Sir, I can't help but notice your cap there. Did you fly in the war?"

Grandpa cast Shannon and I a quick I-told-you-so-grin. "Why yes, sir. I was a waist gunner on this here plane."

"Is that so? Where were you stationed?"

As Grandpa settled into the conversation, I took the opportunity to get a closer look at the plane. They had the doors open and, at the urging of one of the museum employees, my sister and I climbed in to see what it was like from the inside.

Cramped is the best word to describe it, especially the farther back from the cockpit you went. A narrow passage led from the waist gun windows to the tail gun. Being in that space and knowing Grandpa's stories was surreal. Everything he'd told me came to life. I could almost see the ghost of his younger self peering out of the window, watching for enemy planes.

With a renewed sense of purpose, I climbed down out of the plane and went to listen to Grandpa as he spun his tales to what was now a small crowd around him. How incredible, I thought. The people came to the museum to learn about history and here they were experiencing it from someone who lived it. A sense of pride swelled inside of me as I stood respectfully to the side and listened in.

~ ~ ~

The next flight Kent was scheduled for was with a different crew than the last two. They weren't kidding when they said gunners were in high demand.

"Damnit all to hell, Tone!" Wollard hollered when he saw the mission listings. "Why do you get to go up again? None of us have yet!"

Kent couldn't stop the grin from spreading over his face. "They must like my shooting record."

Wollard glowered at the subtle jab at his own shooting ability.

Arnolds headed off the fight he saw coming and grabbed Wollard by the arm. "Well, good luck. C'mon, Wollard. We'll be up in the air soon enough."

Arnolds was right. Two days later, the whole crew including Kent, were scheduled for a mission. Their briefing wasn't until noon, so Kent had the dubious pleasure of explaining to his fellow crewmates exactly what to expect. They'd heard most of it before, but with the first flight jitters, they wanted to hear it all again.

Finally, it was time to report. Captain Cavendish and Lieutenant Grey led the way confidently to the briefing tent. Along with several other crews, they learned about their target and were shuttled to their plane via a large canopied truck.

The crew ran through their pre-flight checks with excitement mingled nervousness. Finally, when the checks were done, the guns loaded, and the bombs secure, the crew strapped in and waited for clearance to take off.

By the tense silence in the radio room where they were buckled in, Kent could tell his crew was more than nervous. To break the tension, Kent started singing. "*My gal's a corker, she's a New Yorker. I buy her everything to keep her in style. She's got a pair of legs just like two whiskey kegs. Hey boys, that's where my money goes.*"

It had the desired effect; Bayer laughed and Warrens demanded, "Who the hell taught you to sing? They should be shot!"

Kent chuckled and said, "Yeah? You think you

could do better?"

"I know I can."

"Then prove it."

As they took off on their first mission together as a crew, they sang their nerves away.

"Alright, fellas," Captain Cavendish called over the coms. "As lovely as your serenades have been, it's time to get to work. Get to your positions and keep your eyes peeled. I want our first run to be as smooth as possible."

The gunners unbuckled themselves and went to their respective places while Barrett stayed in the radio room with Warrens.

As they checked over their guns, Wollard leaned over and asked, "Tone, you got any gum?"

Sighing, Kent dug into his pockets. "Yeah, it's my last piece though."

"I'll get you another pack once we get back."

Kent shrugged and handed over the last stick of gum.

"Thanks a million."

"Look alive, men. We've made the rendezvous point. A flock of P-90s just showed up to the party," Lyndon said over the coms.

With that announcement came the steady rat-a-tat-tat of gunfire from the smaller, more agile fighters. Kent peered through his site, trying to see any enemy planes in range. What he saw made him do a double take. Immediately, he got onto the coms.

"There's something over here. It's matching our altitude and our speed. It's about two miles out, but I don't see any propellers on it."

"You've got to be kidding me," Warrens

responded.

"No, come and see for yourself. No propellers!"

Warrens shuffled back to the waist of the plane and stood next to Kent as he peered out the window. "Well I'll be damned," he breathed when he saw the strange aircraft. "I've got to get on that radio and see what's going on."

The radio operator scurried back to his post to let out the trailing antenna so he could get on the same frequency as the fighters. After about five minutes, Warrens got on the coms and announced, "I've got those fighters on the coms. I'll let you boys listen to what's happening."

They heard the static-filled voices of the P-90 pilots come over the intercom. Kent could make out one voice, a deep southern drawl tight with adrenaline. "No sir, boss! I got him! He's mine!"

Then came incomprehensible shouting and the loud rapport of gun-fire against loud, droning engines. Eventually the noise evened out to a steady hum of aerial fighting.

Cloud cover threatened the view of the aerial battles being waged around them.

"Tone, Wollard," the Captain barked out. "We're about halfway to the target. When we get closer and if this cloud cover stays with us, I want you to get those tin foil canisters out. Maybe we can fool the ground radars draw the artillery fire away from our plane."

"Yes, sir," Wollard answered. "Just let us know when to dump the stuff."

Together, he and Kent retrieved six canisters of shredded tin foil and prepared to pour them out of their respective waist windows. Opening up one of the cans, Wollard stuck his hand into it and pulled out several paper thin strings of glittering silver tinsel. "Makes me think of Christmas," he told Kent. "Boy, what I wouldn't give to be home for the holidays."

"Well, if we get these missions done right, we'll be home before you know it," Kent assured him. "We just gotta stay focused on the job at hand."

Ten minutes later, Captain Cavendish gave the command. "Tone, Wollard, let that tin foil loose!"

With glee, Kent and Wollard each took a canister and poured the contents out of the windows, letting the wind scatter it amongst the clouds. Other planes in their formation were doing the same. Sunlight glinted off of the reflective silver strands, making the unending gray of the sky glitter and shine.

Such an idyllic picture couldn't last though. Even with the hopes of radar confusion, loud blasts of anti-aircraft artillery could still be heard. Flak peppered the sky, tearing through the metal of the plane.

"Damn!" cursed Wollard as a piece of fragmented metal whizzed past his head. "They're trying to kill us!"

"Of course they are!" Kent replied struggling into his flak jacket. When he was in, he tossed the other to Wollard. "Put that on!"

"You're bleeding!" Wollard cried out as he pointed frantically at Kent's chin.

Startled, Kent brought his gloved hand to his face. The chin strap on his helmet was severed. When he pulled his hand away, there was a thin line of blood. "I'm fine. It's just a scratch."

"Grey's been hit!" Captain Cavendish called out. "Barrett! Get him to the radio room. Warrens, make sure he doesn't bleed out. Damn piece of flak about took off his ankle. Barrett, I'll need you up here with me right now!"

"One of those shells punched right through the sealing gas tank on the left!" Barrett replied.

"But it didn't detonate in the gas tank," countered Wollard. "Looks like we get to live another day. I'll keep an eye on it. Barrett, help Grey!"

"I better get a flying cross for this."

"Oh, whine and cry, you Git!" Warrens yelled. "You already call out the airspeeds. Now all you have to do is sit next to the pilot. Just get a move on!"

"Lyndon, where are we in relation to the target?"

"Two minutes."

"Get those bombs primed. As soon as the lead plane drops, we need to drop ours."

"Roger that. Bomb bay doors are opening. Payload is hot."

More explosions sounded, more flak punched through the sheet metal of the plane. There was no safe space to step; nowhere that wasn't getting covered with flak. It seemed like an eternity waiting for the Captain to give the order. "Bombs away!" he yelled into the coms.

"Yes, sir!"

Kent watched out the window as more planes in the formation dropped their own payloads. The sight would never be erased from his memory. This is what happened when you poked a sleeping giant.

When all of the bombs were well below them, the formation continued on its course back to the base. The flak lessened the farther they got from the target. Kent found that in the relative peace, he could breathe evenly again.

"How's Grey?" Captain Cavendish asked.

"Got his leg wrapped. He'll need a medic when we land," Warrens replied. "When we are closer I'll radio ahead and let them know."

"Will you look at this?" Wollard pointed to the holes along his side of the plane. Wind whistled through them. "It's a god damned miracle we weren't killed!"

Solemnly, Kent nodded at the assessment. "I told you it was just awful up here."

The crew were never so glad to be on the ground as when they landed in one piece after their first mission. Grey was taken by the medic as soon as they stopped moving. His ankle was pretty bad, but after a few stitches it would be good as new. The ground crew whistled at the state of the plane.

"Did you fellas aim for the flak on purpose?" one of them asked as he circled around the bomber.

"Shove off," Arnolds replied. "I'd like to see you up in the air risking your neck."

Another of the ground crew came around. "There's 125 holes in this plane. All that flak has a hell of a way of making Swiss cheese out of sheet metal."

"Tell Branson to get his welder out. It's gonna be a long night," the first sighed.

Kent gestured to Arnolds and Wollard. "Come

on. We've got to get through the debriefing."

In the interrogation, Kent told the officers about the plane with no propellers. They listened with rapt attention as he described how one of those "colored boys", the Tuskegee pilots, had gone after it. He hadn't seen what happened to it after that though, so he wasn't sure if it had gone down. At the time, the officers made no comment, just jotted down the information. Later, though, he heard the scuttlebutt that one of those fighter pilots had taken down an enemy plane. Kent hoped it was the one they heard over the coms.

As they headed to their plane after their latest briefing, Wollard caught up with Kent with his typical pre-flight request. "Hey Tone. Got any gum?"

Annoyance gave way to an overwhelming urge to teach Wollard not to ask him for gum anymore. With what he hoped was a benign smile, Kent dug deep into his pockets. Instead of the gum, he picked out a small pack of chewable laxatives the infirmary had given him last week. Tossing the pack to Wollard, he said, "Take as much as you want."

"Thanks. You're a life saver." Wollard popped four of the pieces into his mouth and tossed the package back to Kent who replaced it in his pocket.

Happily chewing, Wollard went about his pre-flight checklist. It was all Kent could do to keep the smirk off of his face.

The mission started off like most of the previous ones. They rendezvoused with the rest of the bombing group and made their way over the Alps towards their target, Vienna, Austria.

The crew talked amicably, their fear and anxiety over running a mission muted by what had become routine. In midsentence, Wollard stopped and grabbed his stomach. "Uh oh," he groaned.

"What's the matter?" Kent asked in mock concern.

"Quick, hand me that ammo can. Empty it out."

"Why do you need the ammo can?" Kent asked, hoping the other fellas were listening in.

"Just give it to me!" Wollard snatched it out of Kent's hand, positioning it on the other side of his gun. He fumbled with his heated flight suit and the clothes he wore under it.

Kent chuckled to himself. "What's wrong, Wollard? You look like something is trying to crawl out of you."

"I think something is!" he cried.

The sound of chuckling came over the coms. "What, did Wollard forget to go to the john before we left?"

"Looks like it," Kent affirmed. "Did you eat something bad?"

Wollard crouched over the now empty ammunition can, his face red with strain. A low, guttural moan escaped his mouth.

"Jesus Christ!" Kent cried out, covering his nose. "That is rank!"

"What's going on back there?" Captain Cavendish demanded.

"Wollard is shitting in an ammo can," Kent replied, his hand still over his nose. He couldn't keep his laughter back this time. Soon enough, all the others were chiming in with their own laughter.

Wollard didn't pay too much attention to them. Once one can was filled, he reached for another, spilling the .50 caliber bullets onto the floor of the plane. They clinked against each other, the noise punctuating the miserable groans coming out of the young man.

When the strange and sudden sickness had passed, Wollard had filled not only three of the ammunition cans, but three of the plastic air sickness bags as well. Kent couldn't stop laughing, so Wollard was forced to toss his mess out his window on his own.

"I'm never eating those powdered eggs in the mess hall ever again," he swore.

The proclamation only made Kent laugh harder.

"I hate to take away from the amusement at Wollard's expense," Barrett called out. "But I think there's a problem with the number two engine. Looks like its leaking oil."

"Shit," Captain Cavendish swore. "Alright then, let's shut it off and feather it. I'd rather lag behind the rest of the group than risk an engine fire."

With that, they fell out of formation, trailing behind the main force and nursing the broken engine. They made it as far as Graz, Austria when the real trouble hit. From the intelligence they were given in their briefing, there was no worry about anti-aircraft artillery in the Graz area. It was supposedly flak-free.

That intelligence turned out to be incorrect. The Germans had shipped in via railway a car with several anti-aircraft guns. Because they were lagging behind and at such a lower altitude than the rest of the formation, the guns were ready for them. Bits of metal burst up at them heavily.

"Damnit! Engine number one is out!" Barrett called over the coms. "Heavy damage from flak. Can you get us up out of here?" he demanded of Cavendish.

Lieutenant Grey answered. "Hold your horses, Barrett. A couple of shells almost hit us up here in the cockpit. We're trying to figure out how to get out of this mess. Hang on."

Kent cast a worried look over at Wollard. If their pilot and co-pilot both got hit, then they were as good as dead. The plane suddenly lurched to one side. Wollard slid over to Kent's side of the waist, trying to catch himself before he tipped out of the window. It took longer than they liked to get out of range of that flak car, but they did it. The bomber shuddered in the air and the remaining engines strained to keep them aloft. Wollard and Kent waited in tense silence for orders from their Captain as the shells exploded around them.

At last, Cavendish's voice came over the coms. He sounded shaken, but determined. "Get anything that isn't bolted to the plane and toss it out. Let the bombs drop, but don't arm them. There's no target and I don't want to rain hell on any innocent people."

"Are you sure?" Arnolds asked. "What if we are just giving weapons to the Jerries?"

"We don't have a choice. If we don't lighten our load, we are going to crash. Everything you can, toss it. Wollard, Tone, get rid of your guns. Any of the duffels, or ammo, send that over too. I'll try to get us over this mountain and landed somewhere safely."

The gravity of the situation hit the crew hard. All of them scrambled to get what they could off the plane. It worked; they limped over the mountain, but just barely. Kent could see the top of the peaks just below his window.

"I'm aiming us for the Adriatic. We are almost to an island called Vis. Some of our boys captured it a week ago, I think. Warrens, get on the radio and let them know we're coming in hot," Lyndon said.

"On it," Warrens answered. Kent could hear the fear in his voice.

"The rest of you keep holding on."

Kent looked at Wollard and asked in all seriousness, "You gonna shit your pants again?"

Wollard glowered at his counterpart. "Shut up. Now isn't the time for wisecracks."

"Suppose we ought to get into the radio room?"

Wollard considered it for a brief moment before giving Kent a nod. "Let's go."

Together, they took their chest packs and made their way to the radio room where Warrens was busy taking notes. Lyndon stared at a map, his brows furrowed in concentration.

Warrens glanced up from his notes. "Where are we exactly? How long until we get to Vis?"

"The rate we are going, maybe 10 minutes." Lyndon nodded at the two waist gunners huddling themselves into the corner of the radio room.

Warrens conveyed that information to the person on the other side of the radio.

"There's a 1,500 foot runway. If you can land on that, come on in," the faceless voice advised.

Warrens looked at Lyndon.

"Captain, Vis has a 1,500 foot runway. Can you make that work?"

Muffled cursing competed with the soft static on the intercom. "That's way too short. It takes 3,600 feet to land a B-17."

"Well, sir, this is what we have. Can you do it?"

More grumbling and swearing preceded the hesitant, "Yes, I can do it. You men get to the radio room and prepare for a crash landing just in case."

At that pronouncement, it wasn't long before Bayer and Arnolds joined everyone in the radio room. They huddled in the cramped space together, waiting in silence, each praying for their survival.

Warrens kept his headphones pressed against his ears, listening to the transmission from the tower on the ground. The plane began its descent, tilting forward and down ever so slightly. They were going in for the landing. Suddenly, Warrens eyes widened in panic. "Captain, we have a problem."

"What now?" Grey barked, irritation and barely restrained fear making the question come out harsher than he meant.

"A B-24 crashed on the runway we are aiming for not five minutes ago. They don't have time to clear it out of the way before we make our landing."

Captain Cavendish didn't say anything for a long time. The crew in the radio room increased the urgency of their prayers. At last he told his crew grimly, "Hold on, fellas."

Kent closed his eyes, imagining the sunrise coming over the desert. He pictured his mother hanging up laundry and his father feeding the pigs.

He thought of Loretta, her smile and that sparkle in her brown eyes. *Please. Let me go home to them. I don't want to die here. Please, just let me go home again.*

The crew in the radio room jolted violently as the plane touched down on the runway. The sound of screeching brakes and the heavy smell of burning rubber filled the air. Kent didn't dare open his eyes, convinced that worse was to come. Suddenly, he felt a moment of buoyancy as the wheels lifted off the ground. A loud bang and scrape as the belly of the B-17 grazed over something in the way. Another jolt as the wheels returned to the earth. Then, everyone twisted as the aircraft spun on the runway before skidding to a halt. Kent waited for several heartbeats before even opening his eyes. The rest of the crew had the same idea. All of them hesitantly raised their heads from their crouched positions to look around in dazed wonder.

The coms sparked to life as the Captain demanded to know what everyone's status was.

Stunned, Warrens, looked over everyone in his radio room. "We're all accounted for, Captain."

Hearing the words broke them out of their shock. Wollard was the first to let out a whoop of excitement and relief. Soon, they were all cheering and hugging each other, simply out of sheer gladness to be alive.

The crew had to wait until the next day for a C-47 to take them back to the Foggia air base. That afternoon, once they'd been debriefed and given temporary quarters until their ride back, Kent took a walk, craving a bit of solitude after such a harrowing near-death experience.

Not long into his walk, he came across a field of grass. A gentle breeze kissed his skin. Every nerve in his body was alive, feeling sensations he had been sure he'd never feel again.

Out of the corner of his eye, he noticed a figure approaching him. It was a man a bit older than himself. He was dressed like a soldier. If Kent wasn't mistaken, he was part of Tito's army, or the Communist-led rebellion against the Axis powers.

The man waved and inquired something in a language Kent didn't understand. The young American replied in English, however it was no use. In a sort of exaggerated pantomime, he pressed two fingers to his lips as though he were smoking a cigarette. After he did this, he removed the metal red star from his cap and offered it to Kent before once again miming the act of smoking.

Not sure what was happening, Kent frowned. Then it hit him. The soldier wanted to trade. He patted his pockets, not sure of what he had on him. As luck would have it, an almost full pack of Lucky Strikes was in his breast pocket. Kent offered them to the man. He took them gratefully and, in the same movement, he gave Kent the red star. Kent dipped his head in thanks. The soldier waved and continued on his way. Kent watched him go, running the small metal red star in his fingers thoughtfully.

* * *

March 6, 1945
Italy

Dear Klove:
Well I guess you are home by this time having a good time. Darn it, I sure wish I could be there too. But I guess my time will come in a few more months. I've got 17 missions now and 18 more to go yet. I sure hope the rest goes faster than the first 17 did. I should be done by the end of May.

Say, you must be getting in good with the CO if you got a ride home with him. Keep up the good work.

Well, I got a taste of the sea the other day when I went to rest camp. I was on the Isle of Capri for seven days. We went out on a boat from Naples. I got to spend the night in Naples on the way back to camp. Rest camp is sure a good deal, a guy feels like he is a civilian again. We stayed in real fancy hotels with real soft beds. The meals were very good and all of them were three or more course meals. They had the band playing at every meal. There is tennis, boating, fishing, badminton, ping-pong and many beautiful things to see on the island. And many things to buy. I spent around $150.00 while there. I sent most of my things I bought to Loretta to keep for me. I sent mother a Cameo necklace, and a bunch of things to Loretta. And not a darn thing to a certain girl at home ha ha! I don't know what she is going to say and I care less. I haven't written to Jane for a long time. I'm not going to either. I guess it's mean but I think much more of Loretta.

You should see our tent floor. It looks like a hog pen. The dust is ankle deep now. We can't get any brick for it unless we buy it with our own money. By the way what kind of pay do you get now for a month? I get $166.00 a month.

The war news looks much better now. It hadn't ought to be very long until the war is over with over here. I sure wish the Russians would hurry up and take Vienna. I'm getting tired of being shot at over that target.

Well, I've got to close for this time so take care of yourself. Good Luck. (Rodger and out).

Love, Kent

* * *

March 24, 1945
Italy

Dear Mother and Dad:
I received your package the other day with the cookies, wash cloths, magazines, and Williams Field papers. Thanks a million, I sure enjoyed reading them. I'll write those people and thank them for the cookies. Also the papers.

Well, I've got 20 missions now and 15 more to go yet. The darn things go plenty slow for our crew.

We moved into another tent today which has a floor in it. Some fellows went home so we got their tent. It sure seems great to stay in a good tent with a floor for a change.

I haven't gotten much mail in the last two weeks and not letter in the last five days. This darn mail is coming slow because none of the other fellows are getting any either. I sure hope I get some tomorrow, *but that's what I thought yesterday.*

The weather here has been plenty good this month so it looks like summer is almost here. If the weather stays good I might be home by the last of June. I sure hope so.

By the way, I was just wondering how much money I have at home. I've forgotten how much I've got at home. How much have I got?

The war news looks pretty good now, doesn't it? But there's still a lot to be done yet before those Jerries are done. I sure wish they would pull out of Vienna pretty soon. I've got about 11 missions over that place, I think.

How did Klove like his leave? I guess he must be going to school some place by this time. I sure hope he gets to go to school for a while.

I noticed in the Williams Field papers that there's a lot of fellows from this outfit stationed there. Boy, it should would be swell if I could be stationed there again when I get back.

Tell everyone hello for me, whoever is there. Have you got the hot water heater in yet? That's what you've been needing for a long time.

Well, I guess I'd better sign off for this time. I'll write some more later. I can't think of anything more to say right now. Write Soon.

Love, Kent

P.S. I think all the mail is coming over by boat instead of by air mail these days. Darn it.

* * *

April 14, 1945
Italy

Dear Mother and Dad:

Your letter came yesterday and I was glad to hear from you. So you got home alright. I'm sure glad you had such a swell time.

I'm still sitting on the ground with 20 missions in. They just don't seem to fly our crew for some reason. I guess they want to keep the good crews on the ground.

How about sending me some canned vegetable soup, nuts (shelled), Velveeta cheese, and some hair shampoo? Darn it all the other guys get packages and I don't get any. I heard you can send all you want now without requests. Is that right?

About that money at home. I know that's what I did with the money in the bank, but didn't I send some bonds home? I can't remember. Dad doesn't owe me anything at all. I was just wondering how many war bonds I have sent home. I've got $675.00 saved up over here since I've been overseas. I'm getting 4% interest on it in soldiers' deposits.

So you don't like California. Ha ha! Why? That's a darn good place. Lots of fun. Yes, I know how those service men get but if you would look in Phoenix some night you'd find the same thing there too. You'll find guys like that anywhere there are service men. Don't you worry about me drinking too much. I don't even touch the Italian stuff at all. And we can't get any American whiskey over here except when we come back from a mission. To tell you the truth, I do smoke but that's no crime is it? You always said I could start *when I reached 21 and if you'll remember, I'm 21 now. Ha ha! Don't you worry. I'll take care of myself. You know darn well that I was brought up good enough to know right from wrong thanks to you and Dad.*

I sure hated to hear about the president's death. He was the best president America ever had and I sure hated to see him go. I sure hope Truman knows enough about the war to lead us to victory. I hope everyone backs him to the limit.

Well, I've got to sign off this time and get this letter out in tomorrow's mail.

Tell everyone "hello" for me. Write soon.
Love, Kent

* * *

The stern looking officer eyed the assembled squadrons in the briefing tent. "Gentlemen, today we extend maximum effort. Five hundred bombers will make their way deep into Germany. We are going to pave the way to Berlin with our bombs. Captain Cavendish, you will be piloting the lead plane. Don't let us down."

Cavendish kept his eyes forward and his face didn't betray a single emotion. "Yes, sir."

Being lead plane made Kent both proud and scared at the same time. It was a huge responsibility and one that came with quite a few dangers. Lead plane was in charge for the rest of the run. In this case 500 other bombers. They had to make sure they dropped their payload at precisely the right time, otherwise, all of the other planes who were looking to them for the signal would be off as well.

There was also the fact of being first in the line of fire for anti-aircraft guns on the ground. All in all, it was a nerve-racking situation. Kent kept his misgivings to himself though. Everything ran like clockwork through the pre-flight checks, take off and rendezvous. The only hiccup was a sudden burst of cursing from Arnolds in the back of the plane.

"What's wrong back there?"

"It's these damned heated trousers! They zapped me!"

Kent laughed. "You've got a short in your pants?"

"Ha, ha. Very funny. What the heck am I supposed to do? It's freezing up here, but I don't want to be electrocuted."

Bayer supplied the answer for him. "Use one of the fur lined Jackets to keep your pecker covered. It would be awful if you made it all this way only to have it frozen off."

There was more banter between Arnolds and Bayer, but Kent let it all fade into the background. Instead, he focused his attention out of his window, on the lookout for enemy fighters. Vapor trails splayed out as far as the eye could see, setting a stunning backdrop to the hundreds of bombers following them.

They were close to the target, maybe about 20 minutes out from it when the flak started.

Kent and Wollard scrambled to get their flak gear on. None of the metal came to them that time. Instead, the plane next to them got hit hard. After a deafening blast from an anti-aircraft gun and the shower of flak, one of the right engines of that plane started billowing smoke.

Kent watched in horrified fascination as the pilot allowed the plane to fall back, probably to ensure they weren't critically hit. After a few minutes, they came back up to the front, sliding between two other bombers, one above and one below. The pilot must have misjudged the space because the bottom of his plane hit the one below him, crushing the glass of the cockpit.

The bottom plane veered erratically. Kent realized that both the pilot and the co-pilot must have been killed instantly. The bomber started to nose dive. Kent couldn't take his eyes away from the scene. A man was sucked out of the top of what would have been the radio room. As he flew through the air, he clutched frantically at his chest, but there was no parachute attached. In a startling moment, the man — was he the radio operator? — looked straight into Kent's eyes. Panic and terror were etched into his face. Kent's own face mirrored those emotions and a wave of helplessness overtook him. Kent thought he could hear the man scream over the din of the guns and the shrapnel as he plummeted.

Within seconds, the man was gone, falling to his death over enemy territory with the bomber going down with him.

Kent cried out and backed away from his window, his breath coming in ragged gulps.

"What's wrong?" Wollard demanded. "You hit?"

Kent shook his head, unable to express what he had just witnessed. It was all suddenly too much. He couldn't imagine a more gruesome death. In that moment, he realized that he would be haunted by that airman's last moments for the rest of his life.

~ ~ ~

We spent hours at the museum. A constant stream of people came up to ask Grandpa questions. He was in his element. In those hours, he seemed more alive, more energetic than he had since Grandma died. The stories he told captivated his audience; they listened with rapt attention. A few older gentlemen who had served in later wars piped up with their experiences as well. They compared military knowledge and traded war stories, much to the delight of the growing audience.

At last, it was time to go. The museum was about to close and it was high time for something to eat. My sister and I walked proudly with Grandpa out of the museum. He grinned from ear to ear when the museum employees asked him to come back any time he wanted.

As we piled into the car, Shannon asked, "Well, Grandpa? What did you think of all that?"

Grandpa adjusted his cap and thought about his answer. "You know, if we get us some banana milkshakes, then I think it will be one of the best days I've had in years."

PART NINE
HOMECOMING

Summer was just about to give way to autumn when Grandpa fell and broke his hip. It was a clean enough break; it only required some screws instead of a full on replacement. After his stay in the hospital, he was moved to a rehabilitation facility in Gilbert, ironically not a mile away from where the family farm used to be.

While he was there, I visited him as often as I could, usually on the weekends.

"Here's the cafe. All I usually have is my tea and toast in the morning, but I could have anything I want. Come on, let me show you the gym. They are really whipping me into shape." he walked swiftly and confidently up and down the carpeted halls; his walker barely touched the carpet. I had to quicken my pace to keep up.

"Why, hello there, Anne," Grandpa greeted a middle age woman in comfortable looking scrubs. "This here is my granddaughter, Kira. She's visiting me today."

The woman smiled at me, "Hello. It's nice to meet you."

"Likewise," I replied, but before I could say anything else, Grandpa was on his way again and I had to jog to catch up. He showed me the gym and introduced me to his trainers. When we'd been around the whole facility twice, we sat in the cafe.

"I'll have a tea, and then whatever my granddaughter wants," he told the waiter.

"Just a tea, please," I echoed. The waiter left and returned with our drinks quickly.

I took a sip and asked, "Grandpa, what happened at the end of the war? Did you come home right away?"

He took a big gulp of his iced tea as he thought about my question. He twisted his glass with his fingers and closed his eyes before launching into his story.

"I remember waiting in the barracks for news."

~ ~ ~

May 6, 1945
Italy

Dear Mother and Dad:
I'm sorry I haven't written sooner but things have been happening plenty fast over here. The war in Italy is all over now and I'm done over here in this theater.
I received the box you sent the other day. Thanks a million for everything. The book of Arizona is OK and so was the Arizona Stockman. The cake was dried out so much I couldn't eat it and the paper was stuck

on it and I couldn't get it off. The candy was real good. Thanks again.

I haven't been getting very much mail lately. I can't figure out what is the matter. I guess the mail service is poor. There was no mail at all today.

Well, it's almost seven pm now and I'm waiting for the news. I think the war will be over then. The last news at five pm said that all fighting had stopped to make peace terms. I look for the peace terms to be through by seven pm I sure hope so.

I might be seeing you in another two months. Keep your fingers crossed.

I've got to close for now.

Love, Kent

May 7, 1945

The war is over!

I might be seeing you one of these days. I hope. Everyone is happy tonight.

* * *

May 9, 1945
Italy

Dear Klove:

I received your letter the other day and I was glad to hear from you. I'm glad you like your new school and I hope you'll get what you want out of it.

As you know, the war is over in Europe. That was the best news I've ever heard in a long time. Everyone was jumping around here like mad the night it was announced. We were shooting flares and all kinds of fireworks that night. I sure wish I knew where and when I go from here. I'm hoping that I'll get to go home on furlough before going to fight the Japs. I think I will if everything goes OK. The way things look now, I'm afraid that I won't get home for another three months. We've got another job to do over here before going home. So I guess I'll have to sweat it out for a while. I finished up with 22 missions when the war ended. My last mission I flew over Linz, Austria.

So you don't like the climate there in Washington, huh? Well I know about what you mean but you can be glad you're not over here now. This place is getting as hot as Arizona weather now.

Our mail service isn't very good these days. I haven't heard from home for a long time now. I can't figure out what is the matter. I get letters from Loretta every once in a while. By the way, what did you think of her? She wrote and told me she went down to see you at the station. She wondered if she passed inspection OK ha! Ha!

As for Jane M., well her mother wrote me a real hot letter answering my last letter to Jane. So now I've gotten her off my string ha! Ha! I'm sort of glad too.

Well, take care of yourself and if you come home on furlough I hope I can be home the same time. Good luck.

Love, Kent

* * *

June 26, 1945
Italy

Dear Mother and Dad:
I guess you are wondering when in the heck I'll be coming home. Well, I'm wondering the same thing and don't know much more than you do about it. All I know is that it just can't be too long now. I want to get home so darn bad and I'm getting so darn restless laying around here doing nothing.

I flew up to Rome today just to get the rest of my flying time in for this month. We landed there to get our Squad Director who was at rest camp for a week. He goes up to Rome about once every two weeks. We stayed on the field there for about four hours waiting for him. We all had a swell time watching all the different types of planes coming in. Lots of big shots came in there while we were there. I saw one plane that was headed for London from there. I sure would have liked to gone with that plane. It's a good thing I never saw a plane that was headed for the U.S. because I'd have gone with it.

Mother, will you write to Loretta and ask her to come over to Arizona when I get home? She wants to but she doesn't know if her grandmother will be in Arizona at that time. I told her that you would be glad to have her come over.

The weather here has been hot as heck the last few days. Tonight it is nice and cool because we had a nice shower. I wish it would stay this way all the time, but it won't. This country around Foggia is all plains. Mostly wheat and fruit country. We are living in an olive grove northwest of Foggia about seven miles.

The dust sure can blow sometimes. This afternoon flying back from Rome we ran into a real bad storm over the mountains. It had us sweating for a while.

Please save all the Life magazines you have until I get home, will you? I want to read every one of them. Any magazine for that matter.

Well, I guess I better sign off for now and hit the sack. I'm plenty tired tonight. Write soon.

Love, Kent

P.S. hope to get home before the 1st of August.

* * *

June 27, 1945
Italy

Dear Klove:

It has been a long time since I've written to you. I hope you will forgive me for not writing. I've been so darn restless waiting around for the Army to send me home. Half of our group have gone home but our squad is the last squad in the group to leave. I don't know how I'll go home but I think it will be by plane. Either on a bomber or by ATC (C-47). I'd rather go by ATC rather than fly in one of those beat up old bombers home. That Atlantic Ocean is pretty big, you know.

Well, how are things treating you these days? Are you still getting good grades in your studies? I'll bet you will be glad when your schooling ends and you get that furlough. By the way, if you are home by the 27th of next month I might possibly be home by that time too. I'm hoping I can be home the same time you are.

But I guess that's too good to be true.

I flew to Rome yesterday afternoon on a B-17. We stayed up there about four hours but didn't leave the airfield. I had two big holes in the seat of my pants. The fellows that had decent clothes went into town. There was a Navy plane there with some high ranking Marine officers on it. There were three Navy enlisted men with the plane.

Did I tell you that I received your picture you sent me? It's a good picture of you. But what is it you have marked out? Are they battle ribbons? Ha! Ha! You Navy guys.

We had to take up all our brick floors from our tents. Now we have dirt floors again. But we won't have to stay here very long so it makes no difference. We had to turn in all our clothes except one pair of each kind. We can't live like that very long either.

We are having a big inspection of our squad today. It's a big one by the Air Force to see if we are ready to move.

Well, I've got to close for now. Take care of yourself and don't study too hard. Write when you find time.

Love, Kent

* * *

The morning Kent discovered he was being shipped home started like any other since the war ended. He began by straightening up his bunk. Then he walked around base trying to look like he was busy or heading somewhere with purpose. He'd discovered that if one of the officers caught you just standing around, they'd put you on KP duty, picking up cigarette butts or some other such nonsense.

That particular morning, however, he was summoned to the orderly tent. There was no getting around it, so he resigned himself to report for duty. When he arrived, the officer at the desk glanced up briefly before he returned his gaze to the papers in front of him and asked, "Are you Kent Tone?"

Kent stood a bit straighter. "Yes, sir."

"Date of birth and hometown?"

"October 26th, 1923, Mesa Arizona."

"Well, Tone. You're going home. Tomorrow you're to act as the flight engineer on Captain Erickson's crew."

"A flight engineer? Sir, I'm a gunner." He wore his confusion cautiously as he didn't want to talk himself out of a flight home, not when others had to take a boat.

The officer looked up from the papers. "It says here you were a mechanic before you underwent training to be a gunner. Is that correct?"

"Yes it is."

"Would you rather wait for the next ship to come to port and board that for home instead?"

That got Kent's attention. "No, sir. I'll be your flight engineer."

The officer indulged in the barest hint of a smile. "Good. Report back here at 1300 hours for a ride down to Bari to pick up the plane that's going back to the States. Here is the flight plan along with a list of passengers. Congratulations."

Kent accepted the paperwork. "Thank you, sir," he said, though the officer wasn't paying any more attention to him. He slipped out of the tent feeling lighter than air. He was finally going home.

Most of his crewmates had already left or had been assigned to different outfits. With glee, Kent packed his things, eager to leave.

Captain Erickson met Kent as soon as he got off the truck in Bari later that day. He was a tall, blonde man with bright blue eyes and an easy smile.

"You're my flight engineer, right?" He asked as Kent retrieved his duffel.

"Yes sir, Kent Tone." Kent slung his bag over one shoulder and stuck out his hand.

Captain Erickson took it with a firm grip.

"Good to meet you. I bet you're as excited to head back as I am. You got someone waiting for you at home?"

Kent smiled. "Yes, sir. She's pretty special."

Erickson's smile broadened. "That's just fine. If we do our jobs right, then we will be with our gals before we know it. Be ready to fly at 0400." He clapped Kent heartily on the back and went off his own way.

Kent reported to the flight line at the prescribed time ready to get going. The names on the flight plan were high ranking officials; Captain Majors, Colonels, and ace fighter pilots. Kent was more than awed at the ranks. He supposed everyone wanted to get home, so he tried not to make too much of a fuss about it.

He did the initial checks and went over the finer points of the aircraft with the ground crew chief who had taken care of her that morning. Before he knew it, they were in the air.

It was the same route he had taken when he'd initially come over seas, except in reverse. From Bari, they went to Marrakesh, French Morocco and stayed the night.

As the others went off to find their barracks for the evening, Kent took the plane to the fuel depot to fill it up. Major improvements had been done to the base since Kent had been there last; for instance, the whole ground was covered in cement instead of hard-packed dirt. It made for taxi-ing the bomber that much easier. After 2,700 gallons of gasoline had been pumped into the various gas tanks, Kent ran through one more check on the systems. The bomber was older and had seen a lot of action. He wanted to be sure it would get them all back home safely.

In his check, he noticed that one of the oil gauges for engine number two wasn't registering properly. There weren't any oil leak that Kent could find, so the best he could figure was that the gauge malfunctioned.

He sought out Captain Erickson in the mess hall at breakfast and let him know about the problem. "Sir, it could take two to three days to get a new gauge and get it installed. I know everyone is anxious to get home, but I am not sure we can if I can't confirm a leak."

The Captain weighed the situation carefully, contemplating his oatmeal and his coffee. After a long, tense moment of internal deliberation, he looked Kent straight in the eye and said. "Let's just go home. If we delay these men any longer, I'm worried they will riot. If you can't find anything wrong, then you'll have to keep an eye on that gage."

Kent couldn't argue with him; he wanted to get home too and was willing to risk it. He'd checked the systems at least half a dozen times and there just wasn't any leak.

They flew nine hours to the Azores and Kent watched that engine like a hawk, praying the whole time. When they landed, they spent the night in the Azores. Kent checked and triple checked the second engine. Still no evidence that anything was amiss.

The next morning, the crew took off straight across the Atlantic — the only deviation from the route Kent had taken to Europe initially. That meant instead of landing in Goose Bay, they landed in Connecticut safe and sound.

After they were safely on the ground, they were taken by convoy to Camp Myles Standish in Massachusetts. They were given a steak dinner with all the trimmings; the Army's way of saying welcome home. Kent ate with gusto, glad to be back in America and knowing it would only be a few more days before he was home.

Kent was honorably discharged from both the Army and the Army Air Corps in October, 1945. Demobilization, they called it. With his sudden newfound freedom, and not sure what else to do, he decided to take Brownie up on his offer of employment.

He stopped over at Brownie's Paint Shop on Canon Drive in Beverly Hills the day after he'd been discharged.

Brownie and Dorothy were in the front office

looking over some paperwork when he came in. "Hello, Mr. Brown. Mrs. Brown."

When Brownie saw Kent, he grinned widely and stepped forward to shake the young man's hand robustly. "Kent! It's wonderful to see you."

"Likewise, Mr. Brown."

"Please, please. Call me Brownie. I've told you, with what you've done for my mother-in-law, there's no need to be so formal."

"How is Blanche?" Kent inquired.

Dorothy spoke up then, her smile genuine. "Mother is doing much better. The blood you donated has done her a world of good. We can't thank you enough."

"I'm sure glad to hear that."

"So what brings you here?" Brownie asked, getting to the point.

Kent shifted from one foot to the other. "Well, sir. I was discharged from the Army yesterday and I got to thinking about your offer to work at your shop. I'd like to do that, if you'll still have me."

"My boy, of course I'll give you a job!" The enthusiasm with which Brownie made this proclamation was infectious. "How do you feel about being my new framework and alignment man?"

"That sounds just fine," Kent said, his smile, growing big with his luck.

"Wonderful. We'll have to send you to training. It's six weeks up in Illinois."

That's when Kent's smile faltered. "Six weeks in Illinois?" He immediately thought about Loretta. He'd only just gotten back and now he'd have to leave her again? "I don't know," Kent hedged.

"Nonsense. It's not too long and all of your expenses will be paid. This training will be invaluable to your success here. What do you say?"

There wasn't much of an option as far as Kent could see. He didn't have a place to live, nor a car to get around in, so if he wanted a job, he'd have to take what he could get. Squaring his shoulders, he looked Brownie in the eye and said, "Alright, I'll do it. When do I have to go?"

Delighted, Brownie assured him, "It'll take some time to make the arrangements. Maybe a week or two, isn't that right, Dorothy?"

His wife gave a nod. "Yes, I'll have to get ahold of them and we will have to set up transportation and lodging for you."

"In the meantime, you'll come here and start learning about how this shop is run. There's quite a bit of work and it'll do you good to understand how it all fits together. Seventy cents an hour suitable for your wage?"

That was a fantastic wage considering he had no idea how to even do alignments on cars. "Yes, that sounds just fine."

"Wonderful. Show up here next Monday morning at eight am sharp and we'll get you started."

"I'll be here with bells on," Kent agreed. The two men shook hands, sealing their agreement. Kent bid both Brownie and Dorothy good day and left the shop with a smile on his face. That had been easier than he thought.

By the end of the day, he'd also secured a small studio apartment and an old Dodge car that he bought on credit. When the sun set, he felt like he was a new man embarking on a new chapter of his life. There was just a small niggling part of him that said this wasn't quite right.

Loretta was thrilled when he told her the news. "Dad likes you. He wouldn't have given you the job if he didn't."

Kent couldn't lie to her. "I know that. I just can't help but feel like this isn't where I am supposed to be."

She cocked her head to the side. "What do you mean?"

He was at a loss at how to explain. "I can't quite put it into words. Maybe I am just a bit homesick. I miss the ranch."

Tenderly, Loretta touched his face. "I understand, but you are here now. You've got a good job, an apartment, and you've got me. Give it a little time and I promise you'll be happy.

* * *

November 12, 1945
Rock Island, Illinois

Dear Mother and Dad:
Well, here I am going to the Bear school. I got here Sunday afternoon at 2:30 pm and started from LA Friday afternoon at 4:30 pm.. I came here from Clinton, Iowa on a bus. Did I have a hard time getting out of LA I tried two times on the S.P. train and every time was turned down because of no room for civilians. I had almost given up until Brownie called

his friend who is the manager of the Beverly Hills Hotel. He had to bribe him to get a ticket (any kind) on a train just so he would get to Rock Island before or on Monday the 12th. Well, he got it OK but it was a drawing room ticket on the Steam Liner. The fastest and best train in the world. Another fellow was to share the room with me. He was to pay for half the room. So Dorothy took me down to the Union Station. I had to tell them my name was Mr. Brown so I could get the ticket. So I was Mr. Brown all the way back here. The ticket came to $143.61 just one way. Brownie gave me $110.00 to get the ticket with so I would have some money to live on back here. So I have to pay him back when I get home. I have $100.00 put away in a checking account at the Bank at Beverly Hills. But Loretta has my bank book and check book. So please send that Army check to Loretta as soon as you get it. She can send it on out to me.

The weather here is plenty cold and wet. I have my long drawers on and I'm still cold. I need a top coat. All I have is a leather Jacket. But I'll make it OK until I leave. I'm boarding at a boarding house at $12.75 a week but I don't much care for it. I only have to stay three weeks but I'm going to stay four or more. I figure I can't learn too much about anything. I can stay six weeks but that would cut me short on being back for Christmas.

Loretta and I had our pictures taken and they were ready the 9th but I never got to see them. I saw the proofs and helped pick out the ones we chose. We took six of the one smiling and six of the sober ones. I don't know which is the best but anyway you will get one for Christmas. Loretta is sending them out.

Loretta and I went up to Ventura the last Sunday I was there. Aunt Oie wasn't feeling too well. I saw Donald the day I left and he was back at his old job.

I've got to close for now. Write when you find time.

Love, Kent

* * *

When he wasn't learning about alignments, Kent got some time away when he went to visit his cousin and his farm. His cousin's place wasn't too far away from where he was staying in Rock Island.

Being back on a farm where he helped out in their dairy and repairing fences made his homesickness even more intense. It competed with how much he missed Loretta. While he was in Illinois, an idea cemented itself in his mind. He wanted to spend the rest of his life with Loretta. He also wanted to be a rancher, like his father. It was what called to him. If he wanted to have both, then he'd have to convince Loretta to move back to Arizona with him. He'd also have to build up more than a little bit in savings to make such a life possible.

When the six weeks of training was complete, he boarded another train back to Southern California, his mind abuzz with plans for his and Loretta's future together.

Over the next few months, he immersed himself in the workings of the paint and body shop, determined to do his best. Brownie's clientele was a dazzling array of stars. From Jack Benny and his black lacquered car to Gorgeous George's orchid colored Caddy, he was constantly struck by the sheer amount of celebrities Brownie not only knew, but had what appeared to be friendships with. When he had said they all came to Brownie's, he meant it.

Every day, he took his old Dodge and picked up Loretta from her high school. They would walk along the beach and talk about their days. Kent would tell her about life on the ranch, hoping he made it sound fascinating enough. He still had to get up enough courage to ask her to leave California.

~ ~ ~

Grandpa paused in his story telling, his eyes wide as he stared intently at something behind me. I turned, but there was nothing there.

"What's wrong, Grandpa?"

He blinked rapidly. "Did you see him? That tall black fella in the doorway? I've never seen anyone so tall before."

I turned again, but there was no one. "I didn't see him. Did he go through the door there?"

He shook his head, "No, he just disappeared right before my eyes. Kira, he was so tall. Taller than the door frame and he was head to toe dressed in black."

There wasn't any fear in his voice, just a mild sense of wonder. "There he is again. Look!"

For the third time, I craned my neck back to look behind me. There was still nothing there. I took a glance back at Grandpa. It was then that I realized something was very wrong. Healthy people don't hallucinate. Was it just his age finally catching up with him? The man was 92, after all. How long could I reasonably expect him to be mentally together? Grandpa watched the tall man in black that only he could see, oblivious to my worry.

It wasn't long after that we returned him to his room, both of us quiet and in our own thoughts. When he was back in bed, I leaned over and kissed his forehead.

"I'll call you tomorrow after work, Grandpa," I told him, trying hard not to let emotions choke my words. My eyes watered, but I kept smiling as bravely as I could.

He beamed up at me. "You always do."

PART TEN
PASSING INTO LEGEND

I got the call that Grandpa was admitted into the hospital in late November. At first, there was a horrible sense of panic as I dropped everything to make the hour-long drive out to where he was. But as I drove and had more time to think, my panic subsided. I remembered the last time I'd seen him in person, only a few weeks back. I'd given him a birthday card that had blueberries on the front of it. He'd gotten a certain faraway look and smacked his lips as he proclaimed that fresh blueberries were his favorite. He then tried to pick the fruit off of the card to eat, but his hallucinations weren't strong enough to give him the satisfaction of actually tasting them.

As I watched him sleep in the hospital bed, I understood that all stories must come to an end. We were simply in the final pages for Grandpa's tale.

Family was called in from all across the country. My sister, Shannon, flew in with her daughter. My cousins drove down from Colorado and California. All of us gathered to say good-bye. We took shifts in the hospital with him, holding his hand and trying not to cry in front of him. For his part, Grandpa did his best to make us all laugh. He put on a brave face during the day. Night time was a different story. He worried and he fought against the inevitable. I took to playing old Hank Williams songs for him to calm him down and lift his spirits. He would sing along for a bit, but when he stopped doing that, I did the one thing that he taught me to do: I told him stories.

Now, I'm not the same kind of story teller that he was. My talents tend to work best on paper. But seeing him struggle and fight and be in so much pain, I had to try. For the first time, I spoke a story out loud to him.

"Grandpa, I know you are hurting right now, but I want you to focus on my voice, alright? Close your eyes. Picture what I am telling you in your mind."

He did as I asked, pain written all over his pale face.

"You are outside on a bright, sunny day. There are some clouds, all puffy white like sprigs of cotton that make it seem as though the sky goes on forever. You can barely look away from it. A warm breeze grazes your cheeks. Do you feel it?"

With his eyes closed and the pained expression lessening on his features, he replied ever so softly, "I can feel it."

"The sweet scent of fresh cut alfalfa fills your nose. Can you smell it?"

A faintly whispered "yes," spurs my descriptions onward.

"In the distance, you can hear the cattle out to pasture. It's such a gorgeous day. The heat hasn't set in yet. The breeze is gentle and it ripples through the uncut alfalfa ahead of you. Can you picture it?"

A soft snore is my answer and with it comes a profound sense of relief. He had calmed enough to sleep.

Over the next few days as he worsened, I continued to describe the scene of the picturesque spring day on the ranch. I drew on all of the tales he'd told me over the last few years, injecting as many details as I could. Each sequence would draw him closer and closer to the ranch house. My story seemed to help with his pain and his fear.

At last he was moved into a hospice facility. I stayed with him that night. When the pain got bad, I whispered my tale about the beautiful day on the ranch as I held his hand in mine. He was no longer aware that I was there, but I like to think that he heard me.

It was a long, rough night. The family gathered first thing in the morning, understanding there were only a matter of hours left.

I held his hand, not willing to let go as each of them filed in to say their good-byes. In between my grief-stricken aunts, uncles, cousins, and siblings, I whispered the final parts of my story to him.

"You're standing in front of the big red door. The wooden slats of the porch squeak under your boots. A wreath of wildflowers hangs over the door, leaving a sweet aroma against the heat of the day. A sense of comfort washes over you. Once you go through that door, you will be greeted by all of the family and friends who have passed before you; Grandma Eva, Grandpa Albert. Most of all, Grandma

Loretta. They are all waiting for you just through that door. When you are ready, grab hold of the brass handle and open it."

There were a few raspy breaths that puffed out through his parted lips. With tears streaming down my face, I leaned in and whispered, "Thank you for the stories."

A long, soft sigh was the only response he gave before passing through the door and into legend.

AFTERWORD

After celebrating 92 years of life, Albert Kent "A.K." Tone passed into legend on the morning of Wednesday, November 18th, 2015. Kent was born on October 26th, 1923 in Mesa Arizona. As a child, he loved to play pranks on visiting family members. His sense of humor lasted his entire life.

He served in the Army Air Force during WWII as a waist gunner on a B-17. He proudly flew 22 missions over Axis-controlled Europe.

When he returned from the war, Kent married his sweetheart, Loretta Brown. They had four children and were married for 64 years before Loretta passed.

Kent never met a stranger he couldn't talk to. If you gave him half a breath, he'd have you knee deep in a conversation before you knew what was happening. Whether you were talking to him for the first time or the millionth, Grandpa had a talent of connecting in a way that is almost forgotten in today's age. He said you have to pay attention to what people say or you might miss something important. In all of his 92 years, he listened as much as he talked.

I've learned that sometimes people become fixated on a certain point of their past. They latch onto the memories and experiences and for them that brief moment shines like gold amongst the tarnished brass of before and after.

If asked, Grandpa would say the best time of his life was during those five significant years between 1942 and 1947. In all of the years after, those were the times he spoke of the most. They were the memories he visited and reveled in most often as he grew older. The storyteller that Grandpa was wanted to share his experiences with the world and, in that way, live on. He wanted to make sure that not only himself, but also that courageous generation of his was not forgotten in the years to come. With his permission and blessing, I set out to give these memories new life.

The result is the book you just read. While the stories were given to me in first person, it felt disingenuous to record them that way. No matter how much I try, I simply can't write the way Grandpa talked.

So I wrote them the only way I could; by taking his stories and turning them into a novel. I did my best to stay true to Grandpa's tales, though some of the details were altered for continuity and clarity. For instance, Grandpa had more aunts and uncles than I have noted; Great Grandpa Albert was from a large, Norwegian family. Including all of them would have gotten fairly confusing for those who do not come from a large extended family.

The personalities of the brave men Grandpa encountered and flew with in the Air Corps are my invention; the most I got from Grandpa were their names (which have been changed) and a few bits of their true nature. The crews he flew with (except for the one he trained with) were completely fabricated, though what happened on those flights is accurate as per his telling.

The letters spaced throughout the text are really the ones he wrote home. Great Grandma Eva saved them. I fixed a few spelling and grammatical errors, but otherwise tried to keep them intact to their original formatting. The original letters have been scanned and included in the appendix.

The song "My Gal's a Corker, She's a New Yorker" belongs to John Stromberg. Grandpa referenced it often, usually with a glint in his eye.

While the stories do take place during one of the most intense points of recent history, I purposefully did not focus on the mechanics and the day-to-day life of a WWII airman. The main goal of this project was to record and honor Grandpa's stories. It would seem disingenuous if I were to insert a lot of historical facts that he left out. To that end, any and all mistakes are mine.

That being said, I would be remiss if I didn't take a moment to acknowledge and thank a few people for their help in making sure the details I did include were accurate. My sister Shannon and her husband Wade did a tremendous job in not only supplying me with the correct military customs and protocols, but also making sure I stayed true to Grandpa's style and voice. Every chance he got, Grandpa always told me and countless others how proud he was of both of you. My friends, Tom and Rachel for seeing this work through its many incarnations from the very beginning to the final edits. Tom also did an incredible amount of work scanning Grandpa's letters so they could be included. Much appreciation to Carla, Brad, and Becca for allowing me to put you in this story. Grandpa was always very impressed by all of you. Also, a big thank you to Gerry for her patience and directness in regards to my lack of grammar.

As Grandpa was quite fond of quoting General Douglas MacArthur, it is only fitting that I end this book about him with one of his favorites. It's something he told me nearly every time we spoke during the last couple of years of his life: "Old soldiers don't die, they just fade away."

It's our job not to forget them.

My grandfather was a tremendous man. I am honored to have known him. I just hope that someday I can tell a story half as well as he could.

APPENDIX

~~*

LETTERS

March 6, 1944

Dear Folks:

Today was the first real day of classification but no tests until tomorrow. They told us today that it is not an I.Q. test but an aptitude test to tell whether or not we are adapted to air crew training. I don't think I have much of a chance and don't feel surprised if I wash out. I did make good grades at C.T.D. thats true but from what I hear that is not needed for these tests. Either you have what they want or you haven't.

The weather here is just like Arizona and I like it fine. There is snow on the high mountains to the north. The ocean is not over four miles from here.

I'll call you over the phone if I find out I'm made a cadet. That will be exactly 13 days from today. Is that O.K.? If I wash out I'm getting a furlough some way if possible. No it makes no matter how hard a fellow works around here he can never get a long enough pass to go that far. Every one here is on the ball all the time. Every Sunday we have a dress parade from 3:30 PM until about 6 PM. Yesterday was my first one to be in. I'll bet there was near 50 squadrons on the field at once and 200 or more men in each squadron. We were the last squadron to pass by the reviewing stand so that caused us to stand at parade rest for darn near 2 hrs. before we could start marching.

245

Yes, I know all about them meeting the Evans. Loretta told me all about it just after it happened. I guess she was scared to death when they asked her that. You can't make me blush any more. Ha!

Tinsley, said to tell you that if he could tell you what he thought about that sour orange, it wouldn't be very gentle man like.

The other day I called Loretta over the phone and talked for 19 min. I didn't think we were talking that long but we did. It just cost $.50 and I had to hunt up change in the barracks so I could pay the phone. I'll remember next time - not to talk so long, or else have a hand ful of coins.

We had two lectures today one by a major and another by a captain. They all told us the danger we would be in while flying in combat. The captain was a bombardier and has seen action in Europe. In fact he said he was the first American to drop the first American bomb on Germany. He was wounded and sent back here to teach new air crew members. He said from now on each of us would have to be trained to meet the enemy in combat. The going is going to be tough and hard going because they have to train us in the shortest time possible and the best trained air-crew member in the world. He said we would be taught the expression "Kill or be killed" a thousand times before we are through. He told us the importance of each member of the crew on a combat mission. Everyone has his job to do just like on a foot ball team and we have train to work together.

The food here is good but most of the time it all don't go around to all queus. If we happen to be the last one on the table, well we have to do with out food, that meal. They told us today that we each are allowed 55¢ a day for food. That don't give us much to eat but after a guy gets to callet you get more to eat. I've first get to make the grade. Tomarrow the I ay for the mental.

I'll have to close for this time.

Love
Kent.

March 8, 1944

Dear Folks:

I have a little time off so I'll write you a line to let you know how I'm getting along. I finished all of my written tests this morning and then this after noon I went to take some kind of coordination tests but they would'nt let me take them today. The other night I hurt my finger while playing catch so they said it would hinder me. I have to go take the test Friday. OK! Well, I don't give a damn any more because after taking the written tests, I'm sure I'm a washout. I am going to try like heck to get back to my old squadron at Williams Field. If not I'm going to apply for Aircraft Mechanic school some place.

The weather here is still good but I'm afraid there's some more rain coming. The wind is blowing just like it does in March. I like the climate here because it reminds me of Arizona.

I guess tomorrow I go in front of an Officer which will ask us all kinds of questions and try like heck to make us nervous so he can wash us out. It's a heck of a fight to keep from washing out. They keep us sweating all the time.

I got a letter from ~~——~~ and he is in Basic training now. He said he is having a hard time making the grade but he is trying like heck to make the grade. When he went through Santa Ana, they only had to made a rating of three to pass but now it has raised up to 7 so you see what I have to put up with.

Did I tell you I got my diploma from K.S. and it is signed by President Eisenhower and Capt. ~~——~~ We had a graduation excersion in which we were presented our diplomas by Capt ~~——~~ He wished us all the luck in the world.

One week from today I can go to the P.X. show or any thing here on the post after duty hours. Being restricted to the barracks would drive a guy nuts in a months time.

My bunks got to be made yet and I've got to shave before 10 o'clock so I'd better close.

Love,
Kent

P.S. We get paid the 15th.

March 12, 1944

Dear Folks:

I have a little time now before we have to go to chow, so I'll write you a line. It sure was good to hear your voices again.

It is starting to rain now so we won't have to stand parade this afternoon (I hope) This will be the last sunday in restriction for me. if I wash out, I think I can have a pass on the week end after washing out. Maybe I won't wash out but I'm sure I will be though. I have passed all my other tests except the interview with the psychiatrist, he said I was too nervous for combat-flying. The reason was because I couldn't hold my hands out in front of me without having them shake. I get one more chance with him, tomorrow. I guess I was lucky because the other fellows washed out right then and there for nervousness. I get scared when I go in there, he is a major. I am going to talk like heck to get him to let me go on.

Monday afternoon. -

I never got to finish last the night so I'll try this afternoon. I went to see the psychiatrist today and they haven't got my grade yet so I have to wait. They are going to call me when they get my grades.

It is trying to rain today so we don't have to parade tonight. Tomorrow our whole flight gets Mess management. (K.P.) I hate to start that stuff again but it won't hurt any of us. We will get plenty to eat anyway.

If I'm still here when you come over, I'd like you to come. But I don't think I will stay here very long after washing out. And if I do happen to make what I applied for. I'll be here for at least 3 months. That is Pilot pre-flight school. I don't care if they give me bombardier just anything to stay in cadets.

I'd better close for this time, I'll write more Wensday.

Love
Kent.

P.S. I've got to get rid of these air mail stamps.

March 16, 1944

Dear Folks:

Well, I'm still an A.H.S. and there has been three lists out so far. About 10 of the old flight 52 has washed out so far. Vassar is still in my barracks and I'm sure he will come through O.K.   , the big shot here and back at Kansas State College washed out today. Most of the fellows washed out on mental. I'm sure I passed the mental O.K. because I'd have been washed out the first bunch. I can't tell you the number but there's plenty of us washed out. Tell Klove not to enlist into any thing yet. He might stand a chance to stay out for some time. He should get all the schooling he can get before he is taken in the service. Thats the only way the army, navy or any other branch has in telling what job you are suited for. As for cadets, no civilian can come into cadets any more. Not even enlisted men here in the states. You have to be over seas before you can apply for cadet training.

I've got to hurry and finish this letter and shine my shoes for inspection tomorrow morning. Tonight I pull guard duty from 10 P.M. until 0200 A.M. All of us pull guard duty at once.

I did'nt care for that kind of hair oil because it looks like it will make your hair grey. And beside they keep our heads clipped so short we do need any thing to comb it with.

I don't think I can make it over there in three days and still get back on time. If I wash out, I'll go to some mechanics school and before I start to school I get a furlough. So that will be better than a three day pass.

I'm getting sun burned from this sun shine my face is red tonight from being out in the sun this after noon. I guess I got plenty white while I was in Kansas. Now I'll get sun tanned again.

I'll close for this time. Next time I write I'll tell you whether or not am washed or not.

Love
Kent.

253

March 20, 1944

Dear Mother,

I am going before the faculty board this morning and that means I'm going to wash out. All the fellows that haven't washed are going to be classified today. Jouetta came out to see me yesterday but this place is no good for entertaining visitors. She got to see the parade and I never marched so I could see it too.

I don't know what they are going to do with me but I'll find out this morning. I think I'll be grounded and sent to Texas, some place. I never dreamed I was nervous.

I won't be able to get a three day pass but when I get to another field I will try to get a furlough.

I've got to go now, I'll write a letter tonight to you and let you know more about what they tell me.

Love

Kent.

Dear Folks: March 20, 1944

I wrote you this morning that I was going before the faculty board. Well, I did and they washed me out for nervousness. They told me that I made pilot O.K. and all that held me back was that they thought I was a little too tense. They kept another boy and myself after they dismissed the others. Both of us was washed for the same reason and the other boy had over 200 hrs flying time. They told us that our asignment was Las Vegas, Nevada gunnery school. He (I mean the Captain in charge of the board) told us that we had had experience on the line so they figure that we will make airel enginner with out going to A.M. school. He said that our job was just as important as a pilot, navigator or bombardier but it didn't take as much strain. They were very nice to us and made us feel much better. I was glad to hear that I was classified as pilot and had passed all the written tests. The only thing that was wrong was my damn nervous tension. One thing I did wrong was, when I made out a folder for them, I put down that my parents didn't want me to fly. I think that had a lot to do with it. I guess I was too damn honest. I put down "They prefer me not to fly."

255

I hope I can get a pass before I leave here. I won't get a furlough for some time to come. Gunners don't get passes while they are training nor do they get paid. When they graduate they will get paid their back pay and get a pass. OK.

Well, if I get on a good ship I might fly all over the U.S. before going across.

I'm sure glad they never grounded me because I thought may be they would because of my nervousness. I'll make a good gunner I think. Come out with Sgts ratings. Then before long you make T/sgt. so what do I care. T/sgt with flying pay is almost as good as a commission. Maybe I can get on a B-29 and all the crew on them are commissioned or have Flight Officer ratings.

The weather here is swell but it still looks like rain. I sure hope it doesn't rain next week end. If I'm here I'm getting a pass.

The rest of the fellows have been classified and about 60 of them made pilot. Vassar made bombardier. Tinsley made navigator. I never thought Vassar would make the grade but he did. He sure didn't have much as far as a student. His grades were poor at C.T.D. They can't say I was too dumb because I passed all the tests. OK.

256

Gunners school lasts about 3 weeks and then I go to an Replacement wing and from there to a outfit.

Ive got to close now.

      Write soon

        Love

          Kent

P.S. I feel like a free man now. No more gigs and plenty of time to myself.

March 24, 1944.

Dear Folks:

I'm in another squadron now, waiting for shipment to another squadron. After I go to another squadron I'll be shipped out to Las Vegas from there. I'm getting a pass this week end but there's not a chance of getting a three day pass.

How are things getting along at home? I'd like to be there on furlough right now. In about three months or less I'll get a 10 day delay in route to Salt Lake City. That means I can take 10 days time getting there from Las Vegas. When I get there I'll be assigned to a combat crew.

I'm sending a picture of our quarters at K.S.C. and some pictures of our old flight 52. The little dog we called G.I. is one of the pictures but I'll send it later. I've only got one of it. The picture of us in flying boots + jackets was taken just before we went up. That is the plane I always flew. I got my log book back the other day. The one that my instructor kept for us. He has all of our grades in it. My grades were all between 80 + 85 and some of the reports he wrote up were pretty good. When I go to Las Vegas I'll send my log books home and you can keep them for me.

I haven't had any letters from you for darn near two weeks. I think maybe the mail man. I'll take it all back. A guy just gave me a letter from you. It took 4 days to get here.

Yes, I got three papers since I've been here and there is always lots of news in them. I knew about the Comming boy it was in the paper. He is a radio operator + gunner, that's the ones they train at Yuma. All the Airplane mechanic gunners go to Las Vegas. All the poor fellows in College now are going back to the ground forces. Around 36,000 of them and all the Classified here at Santa Ana is frozen. They don't need any more air-crew members. Tell K love not to get into the army until they make him. But All the navy deal is a good place to be. That's the only chance to get any schooling out of the service. I think maybe I'll go and see Donalds if I get a pass and find time.

Love
Kent.

Write soon.

March 29, 1944

Dear Mother:

I'm still in this Sqd. 1 yet. I think maybe the gunnery school is full or something. Before I leave this post I have to move to Sqd. 414 for shipment out. I'll stay there at least five days, so I should get at least 2 more week-ends off. Unless I'm on K.P. over Sat. or Sun.

I sure hate that about Aunt Oie & Uncle Harry coming to see me and I wasn't here. Darn it, I came through that gate two times that afternoon and I'm sure they were in the crowd there.

Some of my pals from K.S.C. that washed out are shipping out today + tomorrow. Some go to Denver, Colo. some to Texas and some to South Da.

Thanks for sending me that clipping. I was already informed about the air-crew trainies. Things have come to almost a stand still around here as far as classification is concerned. More and more are washing out and some are not being

Classified. Even the fellows that are Classified are going to have it plenty tough to stay a cadet.

I sure had a sweet time last week-end. The Browns were sure nice to me. Tell Blanch that experienced Brownies' driving while coming back to the base. I thought we were going to start flying any time. He drove from Knots Berry place to here in about 10 minutes. My pass was up at 3 P.M. and I just made it. They wanted to bring me back so they could take me to Knots Berry place.

I hope you have found a helper by now. Thats too much work for Klove & Dale to do. I think he should get rid of those darn cows. It don't pay to work so hard. Why not take life easy.

I've got myself a new pen. My other one is just no good anymore. When I get to Las Vegas I'll send it back. I may get a new one for it. I like this one just as good.

I'll have to close for this time.

Love,

Kent.

April 4, 1944

Dear Mother:

I moved to this squadron yesterday and they put us in tents. Tents aren't so bad in fact I like them because there isn't any cleaning to do much. We have no foot-lockers so we have to live out of our barrack bags. All we do here is wait for shipment and pull a little work once in a while. We have to work on K. P. once or twice while we are here but its not bad. This after noon our commanding officers took about half of us to the theater to see a show. This field is full of wash outs now. There was more than 4,000 cadets pushed out to be sent back to their old out-fits. I sure feel sorry for them because there isn't any thing wrong with them. They are getting a dirty deal.

I sent you a Easter card with some money in it. I want you to get what ever you want with it to make a happy easter for you. Maybe you need a new hat to wear to church Easter Sunday. N love + Dad. I wish you too a happy Easter and don't work too hard.

I think I'll be here for another week end in L.A. Unless some more gunners ship out before Sat.

We have more time off at night for the first time in about 2 months. It sure feels good to be a regular GI. again. We can wear our flight jackets at night with out being giged for it.

I got paid today after waiting four days after regular pay day. I didn't need it but I always like to have my pay on time.

When I get to my next field I'll have you send some of my things back. My O.D. pants + the small work jacket.

I'll have to close for this time, I can't think of anything else to say right now.

Your
Kent.

263

April 12, 1944

Dear Mother, Dad + Klone:

I'm now stationed at Las Vegas, Nevada. We got here about 5:30 this morning after leaving L.A. about 6:30 last night. The field is not bad at all, there are mountains all around us. My barracks are near the flying line so I feel right at home listening to the planes roar. Reminds me of Williams field.

There will be no 10 day delay in Route for gunners leaving this field, I found out this morning. They stopped it last month. So the only furlough I'll get is just before I go across.

Our stay here will be 7½ weeks and the last two weeks will be flying time. We will fire from B-17s and try to hit P-40's + P-39s with camera guns. They will attack us with camera guns too. The 18th replacement wing has changed to Lincoln Neb. so that where we go from here. And from there I don't know. But I do know I'll either be on a B-17 or B-29 bomber. We start to school Sat.

I had another week end pass in L.A. last week. I was on K.P. all day Sat. and when I got to L.A. I was plenty tired. Three of us hitched hiched in together and we stayed at a hotel in Hollywood. Then Sunday I went with the Browns on a picnic. I had a very nice time. I hitched hiched back to the base about 12 that night. I never got back until 4 A.M. and my pass was up at 6 A.M. I still haven't caught up on my sleep.

I'll have to close for now. Here's my new address.   Class 44-23 Sqd 7
                        A.A.F. F.G.S.
                        L.V. A.A.F.
                        Las Vegas, Nevada

Love,
Kent

April 18, 1944

Dear Mother Dad & K love:

I haven't anything to do for about 45 minutes this morning so I'll try and write you a letter. The sky is cloudy this morning and looks like rain. But I doubt if it does rain here.

I went up in the pressure chamber yesterday and my ears are still feeling stopped up from it. We went up to 20,000 feet with out oxygen and stayed there for 12 minutes then put on our masks and went on up to 30,000 feet. Tomorrow we go up to 38,000 feet or higher to see if we can stand the low pressure because most of our real flying will be above 38000 feet.

Today we take a night vision test which I've already taken once before at Santa Ana. I passed it there so I guess I'll pass it here.

There are a lot of new army men in my sqd. and most of them are just kids. They went into cadet training and got about two months college and now they are all picked out and made plain gunners. None of them have been in the Army longer than 2 months. There are a lot that didn't get as far as college. A big bunch came in from A.S.T.C. at Tempe, Arizona.

Will you tell the (Mesa Tribune) where my new address is and take it off of this letter. The mail must be plenty slow around here I haven't got any yet from you.

April 19 - Wensday night.

I did'nt have time to finish yesterday so I'll finish tonight. Your letter came today and I was glad to hear from you. I went up in the pressure chamber today to 38000 feet. It did'nt hurt me any except at 38000 feet I had a slight case of the bends in my right knee. Every body get them some times at that altitude. My ears were O.K. too. One poor boy just could'nt relieve the pressure in his ears coming down and his ear drums broke. Both ear drums. I sure felt sorry for him because he was suffering something terrible. 38,000 feet is plenty high and it means certain death if you do'nt have oxygen. Most of our flying will be less than 30,000 feet.

If you do drive up here I dought if I'd have much time off to have any time with you. You see we are only here 6 weeks or more and part of that time we are 50 miles up in the mountains at a place called Indian Springs. We are up there for most of our flying. And I do'nt know when we are to go up there so you might miss me. This town is a heck of a place to stay in from what they tell me, too.

Now that I've gotten this far I'm going to finish the training out. I figure that it's better to fight up in the air rather than on the ground. I'm going to get all I can out of this gunnery school so I can shoot damn good when ready for combat.

The ground crew doesn't have it so nice and have to work so darn hard. We get flying pay and good ratings and also good training. The pilot + co-pilot are just as dangerous or more than a gunner because he hasn't any things to shoot back with.

I'm glad you got your kitchen floor fixed the way you want it. You must have had a big crowd at the party the way you talked. You must have worked plenty hard.

Well, I've got to clean up before going to bed. I done all my laundry yesterday and it was some job. Damn this army, it takes it so darn long to do anything. They had better not try and charge me for laundry this month.

Love
Kent

P.S. Don't worry about me. I'll be O.K.

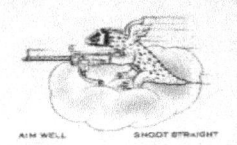

AIM WELL   SHOOT STRAIGHT

LAS VEGAS ARMY AIR FIELD
LAS VEGAS, NEVADA   May 20, 1944

Dear Mother, Dad + Klove:

Im sorry I haven't answered your letters sooner. Tomorrow we go to Indian springs to fly. I have a graduation present for Klove but Im sorry I can't send it until I get back from the springs. The mail has gone out today and the post office is closed. Im glad you liked the card and candy.

We were issued flying cloths and oxygen masks today. We finished taking the written exams yesterday. I passed them all as far as I know. I made 40% hits on the range shooting 50s and 30s. I hit 800 rounds out of 2,000. None of the fellows get over 50% so that's not bad for me. I couldn't hit the broad

269

side of a barn with the shot guns.
We had to shoot them from pick up
Trucks going 35 miles per hour.

I saw _____ this afternoon at the mess
hall. I talked to him for a while. He
knew me the minute he saw me. He
said he might be in charge of our
troop train when we leave. He says
he tries to get one troop train a month.
It will be O.K. if he goes with us.

That card I sent you had air mail
stamps on it by mistake. I first put
one air mail on it before taking it to
the post office. The clerk had me put
on more to make enough to go air mail.
It cost more to send than the package.

I'm on fire guard tonight from 9 P.M.
until 11 P.M. and its almost time to start.

Darn it, I just can't think of any thing
to write. I probably will be flying over
boulder dam and Grand Canyon while
up at the Springs. Also Death Valley.

Well, I've got to close for this time.
                        Write the same address I get
it at the Springs anyway. Love, Kent.

A.A.F. FLEXIBLE GUNNERY SCHOOL
L.V.A.A.F.
LAS VEGAS, NEVADA May 29, 1944

Dear Folks:

Well, I'm back here at Las Vegas again. I fly again this morning and all this week. No, I don't care much for flying in a B-17. Their the roughest plane I've ever flown in. I got sick every time I went up last week, and I mean sick too. There was plenty of guys that got sick. The reason was there was hot weather, rough country and long missions. We had to stay up anywhere from 4 to 6 hrs. at one time. I got to shoot the chin guns, waist guns and top turret. Its fun shooting the chin guns at a target on the ground. I could shoot it straight too. Its the guns that the bombardier uses. You sit up in the glass nose in the bombardiers

seat. The ground was plenty close
to that nose too. We were about 50 feet
off the ground and flying about 150 mile
per hr. This morning I go up for high
altitude to 20,000 feet. We have to
use oxygen for any altitude over 10,000
feet.

All your letters came while I was
up at the Springs but I never took
any writing paper with me. So I
could'nt write back. I did'nt have
much time anyway.

Llove, I'm sending your present today
if I can get to the post office.

Next Sat. we graduate.

Well I've got to go now and get ready
for the flight line.

I'll write more soon.

Love,
Kent

272

Dear Mother, Dad & I love: May 30, 1944

How is every thing at home these days? Is the weather getting hotter yet.? The weather here is hot and the last two days it has rained. Today was the first mission this week because of the rain. I never got sick this time. This time we had lots of fun ups there shooting at real planes. They were AT-6 and they came in just like the real thing. We were shooting at them with cameras in stead of bullets. Did I ever tell you at each student shoots up about $1700.00 worth of amanition. Think of all the money this army has spent on me already.

I am listening to Eddie Rickinbacker over the radio. He sure is laying it on thick.

It wont be long before I get out of this hell hole. I think as soon as I get to my new field they'll give me a furlough. I hate to start out for Fla. and then come right back on that same train.

I'll have to close for this time so I can get this off in the mail.

Love Kent.

June 3, 1944

Dear Mother, Dad & love:

Well, today is the day we graduate and get our wings. We finished flying yesterday and turned in all our flying clothes. We get passes tonight and also get paid flying pay this morning.

I got by this place just getting sick one time that was yesterday. The pilot was flying through the mountains. We were so close to the cliffs that the wings almost touched the sides of them. The mountains were so high that snow was on them. The clouds were all around us and we were dodging them and the mountains too. Boy it sure was rough in those mountains. The air pockets in the canyons caused the roughness.

I guess we are going to Tampa as far as I know. They don't tell us where until we are on our way.

June 5, th

I never got to finish this letter the

other day so I'll do it now. Well, we leave tonight and we go to Lincoln, Nebr..

They gave us passes over the week-end. I never had enough time to go home but if I did I sure would have come. Three of us fellows went to Boulder Dam and on over into Arizona. It isn't as big as I thought it would be. We hitched hiked up there from Vegas. We stopped at Boulder City for a while. That is the best little town I've seen yet. It is clean as it can be and all kinds of green lawns and trees. It doesn't seem possible to see that kind of a place out in the rocks like it is. We got our silver wings but we had to pay for them out of our flying pay. I made Cpl. after a hell of a long time. Well, I'd better sign off for now. I'll write as soon as I get to my next place.

Love,

Kent.

June 24, 1944

Dear Folks:

I'm almost done with most of
the classifying here. Tomorrow I
have to take some kind of a trade
test to see what I know about
airplanes. Then I'll be sent to
another sqd. to wait for shipping.
I think I'll be here from 5 to 10
days. We work on Sundays just
the same as any other day. I got
a lot of new cloths today and had
to turn in all my wool pants &
shirts. They made us send our non-
G.I. shirts home. When I get to my
next field I'll send home for them.

I got to see   again but now
he is in another sqd. He got in three
hrs late on his furlough but they
never said anything to him. The
train was late.

The weather here has been O.K. but
tonight the over cast is coming in
and it might be raining tomarrow.
I sure hope I will be sent out west
some place. I hate this middle west.
Tomarrow night we get passes to town.
We have to be off the streets by 11:30
at night on week nights and 1:30 A.M.
on Sat. nights. Lincoln is a swell town
I think.

We are'nt going over seas now. It
will be from 3 to 4 months yet. Lots of
times the gunners get a five day
pass. I might even get home in five
days from where I get stationed.
I'll have to close for now
                    Love,
                         Kent.

277

June 26, 1944

Dear Mother & Dad & Klove:

Well, I'm still here in this hell hole waiting to be shipped out. I haven't been assigned to a crew yet but it won't be over four days yet. I think I will be shipped out next week some time. The first part of the week. I haven't had a pass yet and I doubt if I ever get one in Lincoln.

We are kept busy most of the time doing detail work around the post. I figure I might get some K.P. duty before I leave this place. Oh! Well, it all comes in a days work.

There is plenty to do on our off time. They have three service clubs and

four P.X's on the field. Also three
theaters and a library too.

Did I tell you I have moved three
times since I've been here. Three different squadrons. Now I've ended up
in Sqd F and I'm living in a tent.
They aren't bad but the bath water isn't
hot half the time. Today the wind
is blowing and this darn tent
feels like it's going to blow away
any minute now.

I got the Mesa paper today and
my name was in there bigger than
heck. Too much bull.

I'm anxious to find out what kind
of pilot, co-pilot, bombardier and
navigator I'll get. I hope they know
their stuff, and also the gunners too.

I sent some socks and under shirts
home today I don't need them any
more. Their to much to carry around
with me. Some of them need mending

but I'm sure you could use them
to work in. They took away one of
my barracks bags so I have to cram
everything in one bag. I can't carry
too much extra junk anymore.

This 2nd Air Force is sure a big
training command. It supplies all
the heavy bombardment groups for
all theaters of combat. So you see they
put through a good many men here.
I will go into another Air Force when
I'm done with my combat training, depending on which theater of war I go to.

Well, I'm about out of ink and no
more around so I'd better close for
this time.
        Write soon.
                Love
                    Kent.

July 7, 1944

Dear Mother, Dad & K love:

I'm here in the service club this afternoon trying to rest a little bit. This field keeps us busy every day of the week if we don't manage to get out of it some how. I pulled K.P. Sat and worked all day Sunday. The way it looks I won't ship out until next week some time.

Your letter came Friday. Sorry I haven't gotten around to answering it but I've been pretty busy.

I went on K.P. Sat morning at 3 A.M. and got off at 7 P.M. Then I went to town with some of the boys and we never got back until 1:30 in the morning. I've been tired the last two days.

The weather here has been hot but today it cooled up a little bit and looks like rain.

I don't have any idea where I will be sent from here. I found out that the 2nd Air Force has two fields east

the 2nd Air Force has two fields east
of the Mississippi river. There is a chance
I'll be sent down to Tenn. or La. What
a place to be sent to, another hot and
damp state.

I was glad to hear that Dick is
still in England. He must be in a
pretty safe place.

I got paid the other day and now
I have some extra money. I bought a
$100.00 bond yesterday and sent it
home. I hope you get it O.K. Keep it
for me, will you? Our Sqd alone
bought 3,000 bucks worth of war bonds
this pay day. Thats pretty good don't
you think? The pay roll was worth
about 50,000 bucks. just this Sqd.

Have you got the grain in yet?
Say, there was a fellow in another
sqd that received a telegram from
his folks that they needed some help
on the farm. And asked him if he
could'nt try to get a few days off to
go home and help. He took the wire
to the C.O. and they are giving him
a 3 months furlough. So if you
get too bad off for help you know

282

what to do. The red cross has to check up and see if he is really needed at home.

Today, being the 4th of July, the guns saluted with a bunch of loud reports at noon time. Then tonight they sounded retreat as usual.

Well, the war news seems to be getting better every day. But I don't like the way the people are acting about getting a new president. Sometimes that will be the biggest head line on the paper. These Republicans are sure strong on that guy Dewey. I wish they would wake up and realize that there is a war on. We get good news broadcasts here, and all kinds of maps discribing the advances made.

Well, I guess I've wound down for this time, so I'd better close.

Write soon.

Love,

Kent.

P.S. I have K.P. again ~~Wednesday~~. Thursday.

July 16, 1944

Dear Mother:

In on a shipping list now and will go out of her some time in the middle of the week. They read it off this morning. It's for B-17s and we think we will go to Alexandria, La. away down south almost to New Orleans. Where theres nothing but swamps and rain.

I was glad to hear that the grain turned out so good. That was a lot of money at one time for grain, wasn't it.

Those pictures came the other other day and the guy sent them out yesterday. Be sure and save one or two of them will you. I don't care what you do with the rest.

That is if you think they are worth
a darn. I saw the big one but
not the small ones. Tell me what
you think of them will you. I don't
think they are worth a darn. My
gold tooth shows up too much.
I've changed my mind, I want you
to save me three little ones. You
can have the rest.

Did you get a #100⁰⁰ bond I
sent home? I sure hope it got
home O.K. I had it insured.

I'm at the service club now
and it is raining like heck
out side now. This is the darn
dest country around here. It will
rain darn near a inch of rain in
about 3 hrs. and in six hours
all the water is gone into the ground.
Arizona would be flooded off the
map if it got as much rain.

I was put on K.P. again sat. but I got out of it. I went over early in the morning and they needed a fellow to help wake up the K.P.s so I helped. They took me off K.P. for helping and I managed to get a sleeping pass out of the deal. So instead of K.P. I slept all morning until noon.

O.K. I'll be careful what I write to the gal. Thanks for telling me, I hope it isn't that bad. Excuse this ink because begers cant be choosers you know. I had to get it from my bunk neighbor. I'm back at the tent now and just got back from the show.

Well, I think I'll have to close for now. I can't think of anything more to say. Write soon.

Love
Kent.

July 23, 1944

Dear Mother + Dad + K love:

I got here fur[?]day morning after a long train ride of three days. They put us busy right away going to school. This is the first chance we had to write. I'm O.K. and this place is not very bad. I'll be here around 10 weeks.

Your letter came the day I got here. You never did say if you got that 100th bond or not. I'd like to know if it got home.

I haven't met my pilot but one fellow we met yesterday and he is a first Lt. and has been flying sub-patrol over the coast of south america for good many months.

Our radio operator is a Staff Sgt. and has been over seas before on a B-17. So now we have to get two more on our crew for gunners besides the bombardier, Nav. and Co-pilot.

This place is sure hot and I mean hot too. It is a real wet heat. The town of Alex. is crowded with infantry soldiers from 3 large camps around here. They say there are about 300,000 ~~~~ soldiers here in a town of 39,000 civilians before the war.

We will fly over the gulf of Mexico most of the time and will have to wear May-West life jackets.

here's my address.

I'll have to close for now, but I'll write some more later. I have so much time now.

Joe,
Kent.

P.S. May get a furlough when I leave here.

ARMY AIR FORCES

Dear Mother: July 25, 1944

Your letter came today, the one you sent
out the 21st. Thats too bad about the well, don't
you think you can get a driller some place. That
will mean you'll have to haul water for the live
stock. I sure hope you can get a well driller.

It rained real hard yesterday after noon and
now its raining again this after noon. But this
time its coming down twice as hard. A cloud
blows up in five minute time, and by that
time you had better look for cover.

I have been going to ground school for 5 days
now and two of them were 10 hr. days. I don't think
I will get to fly this month but I might get a
chance to. We have to take a 14 Physical Exam.
some time next week. Also we get some of our
over seas shots. Only 7 shots and one long needle
in the back for yellow fever. I hate to think of it.

and I went to the town of Alexandria
last Saturday night. You should see the soldiers
in town on Sat. nights. You can hardly walk down
the street their so thick. We took our laundry
in town to have cleaned. We have class "A" passes
and can go to town anytime were off work. Our
food is sure good here, we get three big meals
a day with everything we want. Sometimes we
get 4 meals a day. And theres no limit to the amount
we take either.

289

So you like my pictures do you. I can't help it if I'm thin. How about sending me three of them will you? I've got a certain place to put each one of them, maybe. Be sure + pack them solid.

I'm glad to hear that my bond got home all. I was afraid it might have gotten lost or something. I can't do that any more because I was a little short on cash this month.

That's swell about the knife, I'll get a lot of use out of it. I'll be glad to get it.

I've got some more things to send home before long. I won't be able to take any letters with me over seas. And alot of other things too.

My pilot's name is   or something like that. I have'nt seen him yet. He has been over here at our barracks two or three times trying to catch me here in the barracks. But every time he comes I've gone some place.

I've got to stop for now and go to another class. I'll write some more a little later.

July 16 Wensday Morning

I'm off school from 10th until 1 this after noon. Then I go from 1 until 3 and I'm off the rest of the day. We went out to the pistol range this morning and this after noon we'll go to the machine gun range.

This morning was a funny morning for summer time. The fog was clear down to the ground and it didn't lift until 7:30. It sure looked funny with the fog settled in through the thick swamps. They have some real big swamps here.

I met my pilot this morning out on the range. He went around asking for Tone until he found me. He is fairly tall with redish black hair. He reminds me of John   of Williams field. I seem to like him O.K.

I've got to go to town tonight to pick up my laundry.

I can't think of any thing else to say now so I'll close for this time.

Write soon.

Love
Kent.

ARMY AIR FORCES

July 27, 1944

Dear Mother:

— Well, for the first time of my time in the army, I'm in the hospital. It's nothing serious but a hard cold. I'm almost over my cold but my head kept acking so I went on sick call. The Doc. took my temature and it 100 so he said I had to go in the hospital for 3 or 4 days to rest up. The Doc up here thinks I'm coming down with the meseals but he's not sure. My head is still acking but I think I'll be O.K. in a few days. They sure feed you good here at the hospital. If I hang around here very long I know I'll get fat. I ask them here when I'd be getting out

and they said, "If, maybe 3 days or 3 weeks,"
they didn't know. I hear it's hard to
get out of the hospital after getting in.

They told me I want loose my crew, I sure
hope I don't. I forgot to tell you where my
pilot is from. He's from Saint Paul, Minn.

It sure is hot here, I'm just wet with sweat.

I was talking with my pilot last night
and he said for sure that we would get
at least 7 days leave after graduation from
this field. He said we could a class 4 priority
on the civilian transport plane. So I might
be home about the first or middle of Oct.

Maybe if the war is going much better by
then and they don't need gunners too bad
we will get a few more days leave.

Well, I'd better close for now. Don't
worry about me because I'm OK. I'll be
out in about 3 or four days I hope.
            Love,
                Neal.

July 29, 1944

Dear Mother:

Im getting out of this darn hospital in the morning and Im sure glad to get out too. I just got back from a check up by a Major & Capt. Im still on flying status and I'll fly tomorrow or Monday.

How is every thing at home? Is the well back to normal yet? I sure hope it is.

I can't think of anything else to say right now. Only its plenty hot here. I wanted to let you know Im getting out in the morning. Write Soon.

Love, Kent.

ARMY AIR FORCES

Dear Mother: August 1, 1944

Your letter came Sunday. I got out of
the hospital Sunday morning. This afternoon
I flew from 1:30 until 9:00 tonight. Boy,
did we get tired up there. We were flying
in an 18 plane formation and was it rough
flying. I thought the darn plane was going
to shake to peices. You see the slip stream
from the other planes caused us to fly
through rough air. I got a little sick.
They said they wanted to show the State
of La. what kind of air force they have here
at Alexandria Air Field.

I like my Co-Pilot, he reminds me of
Jack   . He don't give a darn for
anything. He slept most of the time up there
today. We have a bombardier now, I met
him today too. He never flew with us today.

I thought we were going to get paid yester
day but we never. I guess we will have
to wait until the 10th to get paid. I dought
if I can make it until then. I have exactly
20¢ left. I've even barrowed 6.00 already
this month. I'll never send any money home
any more unless I'm real sure I have enough

295

Mother, please send me three pictures and don't say anything to anyone about them. I'll send Loretta one from here. One more thing be careful what you say about Loretta over the phone will you. I've got two on the string and their pretty close together. I don't want Loretta to get med or I don't want to hurt her in anyway. Keep this under your hat, will you.

Monday, I got my flying clothes and also my 64 Physical exam. They gave me three shot in the arm. I've got to go back in a week for some more. I've got the Colera, Tifes & Yellow fever.

I like this field O.K. except for the hot weather. Last night it rained plenty hard and and myself was caught in it on our way to town. We were waiting on the Buss when it started to pour. We got plenty wet before the bus came. I had to take some laundry in to town. I only had a dollar in my pocket book. loned me $... already this month.

Tell Neil hello for me will you. Tell him not to get over heated out there in Ariz. I wish I could be there to see him.

Sure send me those gloves, sweater & socks. I can use them very nicely. It gets cold up there about 25,000 feet.

I sure missed out on another furlough when I left Lincoln. All the gunners that were

296

still there the 20th got furloughs and no set time to report back. Darn it anyway I could have gone on sick call and got off of this shippment. I heard about them but I did'nt believe that it could be true. Now some guys have heard from the fellows that got the furloughs. Darn the luck.

Tomorrow is our day off and am I glad. I'll be able to get some good old sack time. The war looks good does'nt it. I wish the reds would hurry up and get to Berlin.

You asked me about those fellows from Mex. I never got aquainted with them. When we got on the train we spread out all through the cars. I slept all the way to Tucson and then some more out of Tucson. They're not here on this field.

Well, I'll have to sign off for now and hit the sack. I'm plenty tired.

Love,

Kent.

ARMY AIR FORCES   August 5, 1944

Dear Mother, Dad & K'love:

Your letter came the other day, also the knife. Thanks a lot, K'love it's just what I wanted. It will come in handy many times while in combat.

I flew almost all morning this morning and yesterday morning too. Today we went on a bombing mission, bombed the target from 8,000 feet. Our bombardier is a darn good one, he put 9 bombs out of 10 smack in the center of the targets. Our ball turret gunner took moving pictures of the hits from the radio room. It's fun to watch the bombs fall. It wouldn't be much fun to ride one of them down though. I walked across the open bomb-bay on the narrow cat walk. The strong wind coming through took my hat straight up to the top of the bomb-bay. It was a new cap I just got through buying. I thought for sure it was a gone cap. But when I got to the radio room door, I stopped and looked back and there it was resting on top of a bomb. I was lucky it never went right on down, 8,000 feet.

OK. You can give   a picture if you will. No. Don't invite anybody over when I come home on furlough.

Sunday after noon. — I could'nt finish this last night so I'll do it now. I've been to ground school all day today. This morning we went to the machine gun range about 12 miles from here. I fired about 400 rounds of 50 Cal.

The weather has been hot with cloudy skys and rain once in a while. Thats one thing that it really does here and plenty too. Seems like the ground here is always wet. Theres even moss under all the buildings. When flying around here you can see many swamps with muddy water in them. When we fly low enough we can see the crocadiles sunning themselves on the banks.

If you will give a picture that will save me a lot of trouble. If you have'nt already sent them, will you give one. She knows that I sent for three pictures, tell Klove to use some common horse sence. Please.

Boy, you know its no fun to be broke flat. I have borrowed 12 bucks since I got to this place. Still we have'nt been paid. I have hopes we will get paid tomorrow. I can't even buy a coke or candy bar, I have exactly one penny left. Boy, what a life!

We fly again tomorrow after noon and I guess it will be a gunnry mission over the Gulf. Its no fun to go on those missions with guns all around you. I'm sorry I never finished this yesterday but I guess I'm kept too busy.

299

Now its 10:30 P.M. Monday night. We just got back from our gunnery mission over the gulf. We flew out 38 miles from the coast, and our range was 60 miles long and ten miles wide. We could see fishing boats out there and had to watch out and not sink any of them. We flew real low over the water and shot at the white caps on the water. It was a lot of fun. The water was real pretty blue with a lot of white caps on it. I shot out of the nose and the waist of the ship. That the only guns we can use on air to water. Once the waist gun ran away and before we could stop it about 40 rounds went wild out into the water. After we fixed it, it was O.K.

Tuesday morning -
They are paying us this morning. We fly again the after noon and won't come in until 10 P.M.

I'll close for now and mail this

Write soon
Love,
Kent

Hello Neil
Hope the heat isn't getting you down.

300

UNITED STATES ARMY AIR FORCES

Dear Mother Dad & K love: Sept 25-d

Your letter came the other day and
I'm sorry I haven't written sooner. But
I guess I'm just too lazy or something.
There isn't much to write about around
here.

Well, the C.O. of the field told us the bad
news yesterday. He said that we will
get no furloughs from here or anywhere
else. So that's that. He said that we are
headed over seas soon and fast. Of course
he said he felt sorry for us but there
wasn't anything he could do. We leave
here around the 6th I can't tell you any
details only that we are headed for Lincoln.
There we will stay about 4 to 8 days, and
then we pick up a new B-17 and fly it
over. We will get all new clothes and all
the combat equipment we need. So I guess
I won't see you until I get back. I'll
get my 35 missions (only 35 now) in and
come home. I've got a good pilot and he
takes no chances at all.

301

I didn't take out any allotments at all. I've decided to send home what money I get over there. They tried to make me take out a will but there is'nt any sence in doing that. Because I haven't got anything.

You can still write to me through my address here. Then I'll send you my A.P.O. number as soon as I can. After I leave Lincoln you won't hear from me for a long while. You know how it is.

I'll be glad to get the cookies because its' hard to stay on the post. Oh! I forgot to tell you that I'm restricted. You see that fellow 2 nd from the left in our crew picture. Well, he and I went to town Friday night the M.P.s pick up all the G.I.s that stay on the street after 11:30 at night. Well, we were picked up and brought back. I guess we are restricted for a week anyway our passes have been taken and I don't know when we will get them back. Some life.

They had another crack-up here on the post. All the crew bailed out O.K. but the plane cracked up. Thats two in one week.

302

I'm going to send another box of things home. Please keep it for me, will you.

That's too bad Klove never passed the test. Maybe he can find something in my old army tests I took in College. Physics is the most important. Look over them. That's about all they ask you about engines. Hope you pass it O.K. next time.

Gee, I hope you get that well drilled pretty soon. That's too much work hauling water.

Well, I guess I'd better sign off for now. I can't think of any thing else to write.

Write soon,

Love

Kent

Sept 29th
1944

Dear Mother, Dad & K love:

Your letter came yesterday and the cookies should arrive today. Don't you worry, I'll get rid of them without any trouble. I'll bet they are real good.

The weather has been bad yesterday and today. It kept us grounded both times. I'm glad, because we have to fly every day we are here anyway.

We lost our bombardier & Navigator the other day. Our navigator wasn't any good so they gave us another one. He is a 1st Lt. the same as our Pilot. So that makes our crew the highest in rank. They took our bombardier off because we don't need one. Our armor gunner is acting bombardier in combat. All he has to do is push a button to release the bombs when the lead ship drops his. The lead ship does all the bomb sighting.

304

We got our passes back yesterday so now we can go to town again. We were restricted for five days. The radio operator and myself.

Well, in about two weeks I guess I'll be over in England some place. Our pilot is sure that we are going to England. The way we will go will either be the northern or southern route. Northern route takes us up past Iceland and we will stay there about 2 weeks before going on. But the other route goes from Fla. to South America and that way. Looks like a better route. I'll see a lot of country, writer, too.

No there is no chance of getting any kind of furlough or leave now. Not until I come back. They could give us leaves but they won't. That the Air Corps for you.

Well, pay day comes again tomorrow, this time I think I'll send some money home. I've save up quite a bit from last pay day. We won't need any money over there.

The other night our mess hall had some poor chicken salad. About 130 guys went to the hospital with tomaine (??) poison. The meat wagon was going back and forth to the hospital all night taking sick guys out. I was lucky I never ate supper that night. When I got over to the mess hall it was closed up tight. Even the mess Sgt. got sick too. It was good for him.

I'll send you my new A.P.O. address as soon as I get it. But you still can write to me through this field. I won't be able to write until I get over there. And it will take a while to get over here.

Well, I can't think of anything else to say, I'd better sign off you now. Write soon.

Love

Kent

Monday afternoon

Dear Mother:

I want to thank you for the box of
cookies they were very good. The boys on
my crew liked them too.   liked
the date cookies as good as I do. Gee, thanks
a lot. I got another box of cookies & one fruit
cake from Aunt Pie and they were very good
too. They came today so I haven't gotten them
eaten yet.

I got my picture taken the other day in
my blouse but they turned out with too
much light on them so they had to be
taken over. I had to have them taken over
in my suntan shirt & cap. I saw
the proofs this afternoon and picked
the one I liked. I won't be here to pick
them up but they are sending them home
for me. One large one and three small
ones. I know what you will say when
you see them. You'll think I'm thin but
I don't think I'm very thin. If you think

they are very good pictures. Will you give
one? Not unless you think they are
O.K. Tell her I said for you to give me
one.

We have been flying every day now for
the last week and so far no time off. We
are to fly tomorrow afternoon, and then
again the day before we leave. Darn
their hides anyway.

I wired home $90.00 the other day. Did
you get it? I don't want to carry so much
money around with me. I've got plenty
to last over until next pay day. Keep it
for me will you?

Well, it won't be long until we will be headed
across the pond. Darn it I wish they would
give me a furlough first. I think the 2nd
Air Force is mean as heck to do this to us.
Other fellows are getting furloughs.

Well, I guess I'd better sign off for now
but I'll write more before I leave here.
                    Love, Kent.

Oct 17th

Dear Mother Dad & K love:

I'm writing this letter to let you
know that I'm O.K. and feeling fine. I have
an A.P.O. number now it's on the envelope.
It's just a temporary A.P.O. until the army
gives me another number.

I can't tell you where I am now but
it's not bad country. I'm a long way
from home but so far I have n't gotten
home sick. I'd like to be home, sure, but
I'm not home sick. I guess I've been in the
army too long for that.

I bought a lot of things today. Shoes,
gloves, scarf, watch band, bill fold, and
lot other things. Boy, I really blew my
self today.

I've got to go now. I'm O.K. Don't worry
I'll be O.K.

All my love,
Kent

March 6, 1945

Dear Klove:

Well I guess you are home by this time having a good time. Darn it, I sure wish I could be there too. But I guess my time will come in a few more months.

I've got 17 missions now and 18 more to go yet. I sure hope the rest goes faster than the first 17 did. I should be done by the end of May.

Say, you must be getting in good with the C.O. if you got a ride home with him. Keep up the good work.

Well, I got a taste of the sea the other day when I went to rest camp. I was on the Isle of Capri for seven days. We went out on a boat from Naples. I got to spend the night in Naples on the way back to camp. Rest camp is sure a good deal, a guy feels just like he is a civilian again. We stayed in real fancy hotels with real soft beds. The meals were very good and all of them were three or more course meal. They had the band playing at every meal. There is tennis, boating, fishing

310

badminton, ping-pong, and many beautiful things
to see on the island. And many things to buy. I
spent around $50 ºº while there. I sent most
of my things I bought to Loretta to keep for me.
I sent mother a Cameo necklace, and a bunch
of things to Loretta. And not a darn thing to a
certain girl at home. ha! ha! I don't know
what she is going to say and I care less. I
haven't written to _____ for a long time. I'm
not going to either. I guess its mean but I
think much more of Loretta.

You should see our tent floor. It looks like
a hog pen. The dust is ankle deep now. We
can't get any brick for it unless we buy it
with our own money. By the way what kind of
pay do you get now for a month? I get $166.ºº
a month.

The war news looks much better now. It
hadn't ought to be very long until the war is
over with over here. I sure wish the Russians
would hurry up and take Vinnia. I'm getting
tired of being shot at over that target.

Well, I've got to close for this time so
take care of your self. Good luck.
            (Rodger & out)
        Love
        Kent.

March 24, 1945

Dear Mother & Dad:

I received your package the other day with the cookies, wash clothes, magazines and Williams Field papers. Thanks a million, I sure enjoyed reading them. I'll write those people and thank them for the cookies, also the papers.

Well, I've got 20 missions now and 15 more to go yet. The darn things go plenty slow for our crew.

We moved into another tent today which has a floor in it. Some fellows went home so we got their tent. It sure seems great to stay in a good tent with a floor for a change.

I haven't gotten much mail the last two weeks and not a letter in the last five days. This darn mail is coming slow because none of the other fellows are getting any either. I sure hope I get some tomorrow but that's what I thought yesterday.

The weather here has been plenty good this month so it looks like summer is almost here. If the weather stays good I might be home by the last of June. I sure hope so.

By the way, I was just wondering how much money I have at home. I've forgotten how much I've got at home. How much have I got?

The war news looks pretty good now doesn't it? But still there's a lot to be done yet before those Jerries are done. I sure wish they would pull out of Vienna pretty soon. I've got about 11 missions over that place I think.

How did K love like this leave? I guess he must be going to school some place by this time. I sure hope he gets to go to school for a while.

I noticed in the Williams Field papers that there's lot of fellows from this outfit stationed there. Boy, it sure would be swell if I could be stationed there again when I get back.

Tell every one hello for me, who ever is there. Have you got the hot water heater in yet? That's what you've been needing for a long time.

Well, I guess I'd better sign off for this time. I'll write some more later. I can't think of anything more to say right now.

Write soon.

Love
Kent.

P.S. I think all the mail is coming over by boat instead of air mail these days. Darn it.

313

April 14, 1945

Dear Mother + Dad:

Your letter came yesterday and I was glad to hear from you. So you got home alright. I'm sure glad you had such a swell time.

Well, I'm still sitting on the ground with 20 missions in. They just don't seem to fly our crew for some reason. I guess they want to keep the good crews on the ground.

How about sending me some canned veg. soup, nuts (shelled), Velveta cheese, and some ham shampo? Darn it all the other guys gets packages and I don't get any. I heard you can send all you want to now without requests. Is that right?

About that money at home. I know thats what I did with the money in the bank but did'nt I send some bonds home? I can't remember. Dad doesn't owe me anything at all. I was just wondering how many war bonds I have sent home. I've got $675.00 saved up over here since I've been overseas. I'm getting 4% intrest on it in Soldiers deposits.

So you don't like California. ha! ha! Why thats a darn good place. Lots of fun. Yes I knew how those service men get but if you would look in Phoenix some night you'd find the same thing there too. You'll find guys like

314

that anywhere there are service men. Don't you worry about me drinking too much. I don't even touch this Italian stuff at all. And we can't get any American whiskey over here except when we come back from a mission. To tell you the truth, I do smoke but that's no crime is it? You always said I could start when I reached 21, and if you'll remember I'm 21 now ha! ha! Don't you worry I'll take care of myself. You know darn well that I was brought up good enough to know right from wrong, thanks to you & Dad.

I sure hated to hear about the President's death. He was the best president America ever had and I sure hated to see him go. I sure hope Truman knows enough about the war to lead us to victory. I hope every one backs him to the limit.

Well, I've got to sign off for this time and get this letter out in tomorrow's mail.

Tell everyone "hello" for me.

Write soon.

Love
Kent.

May 6, 1945

Dear Mother & Dad:

I'm sorry that I haven't written sooner but things have been happening plenty fast over here. The war in Italy is all over now and I'm done over here in this theater.

I received the box you sent the other day. Thanks a million for everything. The book of Arizona is O.K. and so was the Arizona Stockman. The cake was dried out so much I couldn't eat it and the paper was stuck on it and I couldn't get it off. The candy was real good. Thanks again.

I haven't been getting very much mail lately. I can't figure out what is the matter. I guess the mail service is poor. There was no mail at all today.

Well, it almost 7 P.M. now and I'm waiting for the news. I think the war will be over then. The last news at 5 P.M. said that all fighting had stopped to make peace terms. I look for the peace terms to be through by 7 P.M., I sure hope so.

I might be seeing you in another two months. Keep your fingers crossed.

I've got to close for now.

Love Kent.

May 9, 1945

Dear Klove:

I received your letter the other day
And I was glad to hear from you. I'm
glad you like your new school and I
hope you'll get what you want out of it.

As you know, the war is over in
Europe. That was the best news I've
ever heard in a long time. Every one
was jumping around here like mad
the night it was announced. We were
shooting flares and all kinds of fireworks
that night. I sure wish I knew where
and when I go from here. I'm hoping that
I'll get to go home on furlough before
going to fight the Japs. I think I will
if everything goes O.K. The way things
look now, I'm afraid that I won't get home
for another three months. We've got another
job to do over here before going home. So
I guess I'll have to sweat it out for a
while. I finished up with 22 missions when the war ended. My last

mission I flew over Linz, Austria.

So you don't like the climate up there in Washington, huh? Well I know about what you mean but you can be glad you're not over here now. This place is getting as hot as Arizona weather now.

Our mail service isn't very good these days. I haven't heard from home for a long time now. I can't figure out what is the matter. I get letters from Loretta every once in a while. By the way what did you think of her? She wrote and told me she went down to see you at the station. She wondered if she passed inspection OK. Ha! Ha!

As for _____ well, her mother wrote me a real hot letter answering my last letter to _____. So now I've gotten her off my string. Ha! Ha! I'm sort of glad too.

Well, take care of your self and if you come home on furlough I hope I can be home the same time. Good luck,

Love Kent

319

Dear Mother + Dad: June 26, 1945

I guess you are wondering when in the heck I'll be coming home. Well, I'm wondering the same thing and don't know much more than you do about it. All I know is that it just can't be too long now. I want to get home so darn bad and I'm getting so darn restless laying around here doing nothing.

I flew up to Rome today just to get the rest of my flying time in for this month. We landed there to get our sgt. doctor who was at rest camp for a week. He goes up to Rome about once every two weeks. We stayed on the field there for about four hours waiting for him. We all had a swell time watching all the different types of planes coming in. Lots of big shots came in there while we were there.

I saw one plane that was headed for London from there. I sure would have liked to go with that plane. It's a good thing I never saw a plane that was heading for the U.S. because I'd have gone with it.

Mother will you write to Loretta and ask her to come over to Arizona when I get home? She wants to but she doesn't

320

know if her Grandmother will be in Cuny. at the time. I told her that you would be glad to have her come over.

The weather here has been hot as heck the last few days. Tonight it is nice and cool because we had a nice shower. I wish it would stay this way all the time but it wont. This country around Foggia is all plains. Mostly wheat and fruit country. We are living in a olive grove north west of Foggia about 7 miles. The dust sure can blow sometimes. This afternoon flying back from Rome we ran into a real bad storm over the mountians. It had us sweating for a while.

Please save all the Life magazine you have until I get home, will you? I want to read everyone of them. Any magazine for that matter.

Well, I guess I'd better sign off for now and hit the sack. I'm plenty tired tonight.

Write soon.

Love

Kent,

321

June 27, 1945

Dear Klove:

It has been a long time since I've written to you. I hope you will excuse me for not writting. I've been so darn restless waiting around for the Army to send me home. Half of our group have gone home but our Sgt is the last sgt. in the group to leave. I don't know how I'll go home but I think it will be by plane. Either on a bomber or by A.T.C. (C-47). I'd rather go by A.T.C rather than fly in one of these beat up old bombers home. That Atlantic ocean is pretty big you know.

Well, how are things treating you these days? Are you still getting good grades in your studies? I'll bet you will be glad when your schooling ends and you get that furlough. By the

way, if you are home by the 27th of
next month I might possibly be
home by that time too. I'm hoping
I can be home the same time you
are. But I guess that's too good to be
true.

I flew to Rome yesterday afternoon
on a B-17. We stayed up there about
four hours but didn't leave the air
field. I had two big holes in the
seat of my pants. The fellows
that had decent clothes went into
town. There was a Navy plane there
with some high ranking Marine
officers on it. There were three
Navy enlisted men with the plane.

Did I tell you that I received
your picture you sent me? It's
a good picture of you. But what
is it you have marked out? Are
they battle ribbons? ha! ha! You

navy guys.

We had to take up all our brick floors from our tents. Now we have dirt floors again. But we won't have to stay here very long so it makes no difference. We had to turn in all our clothes except one pair of each kind. We can't live like that very long either.

We are having a big inspection of our Sqd. today. It's a big one by the Air Force to see if we are ready to move.

Well, I've got to close for now. Take care of your self and don't study too hard.

Write when you find time.

Love

Kent.

Dear Mother + Dad:

Well, here I am going to the Bear
school. I got here Sunday afternoon at 2:30
and started from L.A. Friday afternoon at
4:30. I came up here from Clinton, Iowa
on a bus. Did I have a hard time
getting out of L.A. I tried two times on
the S.P. train but everytime was turned
down because of no room for civilians.
I had almost given up until Brownie called
his friend who is the manager of the Beverly
Hills Hotel. He had to bribe him to get
a ticket (any kind) on a train just so
he would get to Rock Island before or on
Monday the 12th. Well, he got it O.K.
But it was a drawing room ticket on
the Stream liner. The fastest + best
train in the world. Another yellow was

to share the room with me. He was to
pay for half of the room. So Dorthy took
me down to the Union Station. I had to
tell them my name was Mr Brown so I
could get the ticket. So I was Mr Brown
all the way back here. The ticket came
to $143.61 just one way Brownie gave
me $10.00 to get the ticket with so I would
have some money to live on back here. So
I'll have to pay him back when I get home.
I have $200.00 put away in a checking
account at the Bank at Beverly Hills.
But Loretta has my chank book and check
books. So please send that Army check
to Loretta as soon as you get it. She
can send it on out to me.

The weather here is plenty cold and
wet. I have my long drawers on and
I'm still cold. I need a top coat. All I
have is a leather jacket. But I'll make
it O.K. until I leave. I'm boarding at
a boarding house at $12.75 a week

but I don't care much for it. I only have to stay three weeks but I'm going to stay four or more. I figure I can't learn too much about anything. I can stay six weeks but that would cut me short on being back for Christmas.

Loretta & I had our pictures taken and they were ready the 9th but I never got to see them. I saw the proofs and helped pick out the ones we choose. We took two of the one smiling and six of the sober ones. I don't know which is the best but any way you will get one for Christmas. Loretta is sending them out.

Loretta & I went up to Ventura the last Sunday I was there. Aunt Dic was'nt feeling too well. I saw Donald the day I left and he was back at his old job.

I've got to close for now. Write when you find time.

Love, Kent,

327

Kira Shay has been telling stories for as long as she could talk and writing them down as soon as she could hold a crayon. While her chosen writing implement has matured, she hasn't gotten past weaving stories that both entertain and make people think. Kira is a co-founder of FSF Publications. She and her husband, Will, currently live in Arizona. You can find more of her work at
www.fivesmilingfish.com